3-

Dr
Alberto

with best wishes

Syb Ruthel

Sep. 30, 2007

EIMONA

A novel by

G. B. PRABHAT

ArcheBooks Publishing

EIMONA

A Novel By

G. B. PRABHAT

Copyright 2006 by G. B. Prabhat

ISBN: 1-59507-142-3

ArcheBooks Publishing Incorporated
www.archebooks.com

9101 W. Sahara Ave.
Suite 105-112
Las Vegas, NV 89117

Hardcover First Edition: 2006

For Kottoppa

Raconteur par excellence
Grandfather
Guru unconventional

"*Eimona* is a chilling account of a future that is almost upon us: sophisticated technology and global finance altering the fabric of human relationships to create a world where each individual is alone in a virtual space and nature is irrelevant unless captured as a computer screen-saver. A timely fable which might make our high-achievers pause and think."

MEENAKSHI MUKHERJEE
India's leading literary critic and
Sahitya Akademi Award winner

"Twenty-five years ago, acclaimed writers such as Salman Rushdie and Anita Desai presented the world with an India wrestling with the simultaneous formation and partition of its national and traditional identities. Today, G. B. Prabhat has provocatively expanded the purview of world literature with *Eimona*, a novel that depicts another psychic partition defining contemporary India. Between the nouveaux riches enraptured with the magic of the stock market and modern media, and those left behind by the new world economy, the reader glimpses a society all too willing to gate its communities and sell off its sense of history. Ultimately, *Eimona* is much more than an essential addition to Indian literature, as it illuminates a brave new world everyone must come to terms with. For we all come from *Eimona*."

KEVIN CAROLLO
Professor of World Literature and Writing
Minnesota State University Moorhead

PRELUDE

"A lost boy has been located. His name is David Johnson. He says he is three and a half years old and claims he is American. He has blue eyes, is dressed in a yellow tee-shirt and blue jeans..."

The announcement was distinctly audible, though unobtrusive, over the soft, civilized bustle of the well-lit, lavish airport.

"I wonder whose child it is," she remarked.

She should have been in her late twenties. Her early pregnancy had not started showing up on her figure—the hourglass figure, which compelled heads to turn.

Her husband, tall and sporting a crew cut, was about the same age as she was. He had an arresting aquiline nose and a mild cleft chin. Under his left eye was a Z-shaped scar. The result of a childhood injury. Women invariably found him attractive, and remarked that the scar was a natural tattoo that complemented his perfect nose and cleft chin.

They wheeled their cart looking for their boarding gate.

For a while, he had noticed through the corner of his eye, two young men and a woman who had been following them at a discreet distance. They couldn't be called young men. They were boys turning into men. When he turned to look at them, they turned away. When they stopped at a bookshop, the two young men and the woman appeared to gaze at the watches in a nearby shop. When he visited the toilet, they stopped to lean on the railings to gaze below, while at least one of them was throwing a furtive glance at his wife.

"This is our gate," he pointed out to her.

His wife looked up. "Yes. This is our gate," she confirmed.

The board said: "No carts or trolleys beyond this point."

He pushed the cart out of the way, and picked up their bags. Just when they were about to enter the gate, he heard somebody say, "Excuse me," and turned around.

The two young men and the woman stood with expectant smiles.

"Yes?" He looked at them quizzically.

One of the young men produced an autograph book and stretched it towards his wife. "Autograph please…"

He was puzzled. Why would somebody want an autograph from his wife?

"Why?" he asked.

The young men and the woman giggled.

"Why wouldn't somebody want the autograph of Nadira?" the other young man asked.

"What Nadira? She's my wife," he said annoyed. But he knew what they were getting at.

The young men hesitated, stared at each other, and then at the woman. "Your wife? Is she not Nadira?"

"Nadira who?" He continued his pretence.

"Nadira…the famous Indian actress…who also won the Miss World title."

This was not the first time somebody made this mistake. People were constantly mistaking his wife for Nadira.

He laughed. "Sorry, boys. Better luck next time."

Without waiting for their response, he turned around to enter the gate with an arm around her waist. Through the glass doors, they could see the young men and the woman arguing. Obviously they were trying to blame each other for the embarrassment.

Many years later he would remember this incident.

"A lost boy has been located. His name is David Johnson. He says he is three and a half years old and claims he is American…"

The announcement was aired again.

"I can't believe people lose their children, especially in such a well-organized place," she said shaking her head. "It's stupid."

"Yes, it's stupid," he agreed.

CHAPTER 1

This happened in Eimona.

Your experience with Eimona is so intimate that you are tempted to look it up on the world map. In vain.

You are not sure precisely where it is except that it seems to be everywhere: America, India, Europe and spreading to the rest of the world.

Its exact extent is unknown, though you know it is massive and expands inexorably every day. The annexation policy of Eimona doesn't seem to be defined by any one individual. It is almost as if it has a diffused consciousness.

Eimona seems a bit like its only historic parallel: the Internet. Like it, everyday Eimona grows without a central authority that sanctions its expansionism.

•

Bharat was glued to the computer screen. The ticker tape indicating the stock prices on the National Stock Exchange showed prices rising every minute.

It would happen today!

Didn't take great analysis or statistics to know that. His hand was impatiently and unconsciously rolling the nameplate meant to be stood on his worktable. "Bharat – Senior Investment Manager" it said for the benefit of his clients.

He glanced sidelong at Mangal who was sitting at the next workstation. Mangal's knuckles that gripped the table were white. He knew that Mangal knew, too, that it would happen today.

The ticker tape showing the stock prices was on its next round. "FI – Rs. 555*," it said. That was the only share price that stood out for Bharat. FI – the stock exchange symbol of Fusion Investments. It was a tiny private American company when Mangal joined it. It was still small, but public in America when Bharat joined it five years ago. When Bharat and Mangal were both offered thousands of stock options every year, and their CEO explained seriously that stock options could make them rich, both Bharat and Mangal had to suppress the urge to say, "Oh, yeah? So you don't want to hike our salary very much. Even though we earned the company fifty million dollars in profit last year." Stock options, then, were an official corporate device of deception. A pacifier.

Then the dream took over.

FI, typified by smart investment managers like Bharat and Mangal, invested in software and information technology companies. And then FI went public in India. Suddenly the stock market zoomed. The daily variation in FI's share price

---

* "Rs." designates Indian Rupees, which are approximately 45 to the US dollar in 2006, i.e. 555 Rupees is approximately $12.33.

equaled Bharat's salary of many years. He, Mangal, and many colleagues were officially rich.

Keshav, who never believed in stock options, had gifted many of his shares, with malicious intent, to his in-laws' families when there were weddings and birthday parties. For his own relatives, he bought nice gifts like flasks and table lamps.

"It's perfect comeuppance," he lamented. "Who the hell thought our company shares would do so well? My in-laws are rich. My own relatives? They own flasks and table lamps. Is there any way of getting the shares back?"

The computer screen now showed FI-Rs. 585. It was only a few minutes back that it was Rs. 555. Bharat mentally calculated his wealth gain in the last two minutes and laughed out aloud at the absurdly large amount. Startled, Mangal looked up briefly, but returned to his trance with his computer screen.

Without speaking a word with Mangal, Bharat was sure that the tingle in his spine was the tingle in Mangal's spine also. The screen dazzled him. He shifted his gaze to look out of the window at the sun-soaked streets of Madras. A Pizza Hut billboard announced exciting new Indian toppings, including spicy *paneer*. A street dog stretched itself and wandered listlessly, stopping occasionally to sniff at the food wrappers thrown into and around a garbage can. Unconsciously, Bharat downed the coffee from his mug.

It would happen today.

•

Pantu-thatha — Grandpa of the Pants — was an ironic sobriquet, a name Subbu's grandson, Bharat, gave him as a three year old boy. Under the inescapable Gandhian influence, early in his life, Subbu took to donning a white *khadar* shirt and a white south Indian *veshti*. Not *dhoti*, which he considered a North Indian condescension. He had never worn any kind of trousers or pants. He had opposed his Britain-bred boss to wear *veshti* to work. When he came so dressed under protest, his boss threatened him with dire consequences. "Then I will quit," Subbu had retorted quietly, but indicating that he meant business. Being a man of conscience, his boss had given in, shaking his head in despair. The issue did not bother Subbu for the rest of his working life.

Many years later, Subbu belligerently turned down speaking engagements at fashionable clubs because they required him to wear trousers. "Fie upon you," he would bellow. "The British have left. The colonial hangover persists. How can an Indian club turn away people for dressing in traditional Indian attire?"

Karna's tale was one of Subbu's favorites for narration, and Bharat's favorite for listening. Bharat was singularly fascinated to hear that, unlike other babies, Karna was not born naked. He was born with *kavacha*, an armor almost integral to his body, and *kundala*s, protective earrings—both gifts from his resplendent father, Surya-the Sun God.

It was only when Bharat was a little over four years old, he realized that the white shirt and white *veshti* were not a part of Subbu's physique, unlike Karna's *kavacha* and *kundala*s.

He asked his grandfather with a furrowed brow, "*Thatha*, why don't you wear pants?"

Subbu was reading the newspaper and replied distractedly, "I don't like pants."

"Why not?"

"Well, I think *veshti* is a lot better," he continued without taking his eyes off the newspaper.

"Oh," said the boy, as if he understood. But he continued

to be thoughtful. He was bewildered how his grandfather felt more secure with a length of cloth loosely suspended around his waist like a towel than in a pair of trousers that clasped the waist reassuringly.

The clock struck eight and shook Subbu out of his reading. "Bharat, time to eat."

"Will you wear pants for me?" Bharat asked with his large doe-like eyes.

"What kind of idiocy is this? No, no," said Subbu, dismissing the question. "Time now to eat. Tomorrow's a working day."

"Will you wear pants for me? Just once? Please?" Bharat asked his question more earnestly.

"No." Subbu's hostility and finality surprised the boy, and himself too. "Come now to eat," he demanded, half expecting a yelp of protest.

Bharat did not protest loudly. A lone teardrop stood delicately poised on the brink of his eyelid, and then rolled inevitably down his cheek. He rose quietly to sit at the dining table.

In a Pavlovian response, Subbu walked into the kitchen to get the dishes. The lone tear seared through him. Had he ever spoken so harshly to Bharat after the death of his son and daughter-in-law? Not that he could recall. Their death had steeled him into the resolution of treating his grandson with the greatest possible kindness. No, it didn't include extravagant indulgence. He hadn't extended it to his son; he was not about to extend it to his grandson. But surely the boy didn't have to understand his private prejudices?

With his mind made up, he went to his wardrobe. He noticed that his hands trembled when he opened the doors. Undisturbed lay his son's trousers in sedate shades of gray and black and blue. The unmistakable odor of his son. The odor that is as distinct as a fingerprint. The odor that emanates from all objects used by a person long after he is gone.

Telling himself that he was doing this only to entertain his darling grandson, Subbu chose a pair of gray trousers and climbed into them clumsily. The wardrobe door was hastily shut to prevent the odor from escaping. Irrational, of course, since the odor had stayed for years after his son's death. His inserted *khadar* shirt stuck out of the trousers awkwardly. In spite of his animosity for the two-legged attire, he curiously stared at his image in the mirror.

"Ta-da-ing..." he made his appearance in the dining room, mocking the background music that accompanied dramatic announcements in Tamil movies.

Bharat let out a whoop of joy and surprise. With the child's instinctive genius for names, he shrieked "*Pantu-thatha, pantu-thatha.*"

Pantu-thatha—Grandpa of the Pants.

The name stuck even though Subbu never wore pants again. He failed to understand why he did not mind this moniker that possessed an object of distaste. Maybe it was because of his acute remorse at having been hostile to the boy. A sort of penitence. No, no. It was perhaps his sense of humor. Or the apathy of advanced age.

Then he became *pantu-thatha* to everybody. His friends, neighbors, all sorts of relatives, Bharat's friends, the corner store grocer, the neighborhood at large. Very few cousins and relatives of his age remembered him as Subbu. Of course, not a soul maybe would remember him as Subramanian. Even to him, his full name represented only a fuzzy link with the past.

Later, when Bharat was a near adult, Subbu tried to introduce him to his father's smell. Bharat smelt the clothes and reported, "Smells of naphthalene balls. The trousers are fraying. Maybe you should get rid of them."

When Subbu stepped out to do his daily shopping that morning, a cosmic question was troubling him. The previous night, Maya, his great-granddaughter, had sought his assistance to complete her science assignment. She had just started her third standard and was overburdened with homework. How Subbu hated homework, tests and assignments which held young children indentured slaves of the educational system. When Maya thrust her notebook under his eyes, he couldn't help wondering how similar the gesture was to Bharat's. Not too long ago, he was helping Bharat with his science assignments. He found it hard to believe that he was helping Bharat's little daughter with her assignments too.

Her teacher had asked the students to figure out, with the help of elders at home, what caused waves and tides in oceans. With an imperfect recollection of his baccalaureate physics, Subbu explained the interaction of winds and waves, and how the moon's gravity affected tides. Maya did not understand gravity. At some length, he taught her what gravity was.

When he was done, Maya pondered for a quiet, long minute—the way she pondered always. She lacked the impetuous responses of children, which was fine with Subbu, who had an aversion to pompously smart children with brimming, inane questions.

At the end of the long minute, she asked, "Why are there no waves in a lake? Or in a bucket of water. Don't the winds and the moon's gravity act on it too?"

That stopped him short.

Why, indeed? Why is there no wave in a bucket of water? Why can't there be a storm in a teacup?

Subbu would turn eighty-four next month. Why had this question not troubled him till now? He was a little ashamed.

That morning, ever since he sent Maya to school, the question tortured him intensely, distracting his attention. But due to sheer force of habit, he unconsciously managed to navigate his way to the mall and to the grocery supermarket, *Foodmania*. They were very lucky to have a supermarket within walking distance of their apartment. Most others had to drive to complete their shopping. Subbu detested driving as much as he loved walking—even in the discouraging Madras weather. For most part of the day, he was walking, outside the apartment or inside.

The question so engaged his mind that with the shopping list in his hand, he asked the first *Foodmania* helper he sighted, "Where can I find a storm in a teacup?"

The helper responded with a baffled, "Excuse me?"

Regaining his composure, Subbu asked, "Where can I find teacups, please?" He had no need for teacups but since his first question contained "teacups," his second question had to contain "teacups" to permit him a dignified recovery.

As he expected, the helper did not say, "Aisle 13," and walk away.

"What type, exactly, are you looking for?" he asked most kindly. Intrusive courtesy when you didn't want it.

"Never mind. I'll come back," said Subbu in a hurry to extricate himself.

After paying for his purchases, when he collected his bags and was about to leave, another helper, in a ridiculous orange uniform, with a plastic grin pasted on his face, looked Subbu in the eye and said, "Have a nice day."

The statement infuriated Subbu. It had become a world of words.

"Do you know me?" Subbu asked the helper.

The helper, who did not expect to have a conversation after chanting his customary greeting, stopped, a little startled. "Sir, were you talking to me?"

"Yes," said Subbu, repeating, "Do you know me?"

"I am sorry, sir, but..." the helper stammered, searching Subbu's face for some sign of familiarity. "No sir, I don't think so."

"Why then do you want me to have a nice day?"

Relieved at this question, the helper said, "It is *Foodmania*'s policy to greet customers this way."

Wearing an innocent expression, Subbu continued, "If your company did not want you to greet customers this way, would you still?"

Not sure of the intentions of the silver-haired gent, dressed in white, the helper replied, "Maybe not. We say what the company policy asks us to say."

"That means you say it like a robot. Without expression or feeling. You are paid to say it. Right?"

"Yes, sir...no, sir." The helper wondered if the man was senile or mad. The old man's firm posture, piercing expression, and studied casualness belied any such possibility.

"Is it yes or no? Do you really care whether I have a nice day or not?"

"Yes, sir. I care."

The old man scratched his head. "How is *Foodmania* doing?"

"Not too well, sir."

"Have there been layoffs?"

"Yes, sir. Some."

"Have some of your colleagues been laid off?" This last question of the old man perturbed the helper. What was he getting at? Was he a corporate spy or something?

Hesitantly, looking both ways, the helper answered, "Yes, sir. Many of my friends have been laid off."

"Is there a chance that you'll get laid off?"

"Yes...yes, sir. That can't be ruled out under current conditions."

"Let's assume that you are laid off. You and I meet at the bus stop. Would you wish me 'Have a nice day'?"

"N...No, sir," the helper responded with greater uncertainty.

"I thought you just said you cared whether I had a nice day or not."

"Sir, I do." The helper's professional earnestness was back.

"Then you must care, whether you are employed by *Foodmania* or not."

"Sir, but it is our company policy to greet you that way."

"Oh, then you are a paid robot. You don't really care."

The helper began to protest once more.

When Subbu was done with the helper, he walked away licking his lips like a lion after it has demolished its prey.

The automatic doors of *Foodmania* swished open to let him outside. Just then he heard a loud, cheerful greeting from another helper near the next door, "Have a great weekend."

The helper wondered why the old man, instead of proceeding outside, started heading towards him.

•

Indu had the air of a rambunctious horse under restraint. It did not help this image that she wore her hair, almost invariably, in the form of a ponytail. She had good taste and was always dressed nattily in western clothes, though her equal opportunity employer permitted Indian clothes. "As long as you have something on," her company CEO would remark, and everybody would laugh obligingly at the boss's joke that stank with staleness. She was impatient and restless with everybody and with herself. A trait that had earned her widespread popularity with her bosses, the respect and awe of her peers, and the ambivalence of those who worked under her. When something did not get done, particularly if it was elementary, her restlessness suggested a racehorse kicking its feet, raring to go.

Many did not know her precise age, though they knew she was very young. Not too long ago, she had joined Paragon Software as a graduate programmer trainee. With lightning speed she had risen to become the youngest vice-president. She managed complex computer programming projects for customers all over the world.

When she was not reading computer-programming books, she was reading or re-reading Sidney Sheldon novels. Somebody commented that it was old-fashioned to read Sidney Sheldon. It didn't matter. For her Sheldon's heroines were an addiction.

Her office had an anteroom with a bed and a wardrobe. When she had to put in long hours, she would shower in the office, change, and be ready for the next round. She would go to bed around midnight and be up again at 3:00 AM.

Her colleagues, who were forced to stay back, cursed her. "Stinking armpits don't increase programming productivity," one of her meek male colleagues remarked once. "Madam enjoys a bed and a wardrobe and access to executive showers. It's okay for her to stay back. What about me? Don't I need a wash?"

When another colleague offered to represent this grievance to Indu, the meek one was petrified. How foolishly he had provided others a perennial taunting opportunity! Indu's irascibility was legendary. Nobody messed around with her. Men found her irresistibly attractive, but nobody made passes. Her one-liner insults, while evaluating her team's professional work, had paralyzed people for weeks. Since she punished herself equally and was technically competent, the others grudgingly tolerated her tough treatment. "Madam" was married, but little was known about her husband. His plight was the subject of much speculation. The office was rife with ribaldry about "positions."

Indu married Bharat nine years ago. Both were twenty-seven at the time. They met when Bharat, as a representative of Fusion Investments, had visited Paragon Software. Bharat's company was planning to invest in Paragon. His boss had asked him to visit Paragon to check out the quality of management. Even though she was not a vice-president then, because of her confidence and presentability, Indu was asked to manage many of the presentations to Bharat and his team. On returning from these meetings, Bharat recommended Paragon very favorably to his boss. Fusion became the largest shareholder of Paragon.

Thinking about this later, Bharat had often wondered whether the extremely positive image of Paragon that he went away with was an exaggerated impression created by the young woman with a perfect figure. That figure was firmly etched in his mind, not so much the figures the woman, her CEO, and the rest of their team presented.

Indu also grew interested in the young man from Fusion Investments. He was not only good looking, he was also intelligent. More importantly, he was a winner. And best of all, she could gather, he was one his firm's most successful investment managers—and, very well compensated.

Even in the slickly managed presentations, Indu could not help revealing her volatile temper. They were tiny slivers, but unmistakable. Bharat became cautious. Though the young woman appeared interested in him, he could not summon up the courage to ask her out. His doubt, his cursed doubt, which was the leitmotif of his life, stopped him from inquiring. Luckily for him, the young woman took the first step.

With a sense of joy, Indu realized that the young man

from Fusion had a very desirable trait. For all his strengths, he was meek. That's exactly how she wanted it. She hadn't been too sure until then whether good looks, razor-sharp intelligence, meekness at authority, and a capitulating instinct could all be part of one package. Bharat confirmed that such a package existed.

Reluctantly, many years into her marriage, Indu had to admit that her marriage was an extension of her office life. She certainly did not enjoy the company of idiot slaves. Just as she required resourceful but servile subordinates at office, she had subliminally desired a meek but intelligent husband. She ran her home affairs with the same iron hand with which she ran her office. Just as easily as she could be filled with certainty and confidence, her husband could be filled with doubt.

Much ahead of Bharat receiving compensation through stock options, Indu did likewise from her company. Paragon Software did very well in its international business. Like Bharat, she became rich beyond her expectations, though unlike Bharat, she had determined to become rich, to win. Stock options and her status were wins at the office, her marriage to Bharat and her almost complete control over their daughter Maya were her wins at home.

Like Bharat, she, too, was waiting for it to happen. But her expectation was filled with a cool certitude, unlike Bharat's expectation, which was marked by nail-biting anxiety. At well-timed intervals, she was taking a look at share prices. Paragon was at Rs. 155; fifteen minutes before it had been at Rs. 140.

Her heart rhythm was not varying with the stock price as Bharat's was.

She was sure.

It would happen today.

•

Subbu had married early. His son, Krishnan, was born when he was in his early twenties. Immediately, Subbu vowed to his wife, Jaya, that they would have no more children. He was just waiting for a safe delivery and a healthy child.

"I want to give all I have to just this one boy," he had explained.

There was no need to explain. Jaya understood him on cue, and was moved by the remarkable dedication of the young father. Instantly, her desire to have any more children dried up. Until she died, her world did not extend beyond her husband and son.

Subbu gave everything of himself to Krishnan. Not in an indulgent way. In fact, his expression of affection was understated. Many times, he was left wondering if he was being communicative enough. His government job gave him the luxury of coming home early on working days, and enjoying pressure-free weekends. He taught the boy his school lessons only when Krishnan came to him with doubts, but took charge of initiating him into history and economics, literature and art.

Subbu's favorite pastime became taking the boy to the public library or to music concerts. It was anathema to him to feed Krishnan with predigested knowledge. He believed in providing broad direction and planting a few clues. He determined way-stations in the boy's journey of learning, but allowed the boy to beat his own path between way-stations. Eventually, the boy would determine his destination and the new way-stations.

Subbu actively recommended *The Picture of Dorian Gray* to Krishnan. After reading the story, the boy asked, "*Appa*, what does one learn? What's the meaning?"

"Everything you need to know is in the story. I don't have to tell you anything."

"But I didn't understand it. Does that mean we shouldn't be immoral?"

"Maybe," said Subbu, not giving in.

"But then Dorian Gray's sins don't affect him when he lives. They get him only after he dies. Right? So maybe it's okay to sin?"

"Maybe."

"Why don't you tell me for sure?" little Krishnan demanded angrily.

"I don't know for sure."

"You are a grown-up. You must know," insisted Krishnan. Subbu gave him a cryptic smile for a reply.

Krishnan's intellect was precocious, but his emotions were a child's. "You don't want to tell me." He stomped out of the room angrily, turning away to hide his tears of frustration.

Anybody who saw Krishnan's professorial demeanor when he was barely eight would not have been surprised that, later, he became a professor of economics. A professor who constantly disproved that economics was a dismal science. His manner was quiet. He conspicuously lacked the high decibel monotone that teachers were either born with or very assiduously cultivated. His lectures were scintillating and generously sprinkled with humor. At the height of humor, his voice dropped so much that students leaned forward, anxious not to miss the best parts. He adopted the technique of telling tales that personalized impersonal economic theories like capitalism, free markets, and mercantilism. Instead of cutting economics classes, which was the universal student routine, students thronged to attend his classes.

When Krishnan fell in love with Sharada, a fellow professor who taught history, it was a most natural act. If Krishnan had been a woman, he would have been Sharada. She had the same scholarly, inquiring mind, the same sharp sense of humor, the same quiet manner. In the first year of their marriage, their home had hardly any noise of inhabitation. Each would be stuck to his or her favorite chair with a book. Conversations were low-pitched and the lighting was soft.

When Sharada became pregnant, Subbu was elated. While he had relished bringing up Krishnan, he did not have the luxury of enjoying Krishnan's company without the strain of chores. Plus there was the distance between man and son that cannot be shrunk, but magically shrinks between man and grandchild.

Every morning he woke up with a lurch of his heart looking forward to the arrival of his grandchild. He was waiting to minister to its every need when Sharada resumed work. But Sharada would have none of it. She was determined to look after the baby, and resigned from her job two months before her due date.

Subbu was a little disappointed that he could not monopolize his grandchild, but was grateful that the child would get a full share of its mother's love. Later in his life, he regretted that he so fervently wished to take care of the child. Maybe that was why it was granted.

He distinctly recalled a day when Bharat, nearly six months old, was playing with his favorite teddy bear while Sharada watched with shining eyes. Krishnan was lounging in his chair poring over *The Brothers Karamazov*, something he had been longing to read for a long time, but had never managed to. Subbu was gazing at the newspaper without reading anything. His mind was taking in the scene and contrasting it with the clamor outside.

Krishnan and Sharada, genuinely affectionate, artistic, understated and phlegmatic—conspicuously incongruous with the world outside. So incongruous that they had to depart early.

•

"Excuse me, Bharat. Do you have a minute?"

"No," growled Bharat like a sage whose penance had been interrupted. "Leave me alone for now."

Now FI's share price was Rs. 600. A short distance to go.

In anticipation, he had retrieved the phone number of Indu on his phone so that he could just press the "Call" button when it happened.

He briefly glanced at Mangal. Gentle beads of sweat had broken out on Mangal's brow. The air-conditioning thermometer indicated 19 degrees centigrade. Unobtrusively, Bharat pulled out a handkerchief to wipe his brow just in case the sweat was showing.

The price of FI dropped to Rs. 595.

"Oh, come on," Bharat said. Mangal gave him a meaningful look.

A presence behind him made Bharat turn around. It was Keshav.

"Not bad, *yaar*, for you guys. Any idea how I can get my shares back?"

"Keshav, beat it," Bharat said menacingly.

"Okay, *yaar*. Take it easy," said Keshav and walked away.

After staying for the five longest minutes at Rs. 595, the price of FI started inching up: 600, 607, 608...609, 610, 611...

Bharat realized that he had been drinking water indiscriminately while waiting for it to happen. His kidneys were bursting. He pressed one hand on his crotch as if to silence it.

611...612.

It had happened!

Simultaneously, Bharat and Mangal thumped the table and said, "Yes!"

Yes. Rs. 612 was the stuff that dreams were made of.

It had happened!

Both he and Mangal were now millionaires. Not rupee millionaires, which was like yen millionaires. They were full-blooded, US dollar millionaires. The stock options that they had derided so much, had been so skeptical about, that Keshav had thoughtlessly distributed to his in-laws, had now made them millionaires.

Indu had to be told. As he reached out to press the "Call" button on his phone, it startled him ringing shrilly.

"Hello," said Indu from the other end.

"Indu…" Bharat was gasping. "It…"

"…happened." Indu completed helpfully.

"Yes."

"So looks like you were watching my company's share price quite closely."

Bharat didn't get it for a moment. He had not been watching the Paragon stock price. It sank into him slowly.

"Indu…really?"

"What do you mean? So you were watching only *your* company's price, weren't you? I was watching both."

"I am sorry," he said, a little guiltily.

When he put down the phone, he couldn't help emitting a low whistle. His indignant kidneys said, "Hello?"

Indu was also a US dollar millionaire. On her stock options.

•

With bags slung from both arms, Subbu paused at the foot of the staircase. Though their apartment was on the

fourth floor, unlike Bharat and Indu and the rest of the occupants, Subbu never used the elevator except when Maya
wanted to amuse herself. She was still thrilled by the prospect
of going up an elevator. The elevator was a play object for her.
Just when they got to their floor, she would command it to go
down. Up and down a few times. Subbu would indulge her so
long as no one appeared to be waiting. After a few times, he
would keep the "door open" button pressed, and would order
her to leave. When there were other people, she would politely press the "door open" button for everybody to get in,
sweetly ask for the floor numbers, shield the switch panel
with her body lest somebody should press the buttons, press
each floor button in order, blush for every "thank you" that
was said, and say a polite "bye, bye" to somebody that might
be left in the elevator when she exited.

To her the elevator was a ceaseless wonder. To Subbu,
every elevator experience with her was a ceaseless wonder.

He took in the height of the first flight of steps, braced
himself, and ran up the stairs, skipping every alternate step.
Occasionally, the Coiffured Man, who lived in the apartment
above theirs, took the stairs, and saw him doing it. Unhesitat-
ingly he said, "Wow!"

Even as he inserted the key, Subbu knew Aaya was home.
She had gone to her village for the weekend. Her slippers
were outside, near the doormat. The sound of running water
was unmistakable, as were the other intimations of the
woman at work.

As he entered, he perfunctorily called out, "Aaya."

"Here, *pantu-thatha*," she called out to confirm it was she.

"Okay. Carry on."

Aaya must be between sixty and sixty-five now, Subbu
calculated. He had brought her from his village as a ten year
old girl to help at home when Krishnan arrived. She helped

with the household work, barely a half-adult herself, and had stayed with them ever since. Jaya jealously looked after all of Krishnan's needs leaving only the chores to Aaya. Subbu was certain that Aaya wistfully desired the duty of looking after the child. Perhaps she shouldn't have been so wistful; perhaps his wishes had a misplaced intensity.

After the accident, when Subbu wasn't tending to Bharat, it was Aaya. And now she looked after Maya and the home. Her real name, Meenakshi, had disappeared from all records except Subbu's memory. She used to call him "*saar*" without complete conviction, until Bharat named him "*pantu-thatha*." She clung on to it as did Subbu and the others, to "Aaya."

Many times, in the presence of guests, Subbu had embarrassed Indu by introducing Aaya as "Aaya." Indu would suppress her rage with a smile when only her lips smiled without the cooperation of her eyes, and explain, "Nanny, you know." She had considered the possibility of "governess" and quickly dismissed it as absurdly regal.

Once later on, flicking the hair from her eyes, she demanded, "Why don't you introduce her as the nanny, or better still, as the *au pair*?"

Subbu rolled the word on his tongue and said, "You know, a name must fit a personality. *Au pair*? No good. Nanny? Worse. Aaya is good."

Knowing this was an unproductive battle, initially Indu stuck to her "*au pair*" and Subbu to his "Aaya." Maya, of course, called her "Aaya." She had a compelling reason. "Aaya" rhymed better with "Maya" than "nanny" or "*au pair*" did, and that was that. Bharat called her "Aaya" loudly, with affection and authority, when Indu was absent. But when Indu was around, he called her, "Aaya" timidly, and consciously limited the need to address Aaya. Indu herself was forced to call her "Aaya" when guests were not around because she could not think of any other name. Besides, Aaya was beyond the age when she would respond to a new name. Her partial deafness was tuned to responding to Aaya, and not to any other name. Aaya lived in mortal terror of Indu.

"Aaya, water…" Before Subbu could finish hollering, Aaya had appeared with a glass of water. This was routine. Shopping at *Foodmania* carefully including a choice of Post cereals, his breakfast favorite. A run up the stairs. Panting for breath. Flopping into the sofa. A drink of water. And a second round of detailed reading of the newspaper after the cursory first round with morning coffee.

Something disturbed his concentration. He had forgotten a tiny bit of his routine. Controlling his rising chagrin at himself for forgetting it—how many times must a man disturb himself before he can settle down to the day's papers—he walked to the niche on the wall near the shoe cabinet, reached into it and shut off the central air-conditioning. In a quick stride, he was opening the windows one after another, his impatience evident in the windows banging open.

With matching impatience, when Indu returned home, she would replay the sequence in reverse. After shoving her shoes into the closet, she would slap the air-conditioning switch on, and go about shutting the windows one after another. She couldn't imagine, why in such hot and humid weather, anybody would deny himself the elementary comfort of air-conditioning.

Even with pollution reaching record levels in Madras, Subbu longed for fresh, natural air, not the recirculated, stale air-conditioned air. Besides, on the fourth floor, pollution wasn't as bad as on the ground floor. The stale air-conditioned air and the perpetually closed windows were not the only things that Subbu disliked about this apartment: The Home. Maya had named it The Home to distinguish it from their weekend beachside apartment, the Second Home. The Home depressed him in many ways. He did not like the antiseptic decor created from pre-assembled pieces, the decor that was in virtually every apartment in the block, the duplex organization, the smell of the room freshener which had become permanent on repeated use, and the neighbors.

The part of the duplex level that annoyed him the most was the bedroom section. Maya had a bedroom to herself. Aaya slept in the passage just outside Maya's bedroom. Next to Maya's room was his bedroom. Across the passage were two bedrooms, one for Indu, and one for Bharat. When Indu moved in and made this demand, Subbu was incredulous, but did not express it. Bharat fumbled, but quickly agreed. A child learns about matrimony from the marriage it observes most intimately—its parents'. Bharat was significantly disadvantaged in this respect. In this and in other marital matters later, his understanding stemmed from consultation with friends or from Indu's proposals.

"I want my space," Indu had emphatically declared. Her bedroom had a corner patio and a wardrobe. She was the only person who had keys to the different drawers and would not brook even Bharat wandering about her bedroom too often without purpose. She was fair to let Bharat have his patio and wardrobe in his bedroom.

A door connected their bedrooms. It appeared locked every time Subbu had a passing glance at it. Maybe it was sensitized to hormone levels and opened automatically when the hormones surged. Where did this mischievous thought come from? Must be the insidious influence of early Sean Connery James Bond movies.

In general, Subbu hated apartments.

The Second Home was an apartment too, but he tolerated it. Because it was built on special soil. The soil on which

Subbu's house originally stood.

He had a sprinkling of the articles of Krishnan, Sharada and Jaya in both the apartments. That's about the only thing that helped his transition from independent house to apartment. These articles—Krishnan's clothes here, Sharada's clothes in the Second Home, his son's cherished book collection here, Jaya's bronze statuette supposedly dating to the Chola period in the Second Home—were his few but strong roots in a rootless apartment existence.

After much deliberation, he had decided to leave the family photograph—his greatest treasure, his guarantor of sanity—in the Second Home. Krishnan and Sharada would smile from it. Their eyes radiated sublime, inexhaustible serenity. Bharat, with a mop of curly hair and sitting on his father, would look at him from a peculiar angle (he had been torn between a moving spider on the wall and the photographer's call, "Readyyyy...smile."). Even though he visited the Second Home only during weekends, Subbu decided the photograph belonged more there than here. That's where Krishnan, Sharada and Jaya belonged.

The most striking part of the photograph was his wife, Jaya. Somehow she managed to convey her great but undemonstrative compassion for her limited, yet infinite, world of her family. It was the only surviving image on paper of her. She was very photography-shy. He could still feel her wriggling against him in the few long seconds when the photographer was peering into the camera to make fine adjustments.

Out of view, he had to squeeze her hand in admonition. She grimaced for a second in pain, and then became photography-ready as best as she could.

•

When Bharat came that evening and broke the news, he was visibly excited. His fair face was suffused with a red blush. He was hardly able to shut his smile. There were many raucous phone calls. He called Mangal at least thrice. He had spent the whole day with him. What world-changing events happened between then and the ride home that he had to call him thrice, Subbu wondered.

Even Indu's armor of composure showed chinks. She did not like to expose them, so hers was repressed gloating. When Bharat exuberantly suggested that they go out for dinner with friends, Indu accepted dinner outside but ruled out going with friends. "Just you and me."

When Subbu's own marriage was contemplated long ago, his mother reported that during the pre-marriage discussions, the whisper doing the rounds in the bride's family was that the bridegroom had a salary of four hundred rupees. A salary that would assure the couple later of a reasonably affluent life.

The numbers that Bharat and Indu were discussing had so many zeroes and so many currencies that Subbu was beyond caring. He wondered if he could write correctly such large numbers.

"*Pantu-thatha*, can you take care of Maya this evening? Indu and I want to go out to eat," Bharat implored.

Quite unnecessary, Subbu thought, the imploring part. What else did he have to do? Maya, uncomprehending, had her left hand index finger stuck into her mouth, as ever. It gave the impression that her hand, hanging limply, was suspended from the mouth by her index finger. Subbu was desperately hushing her to drop her hand since this irritated Bharat. Because it irritated Indu. But Bharat was too distracted.

"Of course, I will take care of her."

"Can I go, too?" Maya asked.

"Not today, darling. Some other day. That's a promise," Indu responded.

Not even waiting for her to complete her reply, Maya ran away calling out "Aaya…" She didn't expect her mother to say "yes", but nobody should blame her that she didn't ask.

When they were leaving, Subbu asked anxiously more than once whether they had taken the keys to the apartment. Bharat was peeved by the repeated question, but Subbu had his reasons. The one thing he would never give up was his sleep. He had to sleep at 9:30 PM, a half-hour after Maya went to sleep, and get up at 4:30 in the morning for his walk. He knew Bharat and Indu would now return only in the wee hours of the morning.

This time, however, they returned at the stroke of midnight. Slightly drunk, Bharat lurched to switch on the light of his bedroom. Indu had gone into her bedroom. He stood staring at the connecting door for a long moment. Then, muttering something, clumsily he climbed into his bedclothes and switched off the light.

The connecting door opened. Indu stood silhouetted. She knew Bharat would have been staring expectantly at the door, willing it to open. Permission was now granted.

Blowing whisky fumes into each other's faces, they made violent love.

He, thinking of his million.

She, thinking of her million.

CHAPTER 2

Early that morning, when he turned over, Subbu knew he had lost sleep. The luminous arms of the timepiece (a winding piece, made in China, bought in the early 1960's) showed 4:15. It was a little earlier than usual. There was no point in trying to go back to sleep. He brushed his teeth for longer than usual since he had earned fifteen more minutes of life that day, lingering on some teeth with the wistful thought of removing the steadfast betel-nut stains.

They were a magnificent set, his teeth. He had a full mouth. There were betel-nut stains, and one tooth was a bit chipped. During his yearly prophylactic visit to the dentist, she would remark, "Good as ever." He strongly believed that betel-nut chewing, the only supposed bad habit that he had acquired during the early years, had turned out to be his savior. People maligned the habit in the 1960's and 1970's since they suspected betel-nut caused severe anemia among other things. However, Subbu had chosen the sensuous pleasure of the sheer piquant taste of betel-nut over the suspected damage it would cause. Later, it turned out that many of the claims were spurious. His constant chewing had ensured a sturdy dental set-up. Except for the one time when a tooth chipped, he had had no other problem.

He stepped into the passage and stood for a moment for his eyes to adjust to the dark. He could see the huddled form of Aaya in the corner. The passage resounded with her snoring. A most intriguing phenomenon. How could one's ears be insensitive to such a deafening noise that arose from another organ within a few inches proximity? Why doesn't a person wake up due to his snoring, while he could wake up by a small shuffling movement that somebody else caused? At least now she was partially deaf (perhaps her snoring had caused her deafness). But she hadn't been disturbed by her snoring, even when her hearing had been perfect. During those days, however, she would wake up if he made the smallest noise.

Since he still had a few minutes to start his walk, he indulged in his favorite pastime, something that he never tired of. His feet were socks-clad in preparation for walking. He could silently sidestep Aaya. Step after step, he walked into Maya's bedroom. The room was at the end of the corridor, and a soft light drifted in through the blinds. The night lamp and the skylight together lit up Maya's face as she slept facing the ceiling.

He sat beside her on the bed and watched her sleep. The gentle flaring of the nostrils, the up-and-down movement of her chest, and her near transparent eyelids. This staring stupor he acquired ever since Maya had been two months old and Indu had to return to work. How the attractiveness of a baby increased with the viewer's age! He was intrigued when his son was born. He was fascinated by his grandson, Bharat, but was constantly distracted by the general challenges of life then. But when his great-granddaughter was born, she held him in a complete, magical thrall. It could be because she came as an unencumbered bundle of joy. Or because she was a great-granddaughter and, therefore, a rare privilege. Or because she was a girl, tender, and so different from the two boy babies, Krishnan and Bharat, he had known closely.

When he laid Maya on her bed, as a two month old baby, after lulling her to sleep on his lap, he would go into the staring stupor that he was in now. The baby would lie with both its hands in the "hands-up" position, clenched fists possessively enclosing a sweet nothing each, with a beatific look incongruous with that position. The transparent eyelids, the almost imperceptible rise and fall of the soft belly, and the baby fragrance of Johnson's baby powder and Bengal gram flour would send him into a frenzy of affection. While every little thing about her was perfect, the most perfect part was the tiny fingernails. It was a hard fought contest between the luxuriant eyelashes and the fingernails. Often he had opened the tiny clenched hands to marvel at nature's best work. He would then have to exercise great restraint to smother her with kisses lest she should wake up. As he had to, now.

The day Maya was born, Subbu had been filled with terror. What if she was named one of the tongue-twisters of the New Economy: Vrimnolika, Karnishta or Avnita? The general principle of naming now seemed to be that the rarer and more unpronounceable the name, the better. At one time, Krishna and Rama competed with Mohammed and Chang for the most used names in the world. Mohammed and Chang were still going strong; Krishna and Rama did not figure in the race at all. It was ages since he had met a young man called Krishna or Rama or a young woman called Uma or Geetha.

He had resolved to fight Indu if she chose a difficult name. He had been preparing for the argument, when Bharat came out of the hospital ward and announced, "*Pantu-thatha*, we have chosen a name for the baby."

Tense, Subbu asked, "What?"

Hesitantly, anticipating to mediate a fight between *pantu-thatha* and Indu, Bharat said, "Indu wants to name her Maya."

Subbu heaved a sigh of relief. Indu wants to name her Maya.

How else should it have been?

Maya. The great illusion that is life. The ultimate leger-demain.

For a moment Subbu was angered that his beautiful great-granddaughter, so real and so innocent, should be so ma-ligned as an illusion. Yet in the next moment, the grandeur of the name struck him. Its greatness, its ability to mock at the meaningless world of self-important humans. Also, the relief of being spared from a tongue-twister. Plus, if you wanted to call out "Mayaaaa..." the name had an infinitely long syllable at its end.

Subbu heaved a second sigh of relief.

"*Pantu-thatha*, what do you think?"

"I think it's a wonderful name."

It was Bharat who now heaved a sigh of relief.

Maya turned eight last month. She was an eight year old angel.

For a while now Indu had been saying that Maya had "problems"—a description Subbu detested and despised. He quarreled with Indu whenever she said this. How could angels have problems? Somebody had to just take a look at her now. Problems?

Suppressing the temptation to somehow wake her up by touching her, he stepped out of her room, and tiptoed down to the shoe closet. Wearing his walking shoes, he shut the door gently behind him.

•

When Subbu left home, the neighborhood showed no signs of waking up. It was too early for Madras to wake up. Some years ago, the morning activities would have begun. The milk-distribution boy would be pedaling his tricycle furiously to deposit one or two wet packets of milk, wet from freezing overnight, at every doorstep. He would be greeted by barking dogs in the independent houses. He would regard them with the scorn of familiarity. In his footsteps would follow the newspaper man, who would reach into his carrier, scroll the newspaper, take careful aim and jettison it towards the doorstep. He would suffer a minor loss of balance at the end of this target shooting, but would recover quickly. The swing of his bicycle, after momentarily losing balance, was a small cost to pay for not having to get down each time. Doors would be opening and closing for commuters to far off factory locations to take an early morning bus or train. Some remaining vestiges of the Old World would be drawing the *kolam* well before the reddish orange of dawn started washing over the sky. This generation would not remember *kolam* as the art of creating intricate patterns on the floor with rice flour. That was then.

Now during his walking hours, although the newspaper man and the milk boy reported for work, Madras slept. The newspaper man reported a significant decline in business.

"Who wants to read a paper newspaper?" he lamented. "Everybody reads on a computer."

Now five in the morning was too early for most people to stir. Except for the young fitness freaks and the odd walkers, who came out only when he returned, most others woke up around seven. All of them came back late on working days, and had to catch up on their sleep. And who commuted using public transport anymore? Everybody had a car, maybe two. Waking up late, they could still report on time. Immediately upon getting up, they threw themselves into a whirlpool of activity. The quiet apartment complex would transform into a bedlam of noise and confusion by seven thirty, only to become quiet and solemn by eight thirty, leaving little indication of the activity hysteria that gripped it a short while before.

Subbu carried a walking stick on his walks. He did not need one for walking support, just to protect himself against stray dogs that were particularly active at that hour. They wandered around in packs. Every summer, they dutifully increased their numbers by a factor of two or three. Within a few days, the pups grew as menacing as the adults and snapped at the heels of walkers without provocation. Some things about Madras hadn't changed.

When he returned home, swishing his walking stick through the air, some signs of life would begin to appear. The young fitness freaks were now out. They would be jogging or walking furiously without taking in the charm of the walk. Mostly it was people from his apartment complex or the neighboring apartment complex.

And then the dogs on leashes stepped out. They diligently took their owners on walks, straining on their leashes to smell something inside the bush while their owners used their feet as skidding brakes, and cried an admonition, "Johnee..." Subbu had concluded that the pet dog's response to anything vertical, such as a lamppost, was watering it. And it didn't matter how many were in a row or how close they were to one another.

One of the regular walkers, with a huge Labrador and a

small Chihuahua type, was a scientist named Praveen whose recent book on astrophysics had caused quite a stir. Leafing through the book in the local bookstore, Subbu was amused by the introduction of the writer on the book's jacket: "Praveen lives in Madras with his wife, children and two dogs, Rob and Jack." Wives and children didn't have names any more. Dogs did. It was completely fair since the man had switched wives four times, had children of each of them, but hadn't changed Rob and Jack during the period. Now, with Rob and Jack in tow, Praveen stepped out. Subbu crossed the road to avoid him.

Subbu's apartment complex was filled with spinsters and bachelors. "Bachelors" and "spinsters" seemed anachronisms. Single men and women sounded a lot better. They were mostly young or pretending to be young—liberated single men and women who were programmed to "enjoy" life no matter what. "Enjoying" life bewildered Subbu. What exactly did it mean?

Aside from Bharat and Indu, he was aware of only two married couples in the entire apartment complex of over a hundred apartments. Aaya reported that one of the couples had already separated. At one time there were more couples who had arrived married, but separated quickly thereafter. Some of them traded places with others in the same apartment complex.

Subbu's apartment neighbors had stopped him on the road and introduced themselves many times, but he felt they did not deserve particular names. His memory for names, particularly of people that he didn't care for, was poor. He didn't know whether this was the gentle intimation of senility or whether it was a deliberate forgetting. His references to the few people he cared to remember were mnemonics. The Coiffured Man who lived one floor above him was one of those up early. His hair, a towering six inches, reminded Subbu of Kramer on the television program *Seinfeld*. The Plastered Hair Man, a young man with premature baldness, had grown long strands of hair which he meticulously plastered over his bald pate, ear to ear. Who did he think he was fooling? When he gunned his green luxury car, a Linda convertible, to life, he would gingerly hold his pate with one hand. The Plastered Hair man was in the apartment diagonally below The Home.

If the Coiffured Man, the Plastered Hair Man and the Pockmarked Man had exchanged their heads, he would have been completely unable to spot their bodies. They all had sculpted bodies and tight-fitting tee-shirts that revealed the pumped-up biceps and triceps. Bulging biceps and triceps had become the counterparts of the woman's cleavage and navel. It amused him sometimes that he conversed at some length with many of the apartment occupants on the most inconsequential topics, but they had not been curious to find out his name. And neither he, theirs.

At a distance he could see the Moon Woman. She lived in the apartment directly below his. She had closely cropped hair that she dyed black. Then her hair color would go through a waxing and waning phase from jet black to a black and dark ochre, then to a tortured black, orange and white, to completely white, reverting dramatically to jet black again. He didn't have to cross the road. The Moon Woman always kept to herself. "Good morning," she muttered before she zipped past.

As he climbed the stairs, he saw the Moon Woman's apartment door was open. She lived alone, and was now walking. He stood there for a second, his suspicion aroused. A moment later, the Coiffured Man stepped out. He was in his bedclothes. His hair was disheveled, making him more Coiffured than ever. Smoothing his hair and suppressing a yawn, he slurred a "Good morning, uncle." As he locked the apartment door shut, he called out, "Uncle, go ahead. I can't run up with your speed."

As Subbu inserted the key to his apartment, the opposite apartment door opened and the Plastered Man stepped out. Subbu knew that this apartment was the Stick Woman's. The Plastered Man was in his bedclothes and his hair was more disheveled than the Coiffured Man's. With a slightly sheepish grin, holding and smoothing his hair desperately, he greeted Subbu, "Hi, uncle."

Subbu returned the greeting with a nod and let himself into The Home.

•

Doubt was central to Bharat's existence.

Thinking back when he was a full adult, he realized that doubt had been his most domineering emotion even as a boy. When he performed onstage on school day in group dances, he would always act on cue looking at the others. Though he had memorized all the steps. During his early years, his strong-willed grandfather handled his doubts. He always felt secure when somebody thumped the table and told him, "That's the way to go." He felt absolutely sure that the questions bothering him must have been bothering humanity for some time now. Surely there were right answers and wrong answers. Why did he have to do all the figuring out again?

He asked *Pantu-thatha* about this.

Pantu-thatha gave him an Irish proverb as the answer. "It doesn't matter how tall your grandfather was. You have to do all your growing up by yourself." To Subbu that was only recasting his belief about way-stations and destinations.

When Bharat grew up, his doubt grew up with him.

Where *pantu-thatha* was an expert, his strong opinions helped Bharat make up his mind. But when his grandfather professed ignorance or wasn't interested, his doubt tortured him. In matters big and small.

When he was in the seventh grade, his class was to go for an excursion to Bangalore. He asked *pantu-thatha* who promptly gave him the reply he dreaded. "It's your choice."

The owl-eyed English teacher, with a pad of paper in his hands, had asked him sternly, "So are you going or not?"

Bharat had fidgeted with his hands in his pockets for a full two minutes. It would of course be exciting to go, screaming and joking with his friends. But if he did, he would have to miss the entire cricket match on TV.

"Do you want to go?" This time the teacher's voice had a rasp.

Cricket match or excursion?

"Sir, I...I don't know. I can't make up my mind."

"You Buridan's ass," the teacher cursed sibilantly.

Bharat slunk away and tried looking up Buridan's ass in reference books. At last, he spotted it in an extended language dictionary. A hungry ass that died of starvation because it could not choose between two identical bales of hay. This stung him, and with face in hands he had sobbed.

The Buridan's abstract ass formed a graphic image in his mind. It was a scrawny ass with protruding teeth, but for some reason it had long prickly hair jutting out of its sides like a porcupine's. It was looking sideways, its face a wry apologetic grin. He was not sure if other people had such graphic images of themselves.

His doubt continued to eat at his vitals until he enrolled for MBA in Finance after his Bachelor of Commerce degree (Subbu helped him with both decisions). At the university, Prof. Chauhan, his teacher of economics, and the guru who saved his life, offered him a palliative. When the professor once, in very personal counsel, began, "In the long run..." Bharat expected him to repeat the Keynesian wisdom: "In the long run, we are all dead." Instead, Prof. Chauhan concluded, "...the majority always wins."

In the long run, the majority always wins.

In the short term, there may be turbulence. It didn't matter. The graph always settled in favor of the decision of the majority.

The aphorism was his salvation, and Prof. Chauhan, his savior. This piece of decisive wisdom provided a quick egress from his tortuous journeys of doubt. When in doubt, which was almost always, he started deciding as the "majority" did.

When he started his professional life in the mutual fund operations, he knew he was trusted with other people's money. What stocks should he invest in? What stocks must he sell? Decision-making became a daily demon to exorcise. He looked to his sides, not inside his analytical brain.

What were other investment companies doing? What were his colleagues doing? His elaborate network of relationships ensured he was in receipt of privileged, semi-official, but accurate information. When all the information arrived, he would whip out his calculator to determine what the majority was buying and what it was selling. If everybody bought pharma and sold cement stocks, that's what he did. If everybody sold pharma and bought cement stocks, that again is exactly what he did. The majority had never failed him. He was now a successful investment manager.

When he was asked whether he would take stock options instead of cash, as compensation, again he couldn't decide. It was Mangal who emphatically said that stock options would fly. Mangal and Bharat knew that the choice of cash or stock was actually theoretical—his company simply did not have enough cash—yet one had to reconcile to his pick. If it wasn't the majority, it was an emphatic personality that saved him. *Pantu-thatha*, Mangal, and now, after his marriage, Indu.

Indu agreed to marry him only on one condition: that her premarital past never be probed. She had hinted at boyfriends, drunken orgies and more. Once more the majority came to his rescue. Bharat asked for some time and consulted Mangal and other friends. Most of them said that they had similar pacts with their wives. After all, their own pasts were not much to write home about. For a tiny moment, Bharat felt cheated since he did not have anything to conceal about his past. And he was ready to tell everything. Prof. Chauhan loomed before him and pointed a mighty index finger towards the majority. It should be all right then.

Indu built this condition into a prenuptial contract carefully worded by her lawyer. The contract had also a catalogue of her assets and Bharat's assets in Schedule B of the agreement. It spoke of the consequences of terminating the marriage.

Subbu hadn't so much bothered about Bharat's choice of Indu. He felt that it was entirely his grandson's decision. When he heard about this contract, he first thought Bharat was joking.

"Since when did lawyers start deciding marriages?" he demanded.

"*Pantu-thatha*, you have been a little out of touch. This is how things are done these days. It's not just with Indu. It would be with any other girl too," Bharat had beseeched.

Till death do us part. A lifetime of sharing begins with an agreement on dividing. Property and cash settlement if the marriage falls apart. Who owns what.

When he was into his fifties, Subbu wrote his will. Much against the advice of a then young Gopalan, the family lawyer. "Very inauspicious to write a will at such a young age," Gopalan had protested.

When Subbu proposed to transfer immediately all his property to Krishnan, and keep a modest sum for his subsistence, again Gopalan had reservations. "Anyway, after your time, the property is his. Why transfer it now?"

"Owning anything is a burden, Gopalan," Subbu had reflected. "I am not doing good to Krishnan by passing on my property. I am telling him that, as a responsible son, he should pick up my burden."

A few days after the death of Krishnan and Sharada, Gopalan came home clutching the draft of the will. His youth worked against him, and he broke down holding onto Subbu's shoulder.

Once more, soon after Bharat graduated, Subbu requisitioned the services of Gopalan. "I want to write my will."

Gopalan was furious. Despite their age difference, he muttered some expletives.

Subbu was firm. He transferred the title of his house, the prized home that he had planned and built brick by brick, to Bharat. He had a sum of money invested in fixed deposits which gave him more than the money he needed for his sustenance. Later, when Bharat wanted to demolish the house and build apartments with a real estate businessman, Gopalan pointed out the folly of transferring property early.

"It is his burden. He should do what he believes is appropriate," Subbu had explained.

"Brave words. Would you have the courage to see your house come down?" Gopalan had asked. Subbu never once visited the site, confining himself to The Home. He saw the Second Home only in the fully finished form, a ready to occupy apartment among dozens of similar looking apartments.

Now as he read the verbose legalese that defined the canons of a modern marriage, his eyes glazed over.

Ridiculous! A piece of the world that he had carefully constructed for himself crumbled. What would Jaya have said? What about Krishnan and Sharada if they had been alive?

"This is all so strange to me. You have to decide," Subbu had declared.

Reflecting later, he decided that the contract was the first point of the estrangement between himself and Indu.

Regarding the marriage contract, there had been only one thing for Bharat to do: Go back to the majority. Ask Mangal. Ask Keshav. Ask at least ten other people who got married recently. Yes, seven had signed such contracts.

Subbu and Bharat visited their family lawyer six times before the contract could be concluded. When Subbu expressed his outrage, Gopalan waved it away with a phlegmatic smile. "Times change. Better to have this contract rather than fight bitterly after a divorce."

Even before his marriage, *pantu-thatha*'s strong will could not help Bharat make all decisions, especially since *pantu-thatha* was not always on the side of the majority. In fact, in many instances he was against the majority. Prof. Chauhan's homily had greater power than the strong will of *pantu-thatha*, and only in cases where the majority did not decisively point in a direction did he summon *pantu-thatha*'s will.

After his marriage, he not only sensed a strong will in Indu, he was relieved to know she was frequently on the side of the majority. Taking a decision, abiding by the iron will of Indu and the opinion of the majority did not create conflicts for him most often. When conflict did happen, he went to *pantu-thatha* or roasted in doubt till events made a decision, not he.

But at all times, whether he was implementing the will of his wife or the recommendation of the majority, *pantu-thatha*'s opinions caused doubts in him. Sometimes mild, sometimes serious. He got the feeling that *pantu-thatha* was in possession of superior knowledge. *Pantu-thatha* was also willing to face the wrath of the world for owning his opinions. Bharat could not help feeling that if he had the same fortitude, he would take the side of *pantu-thatha* most of the time.

He had a compelling experience of this feeling that *pantu-thatha*'s opinions could be superior when he faced the question of religion. Bharat's religion was filled with doubt. Subbu, an agnostic, discouraged him to be religious. However, Indu would not brook an irreligious husband. Nonsense, she said to Subbu's recommendations. The whole world could not be a fool! This view of the majority easily compelled Bharat to embrace religion, at least its rituals. However, when he folded his arms in prayer, quite often he was befuddled by what he should pray for.

To whom was he praying? Is God's benediction reserved only for those who pray? If so, what would He dispense as punishment for not praying? And if everything was His will, why couldn't He get everybody to pray? If He was capable of doing that, then why did He need prayer? Maybe *pantu-thatha* was right about his doubts. When his mind strayed thus, he would open his eyes a chink, and hear Indu's stern admonition, "Mmm..." He would then hastily close his eyes like an errant schoolboy. How did she know he wasn't closing his eyes, if she hadn't opened hers?

To resolve the difficulty of keeping eyes closed for a few minutes, he had a version of the prayer that he called a general prayer. Its supplication was not completely clear to him. Subbu used to read it out aloud from some Sanskrit book, but not because he believed in religion. He had a curiosity for all religions and philosophies without following any. Besides, Subbu adored the Sanskrit language.

Thus Bharat's prayer was the universal invocation, *"Sarve-jana sukinobhavanthu."* Let everyone live blissfully. Sometimes, when he shut his eyes very tight and tried hard to pray, the ass with prickly hair on its sides would appear, with its sideways apologetic grin. To destroy the image, during the palm-folding ritual he would steal sidelong glances through half-open eyes at Indu even though there was the danger of her noticing it. When she finished, he also gleefully did.

Now, during lunch time, as he ate a vegetable sandwich with mayonnaise, a new doubt assailed him. He hated the insipid stuff. He could not help wondering why it had become inconceivable to bring lemon rice with fried yoghurt chili for lunch—like *pantu-thatha* used to send him when he was in school. That seemed like better lunch, or was it? He glanced around him. Most people were eating a sandwich with mayonnaise leaking out. If this wasn't such good lunch, why were so many people eating it? Maybe this was better lunch?

Out of a certain masochistic curiosity, he opened the half-eaten sandwich and stared at it. A bit of mayonnaise was streaking down an uncooked cucumber piece. He shuddered, wrapped up the rest of the sandwich, handling it with two fingers like it was a decomposed insect, and dropped it into the dustbin under his workstation. This, he could eat no further. He stared into the dustbin, and watched with morbid fascination the mayonnaise leak out from the sandwich bag.

A Hamlettian dilemma gripped him. Should he or shouldn't he? He wrestled with his doubt until he felt ashamed of himself. Yesterday he became worth a million dollars. He took a look at the ticker tape. FI-Rs. 621. He was worth more than a million dollars. Surely a millionaire was entitled to liberties in such matters without having to go through this kind of tormenting angst? In an unobtrusive stride, he left the room.

When he returned to his workstation later, he had taken adequate care to smother the scent of lemon rice, fried yoghurt chili, and onion *raitha* that might emerge from his mouth. A generous helping of scented *supari* suppressed all the other aromas.

He felt smug.

It is not often that he managed to triumph over majority opinion, and more importantly, his doubt.

•

"I think Maya has a problem. Her teachers think she has a problem," Indu said, when they were talking after she had returned from her office.

Maya was away at her karate class.

"What did they say?" Bharat asked.

Indu had informed him in the morning that she would be attending the quarterly Parent-Teacher meeting at school. Bharat knew that usually meant he would face her ire when she returned.

Subbu was not in the living room, but could overhear this conversation through the open door of his bedroom. He dreaded this subject. These days the frequency of this conversation had increased.

"Well, she doesn't participate in learning how to use the Internet. All other children just go to their kiosks and hammer away at their keyboards. Learning math, science. Taking tests. Most of them have cleared their year's exams before half the year is over. It is close to half-yearly tests. And Maya's cleared just the first quarter. That, too, not with great grades."

"That's not much to worry about. I am sure she will make it up," Bharat said, battling with a complex mental calculation about tomorrow's investments.

"I believe she insists on playing in the mud, on the slide, or playing catch-catch. Or throwball. What's with her? Every child is playing with every other child on the Net. Very complex video games you know. You must plan carefully, make hard calculations, and move both hands real quick. She can't play simple games like Roboball. When will she play Martial Arcades and such stuff?"

"Don't fret. I am sure she will get around to it." Indu's interruptions forced Bharat to start over on his calculations.

Bharat's preoccupation annoyed Indu. "Bharat, I want you to concentrate on what I am talking about."

"Sure, I am listening. Children learn at different speeds. They make it up as they go along."

Subbu tried as best as he could to distract himself from this conversation.

"Forever she seems to want to play outside. Go for walks. Watch trees. She has taken a fancy to eating gooseberries," Indu continued.

"Where does she get gooseberries from?"

"There's a tree in the school compound. In the next Parent-Teacher meeting, I must ask them to cut it down."

Gooseberries. Subbu could feel the piquant bitterness on his tongue. To smother it, the adept eater would use a mixture of chili powder and salt. Once done, without wasting a moment, you would take a sip of water. The hot and bitter taste would give way to a mellow, mild sweetness. In fact, if your tongue was not well-conditioned you were sure to miss it. Practically everyday, to bribe Krishnan to go to school, Subbu had to buy him two gooseberries.

"Bharat, I don't know what you'll do. Make sure she learns to browse the Net. She must start chatting with her friends. Most importantly, she must learn to take her tests on the Net.

And she *must* remove her finger from her mouth."

Subbu's worst fear was that this conversation might end with a suggestion that they take her to a psychiatrist. Or set her up for an online psychiatric consultation. He had seen both Bharat and Indu log into a site called www.soothe-your-mind.com or something like that. Bharat had told him that it was a paid-for service.

When Bharat or Indu had a stressful day, the opening screen of soothe-your-mind.com would come on: "The best online psychiatrist."

I had a particularly bad day at office.

OH, DID YOU? I AM SORRY. TELL ME WHAT HAPPENED.

A customer screamed. He said he would sue my company.

DID THAT MAKE YOU UNHAPPY?

It did. It makes me insecure.

WHY DOES IT MAKE YOU INSECURE?

Because I may lose my job.

THAT'S OKAY. PEOPLE LOSE JOBS AND GET JOBS.

Subbu decided that he would descend the stairs and go into the living room. With him around, Indu might stop the conversation from going to undesirable ends. Yet even as he was climbing down the stairs, the conversation had ended. He knew for sure since Bharat was barking orders to his personal assistant, BOREBO. An intriguing name, Subbu thought, but the Japanese should be able to explain it by a clever expansion of the acronym.

Some years ago, Bharat had first brought home a pet dog, which was a robot. It did nothing much. Just barked, wagged its tail, rolled over, and responded to commands like "Walk" and "Squat." Compared with that, BOREBO was far more powerful. It looked like a real dog, was a computer, had powerful sensors in its eyes whereby if an unfamiliar figure, whose image it had not stored, walked through the door, it would alert by barking. It was also a phone. Bharat could order it to call somebody by just yelling his name.

Now that the conversation with Indu had ended and did not require his intervention, Subbu had to explain why he had walked down.

"Going for a walk," he announced.

Bharat was sitting amid a pile of papers with steaming coffee in a mug. He had to speak to Keshav immediately about an early morning deal he had to do for one of the financial institutions. As Subbu was leaving, Bharat barked at BOREBO, "Keshav."

Subbu left The Home arching his eyebrows. Why would a man bark at a dog? That, too, an electronic dog?

CHAPTER 3

"We are leaving for the wedding. Maya's asleep," Bharat announced.

Leaving for the wedding. That's the last thing Jaya had told him. He and Bharat had been home that day. Bharat was then about two and a half. He had already been fed and was sleeping. Attending weddings bored Subbu. He was looking for an excuse to play truant. Bharat fell asleep after breakfast and had to be looked after. If he was woken up and taken to the wedding, he would become cranky. Chiding him for not attending even family weddings, Jaya announced before she, Sharada and Krishnan left for the wedding, "We are leaving for the wedding."

Two hours later the doorbell rang.

When Subbu opened the door, he was startled to find a uniformed inspector of police.

"Does anybody here own the car with the registration number..." the policeman proceeded to quote a number.

Realizing the tremble under his knees, Subbu faltered, "Y...yes. That's my car. Why do you ask?"

"Let's go in and talk." The inspector held Subbu's hand and walked him in. From nowhere, a second policeman followed.

When he was seated, the policeman cleared his throat.

Subbu didn't want to even see the bodies. Friends and family pitched in to complete the police procedures, arrange for the hearse, and take care of everything at the crematorium.

To be sure, Subbu had been scared of death, till he was into his fifties. Like everybody else. Perhaps a little more than the others. Until he had his first surgery.

When he was laid upon the operating table, he was under mild sedation in preparation for general anesthesia. He was petrified. His acutely rational mind told him that his fear of anesthesia was his fear of death. His family was waiting outside with reassuring smiles that he smiled back at, when he was being wheeled in.

In his rich baritone, making comforting crooning noises, the doctor had succeeded in bringing some calm. Now, of course, he had work to do. He was moving around in a businesslike manner.

"We are going to administer anesthesia to you," the doctor announced in a festive drawl as if it were a birthday cake that was going to be cut.

Subbu stiffened his knees and hands and his whole body although he was not sure how it would help.

"Close your eyes," the doctor ordered his large, staring pupils.

Subbu obeyed. That did not require much encouragement. Fear and prior sedation forced his eyes shut. He was aware of the movements of the doctor. Something told him that the anesthesia administration had just begun.

In his mind's eye, a black spot appeared quite abruptly. He was able to immediately sense the black spot's omnipotence. Yet, he tried to struggle. He realized suddenly that he did not have a body to struggle with. Just a mind. Even that only for a tiny drop of time. The black spot stood there as if to survey the arena and, in an instant, had expanded to fill everything that existed. This monarch blackened all he surveyed.

When Subbu woke up from his surgery, he was opaque to the discussions about his general condition and the results of the surgery. Apparently everything was well. That seemed minor detail.

His first realization, when he came to after the surgery, was that he needn't have been scared. He remembered nothing at all after the black spot took over. He was very sure that if he had to undergo this experience another time he would not be scared.

He was now curious. About anesthesia. At the first available opportunity he jumped the doctor with his question, "Doctor, how does anesthesia work?"

The doctor was on his way out of the room after his first post-surgical visit. He was a little unprepared for this question. "Huh?"

"Doctor, how does anesthesia work?" Subbu repeated his question.

"What do you mean—how does it work?" The doctor's question contained a bit of outrage.

"How does it work?"

Subbu's insistent tone made the doctor realize that he had to answer the question. "Well, let me try and make it simple. Anesthesia is a mix of several chemicals. Something to paralyze you. So that you don't start moving around when the surgery is in progress. Sedatives to make sure you sleep. Something to make sure you don't have any memory of the happenings. And painkillers for obvious reasons."

Wonderful!

This was what would happen when death arrived. He knew its form. A black spot. There would be no need to struggle. He would not be in charge. The black spot would be. He would willingly surrender control to the black spot. It would unleash on him its potent potion of painlessness, sleep, amnesia and paralysis. The action would be swift. Then nothingness.

Our languages have a serious conceptual flaw, he thought. It was presumptuous to write "died," as if dying were a voluntary action. Everybody was killed. The black spot killed.

Later, when Krishnan and Jaya died, his feelings for death took on a new tinge of indifference. If his son and his wife, inseparable from his personality, had undergone the experience, it was brazen for him to nurse any minor reservation. Ever since, like with Adi Sankara, his favorite philosopher, Death became his constant companion. A companion he chose to ignore with ease. That's perhaps why his companion had stopped his alluring advances. That's why there wasn't any irregularity in his health. Perfect BP, cholesterol and sugar readings. No doctor would suggest a treadmill test since the speed with which he climbed staircases, skipping every alternate step, was by now well known.

While Subbu was no longer scared of death, he was terrified of the devastation of dotage. Of the inescapable destiny of senility. Like diabetics who test themselves periodically for sugar levels, he tested himself for senility. Was he speaking and making a fool of himself? Was he forgetting some elementary, daily routine? Was his short-term memory intact? Could he recall names quickly? Did he still remember his retirement date? Did he obsess over minor details? Was he repeatedly tugging at the door handle to check whether he had locked the front door?

Was losing control over oneself a sign of senility? Only under one circumstance did he repeatedly lose control. Try as he might. Krishnan is sitting in the living room and reading. Sharada is writing on a scrawling pad propped up in her lap. There is absolute quiet. A soft light fills the far end of the living room with more darkness than light. Chitti Babu's *veena* is playing unobtrusively. This was not a frozen, eidetic scene. It was dynamic and living. Subbu would be filled with outrage. Why was that irreversibly destroyed, without decent notice, without anybody's permission? Impotent rage produced only an ache in the chest and occasional tears that did not await his permission. A few times Subbu was caught. It was no more than a tear, and he would flick it away. Not because he was ashamed of it. He had trained himself not to reveal his feelings to Bharat since his tender age. That training conditioned his responses.

The first one or two times Bharat was sympathetic, but following a conversation about this with Indu, he became irritated.

"You know they aren't coming back, don't you?" Bharat demanded once.

"Is that a good enough reason to stop grieving?" asked Subbu.

"Yes. It's no use. We all have to get on."

"Well, I am sorry. I try. Sometimes I am not able to. I am not sure that I want to."

"You'd better watch out. This is becoming kind of obsessive. Maybe you should be seeing a shrink." Subbu knew that Bharat was echoing Indu's opinion.

"Yeah, it's an obsession," said Subbu, his voice hardening.

"It's called affection."

"But how can you grieve so much? I can understand it if it were recent. Or you were young. At your age? For such a long time after your son's death? After all, he was also my father." Indu talking through Bharat again.

"Get out," Subbu ordered quietly. It was not in Bharat's constitution to resist and fight. If Indu had been around, there surely would have been a scrap.

"Okay, okay," said Bharat and left.

So, there was a correct period of grieving. After that period of grieving, you had to become "normal." Occasionally, a clemency petition might be accepted to extend your period of grieving. By a week, maybe two. But after that you *had* to stop. Get on with life. It didn't matter for what, but you had to get on. You didn't have the right to stop and ask for the purpose. If you did have the temerity to ask for the purpose, you were required to go to a grief counselor. There was also a right age to grieve. A right age to lose your father, mother, son, and wife. Then it was the most natural thing to happen. If it happened exactly at the right age, then you were not entitled to even the stipulated period of grief. To ask for extensions was sacrilegious, vulgar. Self-granted extensions to grieving were, of course, the ultimate transgression.

•

It was Saturday.

Weekends meant that they shifted to the Second Home on the beach.

Standing with his feet in the foam of the waves, Subbu took in the ocean. The sea in Madras was grayish, blackish blue, not the greenish blue it was in Mauritius. Yet it conveyed its majestic expanse without doubt.

Jaya had fallen in love with the ocean. She would not let Subbu build a house anywhere but on this beach. It was one of those few times she had insisted on anything.

Of course, Subbu also loved the ocean and the incessant crashing of the waves. By night, the beach was differently beautiful. The infinitesimal movement of the ghostly, disembodied lights on the horizon—ships arriving and departing—was the finest example, according to him, of poetry in motion. On a full moon day, the disembodied lights glided on a carpet of golden filaments.

He had had only one reservation: The fishermen settlement.

It had spread over one end, and parts of it intruded into the urbane colonies nearby. Subbu visited its borders now and then. It was the Dark World. It began where the last burning sodium vapor streetlight stood. The streetlights in the settlement did not work, or if they did, the bulbs were broken during arguments. It was a world of dimly outlined asbestos-roofed houses, dark apparitions, and bodiless voices chatting or squabbling. Splintering glass and high-pitched screams punctuated the steady drone of conversations. Fishermen with bare torsos sauntered in and out. But if a stranger mistook the calm and tried to make an easy entry, he would be stopped before he was barely ten meters into the settlement. Who did he want to see? For what? Where did he come from? Self-appointed custodians of the settlement grilled the newcomer. The speed with which the settlement responded in stopping the stranger was reminiscent of the leaves of the chlamydomonas folding instantly upon being touched.

The fishermen had violent quarrels among their factions, but did not generally bother their affluent neighbors. The womenfolk of the fishermen settlement were employed as domestic help in the colonies. Occasionally, the men strayed into the colonies after a drinking bout, shouting challenges at the rich occupants. When they sobered in the morning, they would be profusely apologetic for their profanities, or lower their eyes in guilt when encountered on the streets, or were blasé because they just had no recollection. Subbu suspected that they used their drunken bouts as an excuse to scream at their rich neighbors once in a while.

Gradually his fear about the settlement disappeared. Also, urban Madras no longer provided "walkable" neighborhoods. Walking was an indispensable part of Subbu's life. He despised the idea of climbing into a car to go somewhere else for a walk. Walking was a birthright, and you had to be able to step out of your house and start walking. Except for the end, which was effectively sealed off by the fishermen settlement, this neighborhood provided the opportunity to walk long distances without the menacing traffic.

And so, he, Jaya, and a young Krishnan built their house brick by brick tending to tiny nuances. Where should the magazine rack be? If the shoe-shelf was in the verandah, where would one sit to wear the shoes? Where would Subbu sit and work so he could stare at greenery in his garden whenever he lifted his eyes? He and Jaya had a brief, but intense argument about what color mosaic the floor should be. He wanted red and she, white. In the best tradition of *The Gift of the Magi*, each foolishly, yet wisely, informed the architect that the choice was the other's choice. They ended up having a white mosaic floor with patches of red, and laughed heartily over it for many years later. The detailed planning of a house—the apotheosis of the inexplicable agony-and-ecstasy experience.

When the police came, he did not want to see the bodies. He did not see his house come down either.

Where that house once stood, now was the apartment

block of which the Second Home was one. Whenever he looked at it, the ghostly apparition of his old home was superimposed on it.

A spirit only he could see.

Subbu never understood the idea of having "fun" during weekends, especially the restlessness. Clearly fun could not be had at home. You had to leave home, if at least only to go to the Second Home, and there to engage in sports, drinking under an umbrella, whatever, but outdoors. You could no longer stay indoors, listen to music quietly, banter with your children, read a book or pick at your garden. Was it John Stuart Mill who had said that it is impossible to work directly for happiness? That happiness was the byproduct of working for something else. If that's so, how could you decide to have "fun" this weekend and "enjoy"? The worst part was that this seemed to be working. Maybe this was soma of the Brave New World; maybe we should stop expecting it in the capsule form.

Now Subbu could see Maya sitting on the sand, a few feet away, assiduously building what looked like a castle. She was absorbed in the process, talking quietly to herself. Her talking was interspersed with little words of advice that she offered herself in a crooning voice: "Be patient," "Make the sand a little wet," "Careful, careful."

Indu was sprawled on the beach along with her friends, men and women, laughing loudly. Bharat had some work at the office and had said he would come to the Second Home in the evening.

A few of the fishermen's boats were bobbing on the sea at the far end. Some things about Madras hadn't changed in decades. The fishermen settlement—much against the vow of some of his elitist neighbors at the time—had not disappeared. It had, in fact, grown.

Subbu decided to head back home.

"Maya, I am going home. Let your mother know."

Maya looked up, but did not confirm whether she was going to let her mother know.

•

Premonition is a powerful human instinct. As Subbu inserted the key to the Second Home, he got this strong feeling and was filled with dread. He threw the door open and realized that his instinct had been right.

Chandra was lounging upon the sofa with a drink in one hand and the TV's remote control in the other. When the door opened, he threw a nonchalant look at Subbu and said, "Hi."

Chandra had gone to school with Bharat, and was a very close friend. He had a key to The Home and the Second Home with which he let himself in. He had an apartment not too far off from the Second Home, but barely lived there. If he was not at The Home or the Second Home, he was at his girlfriend's apartment spending the night.

Chandra's relationship with his girlfriend had been going on for some time. He spoke occasionally of marrying her. Yet, Subbu was perplexed that she lived alone in another apartment. Separate bedrooms were bad enough. Separate apartments? It was supremely ridiculous.

Isn't it ludicrous that she lived in an apartment so far away, he joked once with Chandra.

"Yeah," Chandra replied. "It feels so dumb to drive down for a screw. I wish she lived in an apartment next door or in the same building or something."

Chandra had a decidedly androgynous look. He had fixed his teeth and tweezed his eyebrows into arches. He wore a diamond stud in one ear. Only the tip of his ears could be seen, since his hair flowed to cover most of them. His tee-shirt revealed the compulsory biceps and triceps.

Subbu did not have high regard for Indu's opinion. But she once described Chandra as "a beautiful man" and that pleased Subbu. He could not have described Chandra more appropriately.

As he tried to begin a conversation with him, Chandra "shshhhhed" Subbu with a finger on lip.

Only then Subbu noticed that Chandra was watching a show on TV that featured him. He was walking down a ramp with a shirt that was half open. His impressive muscular torso was highlighted by the clever lighting. His chest was clean shaven. He was followed by man after man, all displaying clean shaven torsos. No trace of any body hair. Subbu slipped his fingers into his shirt and gingerly massaged the gray, gruff hair on his chest. He felt overdressed.

Chandra was a model. For a very long time, Subbu was under the impression that Chandra was jobless since he lounged on the sofa for most of the day. If he went somewhere at all, it would be the gym. When he was slouched on the sofa, he would be obsessing over his waist size or his biceps. At times, he would lie down on the carpet and do sit-ups. This agonized Subbu since this was a genuine Persian carpet that a friend had gifted him many years ago.

"Your job is walking?"

Chandra nodded.

"And smiling?"

"Not always. Sometimes."

"And they actually pay you for it?"

"Pretty decent money, man." Subbu hated it when he called him "man," but hated it even more when he called him *pantu-thatha*.

Subbu had not yet reconciled himself to the notion of walking, smiling, stopping, and giving the audience a lecherous look as being a profession worthy of payment.

Chandra was now walking down the ramp again with his shirt generously unbuttoned.

Subbu asked an absorbed Chandra innocently, "Were there no buttons on your shirt?"

Chandra said indignantly that there were.

"Then why didn't you button up?"

"How would I then display my gorgeous muscles?"

"Then why not remove the shirt?"

"This is a fashion show about shirts, not about muscles."

Presently the fashion show ended and Chandra switched channels. He stared vacantly at an advertisement for a new brand of tamarind. A woman appeared displaying generous cleavage. She stooped without much provocation to dip her finger into various dishes, suck it, and become rapturous. At the end of it, she held up the tamarind packet for prominent display as the camera zoomed in.

Subbu was suddenly in the mood to try and get under Chandra's skin. While he believed that Chandra's biceps were bigger than his brain, he liked him as a sparring partner. He fell, unfailingly, for every taunt. Chandra was a pestilence that you couldn't get rid of. But he could be avoided when required, by moving into the bedroom. The TV and the living room were his territory. He seldom budged. Besides, you could say anything to him. He had infinite patience.

"What do you think the advertisement had to do with tamarind?" asked Subbu.

"I thought it did a splendid job of advertising the tamarind."

"What has tamarind got to do with a woman's cleavage?"

Chandra gave Subbu a look of contempt. "Heard of subliminal recall? Every time you eat this brand of tamarind you'd think of cleavage. It would not be just taste, but titillation also." He licked his lips and shuddered orgastically. "Man! Very clever brand building."

Indu entered the room with Maya. Indu always regarded Chandra like a lizard on the wall. Except that you don't say "Hi" when you open the front door and see a lizard in your drawing room. Nor do you occasionally take it out for dinner with your husband. "Hi," she said.

Chandra returned it and asked, "Where's Bharat?"

"He has some work. Should be back any time now."

"Shall we go out to eat?"

Indu thought about it. "Maybe Aaya has cooked already?"

At the mention of her name, Aaya appeared. "No, I was about to start. Do you want anything special?"

Indu hesitated for a moment. "Why don't you make what Maya wants? Bharat and I have been wanting to go to the new Thai restaurant in Adyar. Shall we?" She addressed her question to Chandra who was quick to nod. Subbu believed that one of the few ways that Chandra could keep himself occupied was by eating out.

Maya, who had been staring at these exchanges from a corner, asked, with finger in mouth, "Mummy, can I come too?"

"Take the bloody finger out of your mouth," Indu ordered.

Subbu felt the blood rising to his head at the mention of the word "bloody." "Look here Indu. Don't use foul language..."

"Okay, okay, *pantu-thatha*. Maya darling, take the finger out of your mouth," Indu said with mock indulgence.

Maya removed her finger from her mouth and repeated her question. "Mummy, can I go out with you?"

"Not today, darling. Maybe the next time."

•

As he was leaving The Home for his walk on Monday morning, Subbu heard the apartment door of the Stick Woman open. From his last recollection, he expected the Plastered Man to step out. Instead the Coiffured Man stepped out and said, "Good morning, uncle. Sorry, I am in a hurry. Got to take a flight." In a moment, he had raced down the stairs.

Going down the stairs, Subbu noticed that the Moon Woman's door was open. The Plastered Man stepped out with his disheveled hair. "Hello uncle," he said, worrying his hair with desperate fingers.

This created serious confusion in Subbu and made him pause. Should the Plastered Man come out of the Stick Woman's apartment or the Moon Woman's? He was very certain of his memory. Today things were different from what he saw last Monday. The world seemed to change very fast.

The Moon Woman was already walking. Her hair had turned completely white. Her glistening white hair gave her a gorgeous halo. In semi-darkness, only her head was evident, bobbing up and down like a ghost head in search of the rest of its body. So today was a full moon day, Subbu smiled to himself. And tomorrow would be a no moon day.

His world with remarkably different laws of nature gave him secret pleasure. He would share this with Maya. She would surely enjoy it. Only he had to warn her, never to signal overtly if she saw a full moon or an abrupt new moon.

As he was returning, he saw another woman at a distance: The Cat Woman. He couldn't recall her name. Dorothy? No. Maria? No. Mary? No, no. Marianne? That's it. It was Marianne. He restrained his impulse to cross the road. She would notice it. And anyway she was brazen. She would cross the road and talk to him.

On seeing him, she slowed down. This was going to be a day that she would talk to him. On some days when she came for a walk with a hangover (he guessed), she would walk past him treating him like a complete stranger. When she stopped to talk, she would either be bitterly complaining or would be celebrating existence.

The Cat Woman's life centered on her three cats. When Subbu once repeated the full names of her cats, Bharat said that the cats were named after three handsome, hunky Hollywood actors. At that moment Subbu was at a loss to recall the full names of the American actors. He had to hazard guesses about the cats' first names.

"Good morning, Mr. Subbu," greeted Marianne, the Cat Woman.

She was the only person who ever addressed him that way. Subbu guessed that she was uncomfortable about addressing him *pantu-thatha* that would, in a sense, establish a grandfather-granddaughter relationship between them. Moreover, she was of Anglo-Indian blood or what was left of it, after many generations of marriages between Anglo-Indian families. She did not know enough Tamil to be comfortable with *thatha*.

"Hello, Marianne, how are you?"

"Very fine." She waited for him to continue.

"How's...Christopher?" Subbu pointed to the cat in her arms.

"This is not Christopher. This is Dennis," she corrected. "Anyway, I don't have a cat named Christopher."

Subbu kicked himself for venturing with the names. "Your favorite? The one you've had for years?"

"Oh, you mean Alan?"

"Yeah, Alan, Alan..."

"Mr. Subbu, how many times have I corrected you? It's

Alan, not Christopher."

Subbu prayed that his forgetting the name was not a sign of senility. Let it be deliberate forgetting, please. She had corrected him quite a few times.

"So, how's Alan?"

"Poor bugger. He's blind and old."

Alan was her favorite cat though he had never seen it. She didn't bring Alan with her on her walks. Possibly nobody had seen it.

"But he's my favorite..." she continued.

"It is touching to see such close relationships between people and their pets," Subbu said, acutely worried that something might show on his face that would break his concocted serious expression. "Do you know why this relationship works?"

Marianne shook her head.

"Because pets don't fight with their owners. Also divorce laws to separate man and pet have not yet been devised."

The Cat Woman winced for a moment, smiled, then she broke into uncertain laughter. Subbu joined her, thereby releasing his hold on his concocted expression. He had often heard that people start resembling other people they live with over long periods of time. He did not know if it applied to pets as well, but Marianne certainly resembled a cat. Her cat look was pronounced when she smiled. She had a Cheshire Cat's smile, a middle-aged, haggard, Cheshire Cat's. She even had bleached whiskers, which disappeared whenever she chose to wax.

Marianne lived one floor above. Subbu's bedroom window and her bedroom window faced each other. Sometimes when the window was open, lying on his bed, he could catch a glimpse of her undressing. Her bizarre body would come to his mind. It was an inappropriately youthful body on a woman of forty-five at least. Her forty-five years protested against the youthful body in the form of ridges and flab at a few odd places. Never having the courage to stomach a potentially ghastly sight, Subbu would move with far greater speed than his age would permit to slam the window shut.

Some mornings between 1:00 and 3:00 he would come awake. He would then hear the moaning of the cats in Marianne's bedroom. A deep-throated moaning interjected by brief shrieks, a noise that made the hairs on his nape bristle. No, this was not the mating call of cats. Subbu, by now, knew all the familiar noises cats could make. This was a noise whose pitch increased steadily to a frenzy. It felt like the noise produced by scratching your nail on asbestos. The sound bored a hole at the bottom of your spine, traveled upwards in a zigzag path, creating ticklish pain on the way, until it came to rest at the base of your neck where it insisted on pulsating. He knew by experience that once it reached this frenzied height, the noise would die down abruptly to quiet before becoming a series of soft, exhausted moans.

These days, he was awakened by the noise only a few times. More often, he awoke, perhaps by a warning premonition, a little before the noise started. Then he would wait for it to start. Mostly it did according to his expectation. Sometimes it didn't, causing him to twist and turn in bed, and finally leave for his walk without going back to sleep. Once earlier, he had hinted to her about these noises. She closed the topic by saying that her cats were well-trained and domesticated. They wouldn't mew their heads off.

The only way he could prove this was by ringing her doorbell while it was happening. And create an early morning racket in the apartment building. Strangely, nobody else seemed to have noticed it.

Marianne had walked a few paces when Subbu heard her

calling, "Mr. Subbu, Mr. Subbu."

Subbu paused, turned around, and waited.

She had her Cheshire Cat smile on.

Still stroking Dennis, she walked up to him and asked, "You are so regular with your walk. Built like an ox, aren't you?"

While Subbu was fumbling for a reply, she said, "See you around," and resumed her walk in the opposite direction.

He stood waving uncertainly.

•

First came the antique furniture. Purchased from all corners of Madras, they cost a tiny fortune. Then came the expensive art pieces, some kitschy, some subtle. There was a particular painting that had a cane frame and four black vertical lines in oil paint. That alone cost a hundred thousand rupees! A rare item by Madras's famous contemporary artist, Cheeku. Everybody thought it was great, so Bharat bought it without a word. Also, in the financial services community, if you were not a bit of an art collector, your peers didn't count you in. It was mounted with the greatest care on the side wall of the living room.

Subbu cocked his head at different angles and studied it. Dab a brush four times in black paint and streak across canvas. And it mysteriously becomes a profound work of art.

Maya gazed at the painting with her finger in mouth and said reflectively, "Bad drawing."

Bharat was furious, partly because he couldn't disagree with Maya. "Do you know how many people wanted it? I had to fight to get it."

Persian rugs, a complete new wardrobe, and expensive curios were followed by the purchase of a ten acre farmhouse plot with an old house a few miles from the Second Home. It cost Bharat close to half a million dollars. He had to mortgage about twenty per cent of his shares to borrow money for the purchase.

At first, Subbu did not understand how Bharat got the money for these purchases. Surely no man could buy these off a salary however big it might be. In one of his patient moods, Bharat provided an exegesis of stock options, how his shares had appreciated, and how you could borrow money for these purchases by pledging your shares.

Subbu was worried. He also realized that his worries were many times naive. He simply may not have understood the current times enough.

"How do you pay back what you have borrowed?" he asked.

"Oh, that's simple. At any time you can just sell your shares and pay back the money," Bharat replied.

"Well, why don't you do that now?"

Bharat laughed. "What? With the stock market rising everyday? Between one day and another, I would lose millions of rupees if I sold my shares now. It is cheaper to borrow money and buy this stuff. Besides, many of the shares that I have pledged are options. I cannot sell them for at least two or three years."

Now Subbu was a little alarmed. "You mean you have borrowed against shares that are not yet allotted to you?"

"They are allotted. Just that I can't sell them now."

"So why don't you buy all this after those shares are yours. Why buy everything now?"

Bharat gave his indulgent laugh again. "For one, these things may not be available then. They are available cheap now. Two years later, I might sell these properties and my shares at a higher price, and have double profit. Besides, if I buy them only then, I would have lost another two to three years of the best part of my life."

This maze of prospective calculations was getting too complex for Subbu. Like the tongue that unconsciously, but constantly worries the tiny morsel stuck between the teeth, this acquisitive habit worried Subbu.

One morning, Bharat's old car disappeared. In its place stood a gleaming red car.

"It's a Linda," he announced proudly.

Subbu knew enough to recognize Linda as one of the three car companies of the world. It was a complex combination of American, Korean and European car companies. Wave after wave of consolidation had left only three car companies. And it was hard to tell which country these companies belonged to.

Braving the thought that this could be senility, Subbu brought up the idea of buying what one's salary could afford. After all, Bharat was drawing a yearly salary of one hundred and fifty thousand dollars, which was a lot of money.

Because of the expansiveness created by his share price, Bharat laughed. Else, he would have been irritated at the subject being brought up again.

"Don't worry, *pantu-thatha*," he said. "The daily variation in my share price is now equal to what I would earn as salary in two years. Do you know I am quite careful? Almost everybody else in my company is buying assets far more aggressively than I am. I am careful. I watch what others do before I make my investments."

Subbu got a doubt. "If your salary is not for acquiring assets, what's it for?"

"Paying the bills," Bharat announced gleefully.

CHAPTER 4

Indu's father, Kamesh, lived in Adyar in an apartment by himself. After he lost his wife, he had been living alone. A cook helped him with his meals. She also doubled up as domestic help washing his clothes and cleaning the house. Indu had been insistent that he live close by so she could look him up conveniently.

When Subbu once suggested that Kamesh move in with them, Indu had given him her cold, businesslike stare. "He's *my* father. I don't think he would want it. I certainly don't want it. He needs his space and I need mine. And don't get too soft. You don't know the trouble father would give us."

Subbu wanted to retort that there was enough space for everyone in the house, but felt that there would be something inane about that answer. He also knew why she tolerated him when she wouldn't accommodate her father. Bharat fooled himself that it was because of a concession he had beaten out of her in the prenuptial agreement in return for the great ground he had to yield. The truth was Subbu was useful in many ways. He kept home, minded the servants, took care of most of the needs of Maya, and made the quotidian purchases ensuring the home never ran out of supplies. And importantly, Subbu played the foil to Indu, who sometimes wanted it. She couldn't trust Bharat to take tough decisions. Subbu knew this use she had for him, though she had never publicly acknowledged it.

Every other weekend, they would drop into Kamesh's house, on the way from some outing or other.

Today, there was an interminable silence after Bharat rang the bell. So much so that inexperienced callers would suspect that the bell didn't ring and would push it a few times.

Initially the insistent blares of the doorbell in quick succession irritated Kamesh, but as time passed, like he became insensitive to the millions of provocations about him, he learned to ignore the bell. His obesity did not permit him to rise from his chair quickly. If finally he managed to get to his feet, his cardiologist's strict instruction that he not move jerkily or too fast prevented him from answering the doorbell or the phone quickly.

When the doorbell rang, he was startled from his doze. He waited to see if it would ring again. Maybe it didn't ring at all. He saw dancing shadows under the door and cursed. So the doorbell *did* ring. He rose slowly, struggled to get his swollen feet into Hawaiian slippers and shuffled with his hands to get his glasses.

Damn! Where were the glasses? Not on the table, not near the TV. He noticed the vague form of the glasses at his feet, something he could not see clearly because his pot belly obscured his view. They must have fallen off his nose when he had dozed off.

Balancing himself with one hand on the centre table, he knelt carefully for he could not bend to pick up his glasses. With the other trembling hand, he picked up his glasses and perched them awkwardly on his nose, half expecting the bell to ring again. It did not. Must be somebody he knew. Dragging one swollen foot after the other, he edged to the door.

"Hello," said Bharat.

"Hello, Dad," said Indu and proceeded to walk past Kamesh into the apartment.

Kamesh had to strain his eyes to see that Maya and Subbu were standing behind waiting for his invitation.

"Oh, come, come!" said Kamesh working up as much hospitality as he could. "Maya *kutty*."

Maya stood her ground clutching Subbu with one hand with the finger of her other hand in her mouth. She was as uncertain about Kamesh as she had always been. Every time she would begin doubtfully, and slowly warm up to him before Indu would say it was time to go. Maya had to start over the next time.

"For God's sake, take the finger out of your mouth," Indu ordered before she stepped in.

"No. Don't yell at her." Kamesh rushed to Maya's rescue.

Subbu watched this with amusement. Not the Kamesh he had known some years ago. Not the Kamesh that got his daughter reluctantly married to Bharat.

Subbu didn't really care much for Kamesh. Kamesh had been the chief executive of a German company's Indian arm when Indu got married. He had unreserved contempt for the likes of Subbu and Krishnan. They were not "winners." With such great intellectual wherewithal, what an anticlimax that Subbu ended up being a government servant and Krishnan, a college teacher. He did not like even their names. Too old-fashioned. In fact, he did not like the name he had been given: Kameswaran. It did not suit his aspirations. As soon as he graduated, he truncated his name to the more elegant Kamesh.

To Kamesh, life was about winning. Sometimes, at any cost. He urged his son, Raj—his older one—and his daughter, Indu to win. Win at school, at college and at work. And so they won. Raj went to the US, graduated with an MBA from Stanford, and was a senior executive with a semiconductor firm. And Indu, how she won. Against all odds. She was a real fighter. They did him proud.

The image of Kamesh, walking around with a bow tie and a liquor glass in hand, during the engagement of Bharat and Indu, came back vividly. The smirk on his face, the murmured apologetic remarks to his friends about what a simpleton family his daughter was marrying into ("but, the boy—he's a winner"), his braggadocio about Indu's achievements in India and Raj's achievements in America, his not so discreet inquiry into the asset base of Subbu's family.

Now, the shirt with a frayed collar, food-stained pajamas, a grimy sofa set, a bedspread that required washing, and hemorrhoids that badly needed mending. Indu was embarrassed and irritated that her father kept inquiring of whoever would care to answer, what one should eat to make stools soft. Whatever happened to his capacity for intelligent conversation?

After they were seated, Indu inspected the dining table. There were some covered dishes with food cooked presumably for lunch.

"Is that your dinner?" Indu asked.

Kamesh nodded. "Cook wanted half a day off. She asked me to manage with the same food for dinner."

"The bitch," Indu fumed. Subbu winced, and Kamesh sighed.

"Indu, please don't use such language." Kamesh's admonition seemed more for observing civilian courtesies to Subbu and Bharat.

"I'll call her just what I want," said Indu. "When I hired her, I had clearly told her that she could not take off for more than ten days a year. Now this is the fourth time in the month that she has taken off."

"No problem for me. I'll just microwave the food. It becomes as fresh as just cooked food."

"The trouble with you is that you can't keep this woman on a tight leash. Now you are consoling yourself that microwaved food is as fresh as new," Indu criticized.

"I have tried reasoning with her," Kamesh drawled. "If she won't listen, what can I do?"

"The problem is you can't manage her. You must be tough and tell her that she'll lose her job if she doesn't watch out," Indu said piously.

"And then do what? If she leaves, who'll cook for me? Not you," Kamesh said with another long sigh.

"Listen, I can't solve every problem of yours. Eat cold food if that's what you will do."

"I didn't want to you to solve this problem. You started it all."

Subbu's mind was racing for some diversion. Luckily, Indu stopped.

The lull was broken by Kamesh clearing his throat. "I received some email from my son, Raj. I am really worried about him. Did I mention it to you before?"

Devastating dotage.

During every meeting, in the last eight months or so, Kamesh had mentioned his son to Subbu. Subbu quickly searched his mind intensely to check whether he repeated himself similarly.

"The boy is two and a half years older than Indu. He is wedded to his job. Every time I raise the issue of his marriage, there's a quarrel. I wish he would at least pick up the phone and quarrel. He writes me nasty email and refuses to talk on the phone."

Subbu knew what would come next. After leaving for the US, in the past twelve years Raj had come to India just once. That too for a period of seven days and somehow endured his father. Most of those seven days, he was out partying or visiting.

"You know what? After leaving for the US, he has visited me just once. In twelve years. That's okay. As long as he gets married. How long can a man be single?" He dropped his voice. "Abstinence for such a long time can even hurt his health, you know."

Subbu suppressed a grin and recognized another unmistakable intimation of incipient senility: inexplicable naiveté.

"I have told him. Marry anybody, any caste from India. Any Indian girl is okay. I'll look for girls for you if you don't find the time..." Kamesh continued.

"Dad." Indu was exasperated. "You have said this a million times to *pantu-thatha.*"

When they got ready to leave, Kamesh realized that he had not spoken much to Maya. He went into his kitchen and produced a packet of Marie biscuits for her. She shrank behind Subbu who told her sternly, "Take it, Maya."

He insisted on hobbling to the car with them. As Subbu was about to close the car door, Kamesh asked, "This *rasthali* banana, does it soften stools or harden it? Every fellow seems to have a different opinion."

•

Maya's love for nature was evident even when she was ten months old. She would lean towards the garden, ready to fall off Subbu's hands if he did not move in the direction of her leaning. Once in the garden, she would stare at each flower. Then she would wrinkle her forehead, knit her brow, and with Herculean labor articulate "*poo*." Flower. She could produce no noise. Just a tiny stream of air.

Subbu had wondered why babies had such a great problem pronouncing this elementary syllable. Krishnan had it and so did Bharat. By experience he knew the remedy. But he offered it only after enjoying Maya's tortured expression in somehow ejaculating *poo*.

"It's okay, baby. Call it *aapoo*, if you cannot say *poo*," he advised her and then demonstrated, "*Aaapooo...aaapooo*."

As inexplicably as these babies could not pronounce *poo*, they could pronounce it with a leading syllable. She looked at Subbu with doubt and outrage. You can't pronounce it differently every day. However with constant reassurance from him, a sense of relief came over the ten month old's face. In a few tries, she could articulate *aapoo* with noise. Her earlier muted excitement at seeing flowers turned to articulated joy as she methodically said an *aapoo* for every flower she sighted. Only after she was three could he wean her off *aapoo* and make it *poo*. He found that he had to wean himself away too since he had started using *aapoo* extensively in conversations with her.

Maya was fascinated by nature's imperfections. The flower that would wilt, the lake with its jagged edges, the withering bark of the tree, the faint autumn yellow that tinged the trees confirming that their green wasn't permanent.

Even though it was a Friday, they had shifted to the Second Home. The gym that Indu went to was close to the Second Home, and she was scheduled to come home early from her office to go there.

When Subbu answered the doorbell, he found Aaya and Maya. Maya had returned from her dance class.

"*Pantu-thatha*, let's go, let's go before mother comes," she urged him.

Subbu had promised her a walk to the nearby park.

She would visit her trees. Each had a name and would participate in a conversation with Maya which to strangers would appear to be a soliloquy. She would stop to scrutinize every flower on every flowering plant. Her final act before returning would be to swing in the rope swing suspended from the banyan tree by the fishermen children. She would whoop with joy when Subbu pushed the swing higher and higher into the air. One of the few situations in which her finger would be out of her mouth, and both her hands would clutch the rope for dear life.

Aaya fidgeted with uncertainty not knowing whether she should be a part of this conspiracy. She muttered some excuse about tending to the cooking, and withdrew from the scene.

Subbu asked Maya, "Don't you have some other class to go to?"

"Yes, a karate class. But I am so tired after dancing. Also, karate is a bore."

Any hopes that they would go for a walk were dashed when Indu arrived a little early. With mild irritation, she slapped the air-conditioner on and went on to close the windows.

"Love you sweetie," she addressed Maya absent-mindedly. Then suddenly remembering, she started to say something.

Maya beat her to it. "Mother, can I please skip my karate class today?"

"Why should you? I have come early so I can go the gym and drop you at the karate class. On my way back, I can pick you up."

Indu had enrolled for classes at the gym, swimming classes, and piano training.

"The child's tired. I thought I would take her for a walk," Subbu interceded.

"Why should you go for a walk now? There's plenty of other time for it. Let her go to the karate class now."

"Why don't you let her off this karate class? Maya finds it very strenuous and boring," Subbu recommended.

"No, no. These days there are wonderful opportunities for people to learn a lot of stuff. Besides, karate is important for self-defense. You need to know things like this."

"Then can I skip my skating class tomorrow?" Maya asked hopefully.

"Not a chance. You are just beginning to pick it up."

"I wonder why people should go to so many classes. You should go if you have a passion for it. An instinct for it. You shouldn't go merely because you can afford it. Or even because you can do it well, if you don't like it." Subbu did not speak to Indu pointedly. He was facing the duplex upstairs when he spoke.

Indu gave him a glare.

"So it's you who's been giving her ideas," she accused. "No wonder her teachers think that she lacks appropriate social skills. She never seems to be doing what other children are doing, and *pantu-thatha* you are constantly encouraging it." Then to Maya, "Why don't you go to the terrace and at least practice your karate steps? What would you do, if you didn't have to go to the class, but couldn't go for a walk?"

At this stage Aaya started developing a tremor. Maya might just say that she would play snakes-and-ladders with an old Tamil board that Aaya had been preserving carefully since her childhood. When Indu and Bharat were not around, they would both play snakes-and-ladders with loud battle-cries. When you were tantalizingly close to the winning square number 100, the largest black serpent lying close by invariably struck you savagely, plunging you into a giddy descent to square number four. Would Maya give the game away?

"Maybe I would paint," Maya said, avoiding the question about practicing her karate steps.

Aaya heaved a sigh of relief, making a mental note to explicitly instruct Maya never to tell her mother about snakes-and-ladders.

Indu gave Subbu and Maya a look of despair. "All right. Go for your walk. I am going to the gym. I am already late." Her urgency to visit the gym led to this quick resolution.

Cheerfully, wearing their shoes, Maya and Subbu left for their walk. Once at the swing, Maya would play hide-and-seek and hopscotch with the fishermen children. Her finger would be out of her mouth then, too. Subbu wondered what Indu would say if she heard of Maya's association with the fishermen children.

•

When Subbu and Maya returned, Bharat was sitting in the sofa with a drink in his hand. Subbu knew he had a drink or two every evening. But this was too early. Also, usually he would look with fervor at the stock quotes of the European markets. Today his face was flushed. Subbu knew something was the matter.

"Wash your feet and do your homework," Subbu ordered Maya and then turned to Bharat. "What's the matter? You don't look all right?"

Bharat took a moment to acknowledge he was being spoken to. "Huh?"

"I said you don't look all right. Is anything the matter?"

Bharat didn't resist. "Do you know Keshav?"

"Your best friend at office?" Subbu asked kindly.

"No, not he. That's Mangal," Bharat said impatiently. "Keshav is the idiot I used to talk about who gifted his shares to his in-laws thinking they might never appreciate?"

"Oh, that chap," Subbu recollected. "Of course. What's with him?"

"Well, he disappeared today," Bharat announced.

"Disappeared? What do you mean? Was he kidnapped?"

"No, no, no. He was fired. For inefficiency. He was called last evening before close of work by the boss. Apparently he was told that his performance was not good. He was asked to clean out his drawers and leave."

"So where did he go?" Subbu asked.

"Don't know. The company won't tell us where he is gone. The chap! I have known him for almost five years. He doesn't tell anybody where he is going. His mobile is disconnected. Nobody answers his home phone. He just disappeared."

"Maybe he would come back to get his final settlement at office?"

Bharat shook his head. "When they fire people, they transfer the final settlement money into your account. They don't want the guy to spend another moment in office. Everything's done. Settled. His name's removed from the records. Kaput. The guy's gone."

This abruptness and finality surprised and also worried Subbu. He was well acquainted with people resigning or retiring, but not being fired. During his entire service, he had seen only one firing. There was a ceremony around it. Notices proclaimed that the person's services were being terminated on grounds of "moral turpitude." The termination was preceded by an inquiry that lasted nearly a month. The poor fellow had to hang around office for some weeks for his set-tlement. Talk about this incident didn't cease for six months.

And the man Subbu saw fired didn't disappear from the face of the earth. With some effort, Subbu was confident he could trace the man today. Except that he hated the fellow. In Subbu's time, nobody had ever been terminated for poor per-formance.

"So what's wrong with Keshav going? I suppose all com-panies do this. And yours is an American company. Why should you be surprised?" Subbu asked.

"A guy can't disappear just like that. He was a part of our scenery, our lives. Nobody, just nobody, wants to talk about it. Everybody pretends that the guy never worked here. They look at me as if I am daft when I ask questions about him. Hell, he was there for five years." Bharat's tone was high pitched as he poured himself another drink.

"There's nothing to be so excited about," Indu announced, appearing from her bedroom. "I am sure Keshav was expect-ing this. He'll surface some place soon."

"But you can't lose friends this way," Bharat protested.

"Don't make friends at work," Indu advised. "That's why I never make friends at work. You never know who'll stay and who'll go. That includes everybody from the chairman to the office boy. Practically fifty per cent of the people who work with me every year are gone the next. You met acquaintances on planes and trains. Now you meet them at work. That's the difference. You talk with them for a while. You smile at them, and offer them what you are eating as long as they sit opposite you. Once the station comes, you say goodbye and keep going. Oops, forgot to ask even the name, was an inter-esting guy, sigh." She stopped to shrug and continue. "Don't get fussed up about your friends at work. Also, you don't know who'll misuse information about you. If they think that they can save their jobs by spilling your secrets, they will."

Bharat became a little tense at this. Does Mangal know too much?

Subbu hadn't realized Indu had come back from her classes. "I am sure..." he started and was interrupted by the doorbell.

Bharat and Indu froze. For a conspicuous second, there was silence.

"Are you expecting somebody?" Bharat asked Indu.

She shook her head.

Bharat looked at Subbu. "I am not expecting anybody either. Did somebody call to say he would be coming?"

Subbu shook his head.

"Then who could this be?" Indu wondered.

The pronounced reaction at the doorbell ringing had initially perplexed Subbu. Later, he started watching it with amusement. He had lived in a world where the front door was always left open. There was traffic through it all hours until it was shut ceremoniously in the night before retiring to bed. Until then, neighbors peeped in without stepping inside to exchange remarks about the latest movie, the current chapter of popular writer Sujatha's novel in *Ananda Vikatan*, and the local MLA's reprehensible mischief. Numerous callers, from the spinach-selling woman to the milkman, would constantly darken the doorway. Seldom did the doorbell ring. The arrival at the doorway was so noisy that it would summon you from inside, if you didn't already notice the person because you were sitting in the hall.

Knowing that Indu and Bharat would take a few more seconds to thaw out of their inexplicable petrifaction, Subbu got up to get the door.

It was Chandra.

He didn't bother to greet anybody. He just sat himself on

the sofa and started switching channels.

"You didn't say anything," Bharat complained to Subbu.

"What can I say?" sighed Subbu. "The moving sword cuts, and having cut, it moves on."

Bharat looked frustrated by Subbu's comment.

Chandra perked up. "What's this about?"

Bharat repeated the Keshav story to him. "Keshav was a good guy. He may not have been a great performer, but he had a terrific sense of humor. Liked to meet him now and then. Cleaned out his drawers and disappeared. Another fellow has even taken his desk."

"Cool," said Chandra.

Subbu did not know what was cool about this. So he asked Chandra, "What's cool about this?"

Chandra was surprised. "What's cool about what?"

"You said, 'cool' and I assume you said that about Keshav getting fired."

"Oh, that's just an expression, man," drawled Chandra.

"I thought you used that expression only to describe good things," insisted Subbu.

"Well, not really. God, sometimes it's so scary. Keshav must be feeling a little lonely and scared," remarked Chandra.

Subbu was pleasantly surprised by the rare flash of brilliance.

"Fear and loneliness. And for some, money. That's what's left, isn't it?" Subbu asked in the general direction of Bharat and Chandra.

Chandra grimaced. "Don't start lecturing, *pantu-thatha*."

"You don't want to face it, do you? Or perhaps you don't even think of it," Subbu persisted, but quietly.

"How can you say that? About loneliness and fear?" Chandra impugned.

"Of course, you are lonely. We all started out by having

cars and houses full of people. Then it became one family per car and house. Now it is one person per car, per apartment and..." he stole a furtive glance at Bharat here. "...one person per bedroom."

"Well, it gives us all privacy. It gives us space," argued Chandra while Bharat watched with doubt.

"It may as well, but it also makes you afraid. Loneliness and fear. You are afraid all the time. What's the one thing you are sure about? Your job? Your wife or husband, granting you have one. Your children? Your wealth?"

"This is all too deeply psychological," remarked Chandra. His desire to conclude this conversation was evident.

"The problem is we think this has to do with psychology. And then you keep going to shrinks. Has it struck you that the problem could have something to do with economics?" Subbu teased.

As ever, Chandra fell for the taunt. "Economics? How?"

"All this talk about capitalism. The survival of the fittest. Of selfishness. There's nobody to save you. Not the government, not charity. You are responsible for your survival. All very good for business. But we work with it all day. It seeps insidiously into our blood. We then carry it home. There's nobody to save me. I have to be independent of every other person. We create defenses, boundaries, moats. We then become utterly selfish. Nobody exists, but me. Nobody is knowable, but me. Quite solipsistic you would say, wouldn't you? Before we had global capitalism, when there were many safety nets, we didn't have much of this problem, did we? Plausible?"

Chandra pouted his lips and said, "Very complicated. Interesting word you used. What's it? Solip... Oh, forget it," and switched to his favorite channel. He critically appraised the male model on the ramp. "Good biceps. Needs a bit of tightening around his waist. But cool hair. And cool earrings. Can I get a drink, please? Bharat, where's your hospitality?"

Bharat apologized and poured him out a whisky, the doubt still remaining on his face.

Subbu decided that their sparring had concluded for the moment. He had silenced Chandra. But the victory was bittersweet.

Of late, things had started troubling Subbu. Earlier he was insensitive to the goings-on around him. Aversion would show up occasionally. Lately, even though his insensitivity was still strong, the aversion bit was growing. He rose to go to his bedroom, but Chandra's voice stopped him.

"Hey, man. I have been thinking about it. You said something about a sword when Bharat was talking about Keshav getting the sack. What did you mean? Moving sword?"

CHAPTER 5

Maya badgered Subbu into joining them on the shopping trip. Her long-standing wish to go shopping for toys had been granted by Indu. She needn't buy anything with electronics in it. She could buy just old fashioned dolls in different garbs, a house-building kit, whatever. Subbu was intrigued by this expansiveness of Indu. It didn't require much probing.

Indu was given a substantial raise after her performance review—a continuation of her winning streak. Her father would be happy. More importantly, she had also cashed-in some of her stock options. She would soon have nearly a quarter million US dollars cash in the bank. Sensing her mother's mood, Maya made a submission that her boon be granted. Under normal circumstances, this request would have been viciously turned down with a possible chiding to Subbu about how he did not teach the child proper priorities. But today,

Indu readily agreed.

Bharat felt a little envious of Indu. She did not bother to check with him, or for that matter with anybody else, whether or not she should sell her shares. She simply felt that she was worth close to a million and a half dollars in stock and that it was a prudent time to convert some of that into cash. Bharat had been dithering painfully over just such a decision of his own for some time now. His colleagues didn't sell and urged him to hold on, too. Fusion Investments shares were still undervalued, they told him. And anyway the shares were still on a roll.

Bharat offered to drive them to the toy store in his new Linda. Initially, Subbu thought he wouldn't go. He later gave in to Maya's fervent pleas.

Maya reveled in shopping for toys, particularly without adult interference. She picked girl and boy dolls, man and woman dolls in attires that were Indian, Chinese and Japanese. Many of these attires could be changed. She bought a doll house that could be assembled. It was complete with tiny cots, dressing tables, a crib, a baby and a tiny feeding bottle. When she saw the tiny feeding bottle that could squirt a minuscule jet of water, Maya squealed with excitement.

The salesman, who materialized with a "May I help you?" tried tempting her with all sorts of electronic contraptions. Disks of the latest three dimensional games, an extremely sensitive joystick that would allow intricate motion control, and a digital assistant that would help her with her mathematics lessons. Maya spurned his offers with great disdain. The salesman just couldn't understand. With her finger out of her mouth, Maya ran from counter to counter picking dolls in human form making sure that they were mute.

When they got into the car, Indu threw an unwelcome surprise at Subbu. "Remember Anushita, Bharat?"

While Bharat tried to remember, Subbu was held in temporary thrall by the name. He mouthed it without sound.

"No," said Bharat.

"My colleague, Anushita?"

"Oh, yes. She traveled with you to Japan once, didn't she?" asked Bharat.

"Same female. She's having a party this evening. Apparently some important speaker has turned up from America. This lady is an expert in marital harmony. Anu has been pestering me to attend the party. She assures me that the speaker is much sought after in the US."

Subbu became alarmed. "Would you drive past The Home to get to this place? Then you can drop me and proceed to the party."

"Don't worry, *pantu-thatha*," Indu placated. "We are going to stay only a short while. I have to get back home by eight. I've invited people to celebrate my raise."

The time was nearing seven. Shouldn't be too bad, thought Subbu. And if she was organizing a party, Indu started preparations early. She would leave quickly.

•

Anu's house had a large hall, which had obviously been rearranged for the party. An impromptu bar had been set up in one corner. Round tables and chairs were positioned around it. Light from the arc lamp reflected off the constellation of jewelry on the men and women, creating a spectral dazzle. Men wore short hair. Women wore short hair. Men wore long hair. Women wore long hair. Hair was slicked back with gel or was shampooed and fluttering in the draft from the air-conditioning duct. The soft buzz of conversation was interrupted regularly by staccato laughter and loud back-slapping.

Anushita, the dutiful hostess, welcomed them in a strapless evening gown. Subbu worried that the gown didn't have adequate support.

"Come on. Come on in. Join the fun," Anu cried. "Meet Tarun."

Tarun, a gray-haired man in his fifties, with a salt and pepper beard eyed Indu lecherously. A reptilian tongue whipped out of his mouth and licked his lips. He picked her hand up, kissed it with an unusually loud smack, gave her a hug around the shoulder, and extended a hand to Bharat. "Hi, I'm Tarun."

After Bharat had shaken his hand, trying not to worry about the loud kiss, Tarun turned to Subbu. Viewing him like an antique, he extended his hand to Subbu. "Hi, I am Tarun."

Whisky fumes assaulted Subbu's nose. It was barely seven and this Tarun already had an unsteady gait. It occurred to Subbu that the last time Tarun urinated, he might not have washed his hands. So he shrank away from Tarun's extended arm, hastily joined his palms and said, *"Namaste."*

Tarun said, "Wow!" and turned to Indu. "I'd like you to meet some really exciting people. Dhruv, Riddhima and Vinty." He led her away into the crowd.

"Hello, Bharat," greeted somebody and led Bharat in another direction.

The silver-haired gent in white shirt with sleeves folded to the elbow and in a starched *veshti* invited many curious stares. Some women were startled into remarking, "cute!"

With Maya clutching his *veshti*, Subbu made his way to one of the round tables. He was careful to select an empty table. A uniformed bearer extended a tray full of colorful drinks which Subbu watched with curiosity for a moment before saying, "A glass of water, please. No ice. And orange juice without ice for my little friend here."

The bearer disappeared and appeared a moment later with their drinks.

Managing an impossible combination of a frown and a smile at the same time, Subbu started gazing. Most men had managed to bare their biceps and triceps and the women, dutifully, had artistically cut holes in their dresses to reveal navels.

It seemed to Subbu that nobody seemed particularly interested in any one person. Except for one or two engaging conversations, most people were flitting around. From one to another after two-to-three minute interludes. It was almost part of the stride. They did not pause to talk. They spilled words occasionally while they were gliding. It all reminded Subbu of Internet browsing and channel switching on TV.

"Please do come home some day." I am not going to give you my address or telephone number.

"Sure, we will." I am not going to ask for it.

The haiku version of such an encounter was waggling three fingers in greeting, working up the most cheerful smile on the face while your feet took you rapidly away from the person you were greeting. The other person reciprocated with equal grace.

Soon there was a commotion in one corner. A crowd had gathered. Subbu asked Maya to stay at the table, and took a peep at the centre of the crowd. There stood a man and a woman slinging drinks and insults at one another. Anu entered the scene to part them in as urbane a manner in which such a parting can be accomplished. She settled them down at different tables. Later, going back home in the car, Indu would sniff, "Husband and wife. Ugly brawls in public. Terrible." Bharat would agree. "Terrible."

Anu requested people to take seats, which they did around

the various tables. Everybody avoided the table at which Subbu and Maya sat. After a brief introduction to the prowess of the guest at marital harmony, Anu announced, "Jane from Atlanta for you, ladies and gentlemen."

Jane was tall with short blond hair. She was dressed in a flowing gown. A thin necklace suspended a rock-sized diamond. The curls over her lips, highlighted under the powerful arc lamps, betrayed her surgery-enhanced face. She must have been in her mid-forties.

"Good evening," she cried. The crowd responded by greeting her back. She refused to take the podium, choosing to walk around, talking through a cordless microphone that was clipped to her dress.

"Okay, let's start." Jane started with a single clap. "How many of you here say 'I love you' about five times a day to your husband, wife, girlfriend, boyfriend, as the case may be?"

There was a hushed silence.

"Four times a day?"

No response again.

"Three times?" Jane had started enjoying this now.

Guilt shaded the faces of the audience.

"Two times?"

A few hands went up. Most people shifted uneasily.

"Once a day?" Jane continued with concocted disbelief.

Abject contrition hung over the crowd while a few more hands went up. Most could not meet the stare of the matrimony evangelist from Atlanta.

Subbu stared back at Jane when she looked at him. For some reason, she shifted her gaze immediately.

"I think I made my point," Jane announced triumphantly. "The problem with most of us is that we do not express our love. To spouse, to even children. Think of it. Think of it, carefully."

Subbu thought of it. He had not said it once. During his entire lifetime. Not once to his wife. How would she have reacted if he had said it? Worriedly, she would have told him, "You were all right even an hour ago. What happened?" and felt his forehead for signs of an insidious fever. If he had said it to Krishnan, his scholarly son would perhaps have moved away terribly abashed, and Subbu himself would have wriggled in embarrassment after this grandiose declaration. He had certainly had his share of arguments with his wife and son, only for each to pull the leg of the other who got angry. Their exact miming of each other would cause peals of laughter. It had not remotely occurred to any of them that their tripartite relationship was questionable in any way.

Jane continued her harangue: "I said 'I love you' once a day to my husband and my first marriage broke down in six months. I said 'I love you' twice a day, and my second marriage broke down in twelve months. Now I say 'I love you' three times a day to my husband, and my marriage is more than eighteen months old. What does this prove?" She paused for effect. "That the number of times we say 'I love you' is inadequate at all times..."

The audience applauded the marital harmony expert.

"It's not that marriage has become an irrelevant institution. It's still very important. It's just that we don't know how to manage it..."

Subbu found this highly tedious.

Indu was nodding in agreement vigorously and even making notes.

He agonized over the "I love you"s he was likely to hear from her for the next few days.

Maya was tugging at his *veshti* saying, "Boring. Let's go home."

Fortunately, the compulsion to go to the next event made

Indu rise.

Bharat followed, with the corners of his mouth hurting from smiling without mirth. If he did not feel like smiling at parties, why did he?

When outside, Indu asked promptly, "*Pantu-thatha*, how many times did you say 'I love you' to your wife?"

"Not once."

"I can't believe that."

"That's the truth."

"Then it's too bad," judged Indu with her newly minted wisdom.

Soon Indu and Bharat were out of earshot leading the way to the car.

"A world of words," muttered Subbu.

"What?" asked a surprised Maya momentarily removing the finger from her mouth.

"Nothing," said Subbu.

●

On his morning walk, Subbu tried avoiding Marianne. Adroit as ever, she cornered him.

As she was approaching with the cat in her arms, his mind raced. What was the cat's name? What was the damn cat's name? Melville? John? Christopher? No, it was certainly not Christopher. That's the name that made her mad. Alan? No, that's the blind one. Then what the hell was it? He got it. Dennis. It was Dennis. He felt triumphant.

"Good morning, Mr. Subbu. How are you?"

"Good morning, Marianne. I am fine. How's Dennis?"

Instead of warming up to him, Marianne frowned. "Mr. Subbu, you don't seem to remember much. This is not Dennis. I left him at home with Alan. This is Prince. See, he has these brown stripes that Dennis doesn't have."

"Yeah, I can see them," he said. Though he stared very hard, he couldn't see what brown stripes she was talking about. Good God, one more name to remember. Prince. So it's Prince, Alan and Dennis. He told himself that he must note it down somewhere. Then he felt irritated. Why should he remember some stupid cats' names? Why is that so important? Stupid cats of a stupid woman.

"Mr. Subbu, did I tell you? From last week, I became a consultant?"

"Well, what do you consult on?"

"Advertising, marketing?"

"Oh," said Subbu. "Who do you consult for?"

"Anyone who needs my services. I have clients, you know."

"What happened to your job?"

"Oh, I gave it up. It kind of got boring, you know. The same thing over and over again."

"I know the feeling. Good luck with your consulting."

"Why don't you drop in some time? For a drink, maybe?"

"I don't drink," said Subbu.

"Not a drop?"

"Not a drop. Never have."

"Wow!" said Marianne. "No wonder you are built like an ox. How old are you?"

"I am going to be seventy-five," Subbu lied with a straight face.

"I can't believe it. Anybody would rate you fifty."

This was not the first time Subbu heard the word "consultant." Many people had told him that they were consultants. He did not understand this designation. During his days, people were professors, general managers, sales managers and surgeons. These days many people who had a job were designated a "consultant."

95

He was a little late from his walk since he left a little late. Also, he stopped for a while to gaze at the rain clouds that were gathering in the east. There must be some depression over the bay. Somebody whirred past him. The moon was black and white today.

It was almost seven when he came back to the apartment complex. The frenzy of going to work had taken over. Coat tails flying, half-eaten sandwiches in hand, shoes being worn on the walk, office-goers struggled to beat time as children stumbled down the stairs sleepy-headed to clamber into the vans waiting for them and impatiently honking. It appeared to Subbu that he was moving in slow motion, deliberate and without purpose, while the environment around him was a haze of color. It suggested to him an absurd reversal of Charlie Chaplin sequences where Chaplin would be moving at top speed while the environment was placid.

Getting inside The Home, Subbu ached to turn off the air-conditioner and open the windows. He would have to wait. Indu was not gone yet.

Bharat was barking that morning's commands to BOREBO and sipping from the coffee mug.

"Hey, Bharat. I met this Marianne on the way."

"Which Marianne?" asked Bharat.

"She lives in this block. One floor above," Subbu said with mild irritation.

Bharat shrugged. "I don't know many people who live here. Never seen most even once. Anyway, what's with her?"

"She says she became a consultant. What's a consultant?"

"Oh, she must have lost her job. Anybody who loses his job becomes a consultant."

•

Both Indu's company and Bharat's company required them to undergo an annual medical check before they could be covered for medical expenses. Since Subbu was a dependant on Bharat, he had to undergo the tests, too.

That afternoon they visited their general physician. There was a long queue. Bharat sat in a chair clutching the test results, while Indu flopped in the chair next to him. Subbu stood by the window gazing at the street below. It was going to take at least forty-five minutes before their turn.

In a few minutes, Bharat with his chin tucked into his neck had gone to sleep. So had Indu except that her head was lolling backwards and she had her mouth open a slit. She was even snoring softly.

Weekdays were for work. You worked late, sometimes not even returning home for the night. Weekends were for partying. No sleep till two in the morning. The connection between nighttime and sleep had become very slender.

Bharat and Indu spent the whole day nodding in sleep when they got five minutes at a stretch without programmed work. In cars, at beauty parlors, and sometimes on toilet seats. Subbu sighed at Bharat's gentle snoring.

Earlier, we begged for food. Now, we beg for sleep. One way or other, we are still beggars.

"Bharat," the attendant announced. No response as Subbu watched with concern. "Bharat!" in a sterner tone woke him up. He shook Indu awake, who woke up with bleary eyes, stretching herself.

"HDL is not high enough. LDL is a little high. Mr..." the doctor paused to locate the name. "...Bharat. Mild cholesterol problem. Does it run in the family?"

Bharat turned to Subbu.

"Not that I know of," said Subbu. "Of course, we never tested."

"Not to worry," said the doctor. "We'll try some dietary changes. Avoid fried food and red meat. Shift to olive oil, if you like it. Plenty of leafy foods. Tea and apples are said to help. Let's watch for about three months. If that won't work, we'll put you on cholesterol reduction drugs. No great bother. Many people your age take these things daily."

He examined Indu's results. "Your cholesterol is normal. Your sugar is borderline. Family history?"

"Father's a diabetic," Indu confirmed.

"Well, you have to be careful. Not yet time for medicines. Avoid direct sugar in food. Take long walks. Cut out liquor...all right, all right. Reduce intake if you can't cut it out. Same thing. Let's watch for three months."

He then turned to Subbu. "Yes, sir. Let's take a look at your readings." For a long time, he stared at the papers over his glasses. "Except LDL, which is also only very marginally above normal, everything's perfect. Can't find a thing wrong. Ever done a treadmill?"

"Doctor, we live on the fourth floor. Never once taken a lift. I usually run up the stairs, not walk. Do you think I need a treadmill test?"

The doctor laughed. "Oh, yes. I remember now. You've told me that before. No, I don't think you'll need a treadmill. That would be a waste." He turned to Bharat and pointed to Subbu. "Your father?"

Bharat shook his head. "No. My grandfather."

"Oh. Yes, you've told me that last time. Well, even I don't have his readings. Good luck and see you after three months."

On the way, Indu wanted to stop by and see Kamesh. She had been waiting to announce her latest raise to her father. She waited impatiently as he took his usual time to come to the door.

Kamesh heard out Indu's description of her achievements

and her quantum raise.

When she was done, he said, "My computer's not working. The technician came and set it right. It worked as long as he was here. The moment he left, it's complaining of some memory problem or something. Now he says he will offer only telephonic assistance. I can't hear well over the phone. Can you get somebody to see it?"

"I have to call the same number as you do," said Indu with irritation.

Kamesh turned to Subbu. "You know email is the only way to keep in touch with my son. My computer's been down for the last week. Now I don't know what he is up to."

"Dad, you haven't said anything about my promotion."

"That's good," said Kamesh listlessly. "Subbu *saar*, I may have said this to you before. This chap, how long will he remain single? Look at Indu, she's married. Settled. I have now told him, not any Indian girl, any girl is okay. Whether she is American, Spanish or German. My tummy's gone. Been having problems for the last three days." At the mention of "tummy," Indu braced herself, but the storm blew over. "My computer's down, my feet are swollen," continued Kamesh. "What am I to do?" and laughed weakly.

Subbu smiled politely.

Kamesh fell silent while Indu stared expectantly at him.

"Dad." Indu broke the silence since Kamesh seemed to have no idea of doing it. "You haven't said much about my raise."

"I told you, it's wonderful," said Kamesh before falling silent.

"What is it, Dad?" Indu asked. "What's wrong? Is it one of those days?"

Her father continued his silence.

"Look. You have a fully furnished apartment, a cook and a

chauffeur. What are you complaining about?" she demanded.

Her father looked away.

"Loneliness, is that it?" Indu demanded again.

Kamesh nodded. He had been staring at his feet all the time.

"You asked both of us to focus on winning. And on success. Your son is winning. So am I. We did your bidding. Now you don't have a kind word for us. Don't complain about your loneliness. You are so full of self-pity, so self-centered."

"Don't talk to your father like that," chided Subbu.

Indu now directed her ire at Subbu. "Stop lecturing, *pantu-thatha*. Why am I always wrong? It's not just me, is it? The young are always wrong, the old are right. Isn't this about that?"

"They live in dread of all appeals that might interrupt their long communion with their own desires." Subbu's tone revealed his muted provocation.

Indu whirled around. "*Pantu-thatha*, I am sure you didn't think that up. Somebody else said that."

"Even if I gave you another century, you wouldn't discover who said it," Subbu said with bitter jubilation.

He felt that a sneering remark from him entitled the other also to one. In fact, he quite enjoyed the provocation he caused and the ensuing debate. All along Indu appeared to tolerate him; maybe tolerate was the wrong word for toleration takes effort. Thanks to adequate space and money and very little time, Indu's world and Subbu's world did not intersect most of the time. If they did, they did so with the spark of sneering remarks sizzling and arcing through the points of contact.

•

Frankly speaking, Bharat did not like living in apartments. He had always wanted an independent home with a garden to tend to. He still carried memories of the old house where the Second Home now stood. Under the pressure of Indu, and the advice of his friends who considered retaining an individual house within city limits the greatest of follies, he demolished that beautiful house and converted it into an apartment complex. The sale of the remaining apartments left him significantly richer. He used most of the money to buy The Home that they had lived in on rent for a long time. Then, an independent house had seemed difficult to maintain. After the demolition, much as he yearned for it, an independent house remained an unreachable ideal.

With his stock options, things changed. On his half-a-million dollar farm, he could now have an independent house and lots of space around it. He could walk around, on a walking track, listening to music as he pleased. If he said this to Indu, she might dismiss his desires as philistine, like she dismissed Maya's.

"*Maharajah* wants so much space around his house that he could walk around," she once said.

She could never understand the long walks he wanted to take (but never took), by the seaside, with no particular aim. She could think of a walk as only an exercise. And anyway if you wanted to exercise, you went to a gym.

When the real estate salesman (whom Subbu insisted on calling "a broker") brought Bharat first to see the property, he instantly fell in love with it. One part of the land was a wooded wilderness. The other end had a flourishing orchard of guavas, papayas and pomegranates. Between the two spots was white, pristine sand—amorphous and caressing the feet.

Bharat longed to own this Eden. The price scared him a bit. As he drove back home, and as his love for the place oozed out of his heart, the ass with prickly hair and its sideways grin bothered him. Much as he tried, he could not shoo it away. He agonized over four sleepless nights and made up his mind only when five of his colleagues with much less stock options bought bigger farms.

The farm did have a house which was dilapidated. The architect was clear. There was no point in attempting a renovation. The existing house was falling to pieces. Bharat was glad that the architect had resolved his dilemma. Now he could charge forward with his desires.

The house had to be at least five-thousand square feet. Everybody would get in everybody else's way if there were less than that. It would have to have marble or granite flooring. He poured out the tiny details that had been gathering, one at a time, for the past few years.

When the architect revealed his first-cut plan, he announced, "Mr. Bharat, this is going to cost you nothing less than sixty *lakhs**. And this is minus landscaping and other costs. Is that okay?"

Sixty *lakhs*. A hundred and forty thousand dollars, nearly.

Bharat asked to be excused briefly from the meeting. He called Sunil on the phone. Sunil had become an important character in Bharat's life after he got his stock options. He was his relationship manager at Bharat's new found multinational bank. The bank fawned over Bharat since he was a "high net-worth customer" in the bank's language. Sunil had been named to take care of the entire asset management tasks of Bharat. When Bharat finally made up his mind to buy the farm, Sunil mortgaged a large portion of his shares, and almost instantly produced half a million US dollars cash in his account. At any time, in the past, his bank account had con-

* One *lakh* equals 100,000 Rupees

tained no more than twenty thousand dollars. It was a heady feeling, having so much cash all at once—cash that could flow like a clear stream, frictionless, and get those elusive dreams.

"Hello, Sunil. Bharat."

"Hello, sir. What can I do for you?" Sunil asked enthusiastically.

"I need some money for building a house on the farm that I purchased. Do you think you can organize some money?"

"Sure. How much?"

"About sixty *lakhs*."

"One moment, please." Bharat could hear Sunil punching on the keyboard. After a minute, Sunil responded. "That would mean pledging another ten percent or so of your shares. Is that okay?"

Bharat had quickly calculated that he would have to pledge ten percent. Except he didn't know whether the bank would give him money for building a house.

"Sounds okay. How long will it take to raise the money?"

"Twenty-four hours. Less, if required."

Bharat whistled. This was great. "Thanks. Will let you know." He confirmed to the architect his intentions to build the house.

"Excellent," the architect nodded. "I will need you to come every weekend for about an hour for a review at site."

Bharat tried to get Indu engaged in the plan for the house and the farm. Besides saying that she would like a gym, Indu was clear "it was his farm and house." She cared to mention her requirements of a gym only because of Bharat's threat that they may spend more weekends there than at the Second Home.

Subbu flatly turned down the request to be involved. "All property is a burden. Only now I am relaxed after giving everything away to you. Besides, these numbers of acres and *lakhs* really faze me. Leave me out of this."

This made Bharat very angry. Nobody would help him. Nobody would rid him of his doubts. He had to depend only on the architect. He asked as many people as he could, and everybody confirmed that the architect was an excellent professional, and therefore he didn't need to look beyond the young man for assistance. That pacified Bharat, somewhat.

•

That morning, after the weekly review at the farm, Bharat drove back to Madras. He had to stop at The Home and pick up Subbu before both of them went shopping. *Pantu-thatha* had to purchase some new *veshti*s and had been pestering him for some time now. His favorite *veshti* shop was in Nungambakkam from where he had been buying for the last forty odd years. He couldn't be persuaded to buy his *veshti*s from anywhere else.

The East Coast Road was easily one of the best-laid roads of Madras. It invited you to step on the gas pedal. The Linda was a sleek animal. It packed the power of a cheetah, but without its jerky motions. The engine was so noiseless that if it were not for the blurred countryside on both sides you couldn't be sure that the car was working.

Subbu was waiting impatiently near the gate.

"I am sorry. Got a little delayed," Bharat apologized as he held the door open.

Bharat wanted to buy a new suit. Fusion Investments' CEO from New York was visiting their office next week. Bharat had to make a presentation to him. He had outgrown most of his suits. Just a jacket wouldn't do for this presentation. He craved to grab the attention of the big man while he could.

The suit he found was more polyester than wool, ideal for Madras weather. Bharat had baulked a bit when he lifted the lapel of the coat and discovered the price tag. Manicini's, Made in Italy, Rs. 175,000, it said. Well, he consoled himself, if it had to be Manicini's he had to pay Rs. 175,000. He checked his wallet to make sure that he had brought his credit card which had a limit of Rs. 250,000.

In the fitting room he tried the suit fastidiously. One of the buttons was about to come loose. This was an outrage. You pay so much for the best Italian brand and they don't care to stitch the buttons on properly.

"No problem, sir," the store manager mollified. "We will have the button sewn in five minutes."

"Munuswami," the manager called.

A sweaty, dark tailor emerged from the recesses of the shop and returned the suit five minutes later with the button firmly sewn. Subbu watched with interest. What did it matter whether it was Manicini's or a local brand? Finally tailor Munuswami or Kuppuswami was involved in the making of the suit.

Not too long ago, Bharat wasn't earning much beyond the price of the suit in a whole year. Now not only did he earn far more in a month, the price of this suit was a tiny fraction of his stock holdings which were now in excess of a million and seven-hundred and fifty-thousand dollars.

The two men finished one round of purchases and walked towards the Linda to put everything in before they resumed.

Subbu asked, "How much less would the suit have cost if you had contracted directly with Munuswami to stitch it for you?"

This question troubled Bharat. "Much less," he had to admit.

"So why did you pay a lot more?"

"Oh! You pay for the brand."

Wearing a stupid look, Subbu asked, "What does paying for a brand mean?"

"Well you pay for the style...the cutting..." Bharat stammered. "*Pantu-thatha*, I don't think you'll understand."

Subbu wouldn't give up. Peering intensely at Bharat's face, he asked, "Now Munuswami knows all that because of his contracting experience with Manicini's. I am sure he moonlights."

Ignoring Subbu's remark, Bharat bent down to open the car door. He could not help admiring the incredibly consistent sheen of his Linda. Its gleam was an imperial announcement of its presence.

As soon as he placed the suit carefully in the back seat, he felt the tug on his trousers. He turned around to face a dirty urchin.

Engrossed in thoughts about his new suit, Bharat had not noticed the boy trailing until he was close to his car. The boy should have been about eight. He had large brown eyes and his hair was bleached by dirt and grime. Through a tear in his shirt a part of his rib cage was peeking out.

The boy's brown eyes and his rib cage stared at Bharat. Bharat's light colored trousers had tell-tale smudges where the boy had tugged.

"How dare you soil my trousers?" Bharat was incensed. He had an important post-lunch meeting.

The question passed over the boy's head. "*Saar*, many days since I ate. Give me something."

The brown eyes bored him. Bharat tried the mechanical shooing. "No change. Go away."

He then became conscious of the boy's posture. The boy stood with his hands on the hips with raised eyebrows conveying disbelief. He almost had a swagger.

106

"Really? You have no change?"

For a moment, Bharat paused admiring the boy's gumption. Then chiding himself, said, "Of course. Do you want me to turn out my pockets for you?"

"Well if you don't have change, give me ten rupees, a hundred rupees—whatever note you have."

"You deserve a sound thrashing for talking irresponsibly like this. A hundred rupees? You must be joking. If you talk this way, do you think anybody would ever give you anything?"

Bharat started walking away. Subbu who had a curious smile on his face took a second to break out of the stupor and follow his grandson.

The boy's brown eyes, his hair bleached by dirt and grime, and his ribs under the shirt, followed Bharat.

Particularly the exposed ribs.

To escape, Bharat pulled out the shopping list and gave it to Subbu. "*Pantu-thatha*, check what else we have to buy."

Subbu took the list but did not read it. "Do you know that a Tamil poet has called children 'pieces of God'?"

There was no reaction from Bharat.

Subbu continued, "Pieces of God begging in the street."

"*Pantu-thatha*, please check what else we have to buy," Bharat repeated his order.

"Why do you think children beg in the streets?" Subbu asked.

Bharat was irritated. He knew if he did not answer this question, it might branch ominously like a hydra into a dozen other questions. "It happens in capitalism. When you choose to make rewards proportionate to the value people create, inequality is the result. Nothing wrong with it. Otherwise we would have had communism or some variant. Which has definitely proved ineffective."

"So what happens to the people who begin on capitalism with nothing in their pockets?" Subbu asked innocently.

"Are you feeling hungry? Shall we get some lunch?" tried Bharat.

"You haven't answered my question," Subbu insisted.

"Oh, well. I guess, eventually, the overall prosperity would improve, lifting everybody over the poverty line. What do you want to have for lunch?"

"When is 'eventually' for this boy?" Subbu continued, wearing his stupid expression.

Bharat chose not to answer.

"So you feel that your capitalism theory explains why children are begging?"

Bharat threw up his hands. "Exactly. Hasn't it helped reduce poverty everywhere? In America? In Europe? Now, can we get something to eat? Please?"

After lunch they came back from their shopping expedition laden with bags that contained a motley mix of goods: milk, green gram, fruit juice, sanitary pads, and cereals.

At first, Bharat did not notice it. He was so laden with bags that he was anxious to unburden himself. Also the bags obscured his view.

It was Subbu who noticed it and exclaimed. Then Bharat also saw it.

There was a gash on the side of his car about four feet long that exposed the steel under the paint.

Now the paint was not so incredibly consistent. The Linda looked a little less imperial.

The steel under the paint seemed somehow like exposed ribs under a torn shirt.

CHAPTER 6

Saturday morning, Chandra let himself into the Second Home quite early. When Subbu returned from his morning walk, as usual, he found Chandra watching TV. He had had a haircut, and had tweezed his eyebrows thinner. A glittering diamond in his ear indicated he had changed his earring, too.

"Hi, *pantu-thatha*," he greeted.

Subbu started worrying. "Chandra, nice haircut. When did you get it?"

Chandra raised his head, caught Subbu's expression, and shook his head. "Man, I know where you're coming from. I got this haircut yesterday, okay? And I had a shower immediately. And for your information, I already had a shower this morning. Brushed my teeth and used breath freshener, okay?"

"You are a sensitive chap." Subbu grinned evilly. "You made my morning. Let me see what's in the papers."

Subbu flopped into the chair and, much to the irritation of Chandra, started reading aloud. He always read the "Matrimonial" section first in the weekend edition. It provided unceasing amusement. The advertisement space for matrimonials had been shrinking dramatically, but still occupied half a page.

"Girl, 31...how can anybody call herself a girl at 31?...employed in multinational bank, IT department seeks Java compatible husband. Boy, 40, seeks girl, preferably J2EE proficient, working knowledge of real-time operating systems desired...Wait a minute? Are these employment ads or matrimonial ads? Okay, they *are* matrimonial ads."

He turned the pages to the "Classified" section. "Hmm. Attention Mothers... The best birthday gift for your teenaged daughter is...breast enlargement implants...act before it's too late..."

Bharat burst in, shutting off his phone. "Thorough rascals," he exclaimed.

"What happened?" Subbu asked.

"I called Linda. They have a twenty-four hour service, but some uncultured idiot answers the phone. When they sell you the car, they tell you, if there's a problem, they'll pick up the car. And they'd give you a replacement until they set it right."

"So?"

"This idiot on the phone, like all customer service representatives, says I have to drop off the car. They pick up only when it has a mechanical defect. Since the car can run, you've got to drop it off. And he says that they discontinued the policy of giving a replacement. And I ask him, how can they do that? Without informing customers. And I am a high net-worth customer. And this is a high-end luxury car, damn you. Where's customer satisfaction?"

"What did he say?"

"He says, sir, this is the best we can do. You don't like it, you can shift to Excel Motors or Kelly. They treat customers like pigs. He's right. Excel and Kelly treat customers quite badly. I threatened to sue him. He says I am welcome to do what I please."

"Are you going to sue him?" Subbu asked.

"Waste of time and money. When there were twenty car companies and a thousand models, that worked. Now with three companies, each worse than the other, there's nothing we can do."

"But I thought you said consolidation was good. You earned a lot of money through this kind of merger, didn't you?"

"I did. I did," Bharat said impatiently. "If I could do something to reverse it, I'd do it now."

"Forget the ideology. What would you do with your car?"

Bharat sighed with resignation. "What can I do? I drive my car down for repairs and ask Indu for rides until my car comes back."

Indu spoke from inside her bedroom. "No late leaving. Until weekend, I leave at six. You are welcome to join me."

"Six? Indu, you are crazy. Please, make it eight."

Indu dismissed Bharat's plea. "I leave at six. If that doesn't work for you, too bad. Get a ride from Mangal."

"Mangal's out of town. Okay, okay. I'll join you. Need to get up at five. Crazy life."

Maya appeared in her nightdress. It was clear that she had brushed her teeth and washed her face. But she hadn't drunk her milk yet. If she had, then there would be a tell-tale moustache, which always got on Indu's nerves.

"Daddy, can I use the Internet?"

"Yes," replied Bharat with ambivalence. "What do you

want to do?" Let her chat, he prayed. Let her look at 3D games. Look up toy sites. The latest child thrillers. Anything, anything, but chess. Oh, please, please.

"I want to play chess."

The blood rushed to Bharat's head. Patience, he told himself, you need patience to handle a problem child.

"All right. Come over."

Maya settled in her chair and started looking for the chess program. She played a decent game of chess, but not a brilliant one. She could not beat the program yet at Level 5, the last but one level, but she knew she was progressing steadily. Last week, she was still losing at Level 4.

"Look Maya, many of your friends are chatting. Do you want to?" asked Bharat.

"No," said Maya with determination. "They are asking each other silly questions and giving sillier answers."

"Maybe it's great fun. How do you know? Why don't you try?" Bharat urged.

"Oh, I have seen them chat. It's quite boring."

Subbu stealthily made his way into the room. He followed Bharat a few steps behind. At some stage, Bharat's cordiality could turn hostile.

"Maybe you should take a look at these new space games. They are quite cool, you know."

"Daddy, I can't concentrate if you keep talking."

Bharat gripped the chair hard, and Subbu could see his knuckles turning white.

"Why the hell don't you try some other game?" Bharat asked through gritted teeth.

When Maya looked up in alarm, Subbu intervened. "Why don't you leave her alone? Let her play what she wants."

"You don't know how to handle a problem child, *pantu-thatha*."

"Don't call her such names." Subbu was enraged. He pulled Bharat aside to let Maya return to her game. He then whispered viciously, "There's nothing wrong with her. And don't keep saying such things in her presence."

"You are partly responsible for this, *pantu-thatha*. You don't see her problem. You don't want to see her problem."

"She has no problem."

The maid entered the room and started swabbing with little concern for this animated conversation. Her swab touched Bharat's foot and he got diverted. "Can't you see we are talking?"

"Well, I have to go to the next house. I can't wait forever. Why don't you finish your conversation in the next room? I've already swabbed it," she retorted nonchalantly.

"What cheek! And always getting between my legs," Bharat exclaimed and stomped out of the room.

For a few years, at the Second Home, they had a maid to clean the house since Aaya was too infirm to tend to house cleaning. The servant came from the fishermen settlement. She was never the same person. Every few weeks, Indu or Bharat would get into a noisy argument with the maid. Following the argument, the services of the maid were terminated. Sometimes the same person returned after a break of a few months—the sheer effect of circulation in the stream of servants.

This servant maid was quite new. It took a few minutes for even Subbu to recognize her. But he was grateful for her intervention. It ended the argument with Bharat. Jaya and Sharada also had arguments, mild-mannered though, with domestic help that they constantly replaced. Some things didn't change. The arguing, churlish maid was a slender thread to the past, an unchanging fixture through the times. A connection to a past that Subbu cherished.

•

When Chandra walked in the next morning, Subbu was reading.

"Quite early for a Sunday morning, don't you think?" asked Subbu.

"Yeah, my girlfriend woke me up early. Didn't have much to do. Had some coffee and a shower. Is Bharat up?"

"On a Sunday morning? You must be out of your mind. Why don't you spend the day with your girlfriend?"

Chandra rolled his eyes. "Spend a whole waking day with her? We'll get on each other's nerves. Sometimes I think she is pretty dumb. But I can't say it, you know."

Subbu nodded. "I understand." Even though he didn't, he felt he lost nothing by this comment.

Chandra watched TV for a while and yawned. He walked behind Subbu to peer at what he was reading. Subbu shut the book, lowered his reading glasses, and waited for Chandra's question.

"Yeow! What's that? Hebrew?" Chandra asked.

"No, it's Sanskrit. Kalidasa."

"Sanskrit? It's extinct," pronounced Chandra.

"It's an extinct language, and it's the best language."

"I don't know," Chandra said, arching his tweezed eyebrows.

"No, you *don't* know," Subbu emphatically replied, then returned to his reading. After some time, Subbu saw Chandra shifting uneasily but decided to ignore him.

"*Pantu-thatha*, I got to take a pee. Can I could use your loo?"

The problem with The Home and the Second Home was that all bathrooms were attached to the bedrooms. Chandra usually used Bharat's bedroom's toilet, and Bharat didn't

114

seem to mind. Today Bharat and Indu were still sleeping. It was only seven. Couldn't wake them up. Couldn't wake up Maya either.

"Yes, okay," said Subbu, even though he hated it.

Chandra had never been inside Subbu's bedroom, so he had to be ceremoniously led there, whereupon Subbu patiently waited outside until Chandra came out of the bathroom, drying his hands with the towel on the towel stand. Subbu made a mental note to change the towel.

"Hey! Who's this?" Chandra remarked at the family photograph.

"The baby with the curly hair? That's Bharat," said Subbu.

"Wow! He was quite cute then. Well, he's cute now too. The girls, they love his chin. Wow, he's had this chin even when he was a baby."

"It's a tradition in our family to keep the chins we were born with. I don't know about yours," said Subbu.

Chandra glared at him.

"And these?" he asked pointing to the others in the photograph.

"My son Krishnan, my daughter-in-law Sharada, that's my wife Jaya. And that's me."

"Hey, *pantu-thatha*, I must say you were quite good looking."

"I *am* good looking," Subbu corrected.

"What's this?" was Chandra's next question.

"That's a bronze statuette. Goes back to the Chola period, I am told. My wife brought it from her home."

"Who is Chola?"

"Some tribe that ruled us at some time," Subbu answered wryly, gazing at the towel he could see through the bathroom door that was a crack open.

"Oh."

Subbu started drumming the book in his hand, inching towards the door.

Chandra was not ready to budge yet.

"And what is this?" He picked up a small glass bottle that seemed to have a curious mixture of soil and rubble in it.

Subbu hadn't wanted to see his house come down. When the demolition was going on, he summoned Gopalan to get him some soil and rubble from the site. The soil, and the walls of his house, all exuded a special aroma. Very faint, but exquisite. He feared that this aroma would disappear in the new building that would appear in place of his house. And his fear was right. The smell just disappeared from the Second Home.

He had tucked away the bottle behind the family photograph and didn't expect anybody to notice it. Once in a while, he opened the bottle and smelled it. It would at once conjure up for him his house with nuanced detail as surely as Aladdin's genie appeared every time he rubbed the lamp—so much so, he often wondered whether the soil or the rubble had some narcotic properties.

"It's special soil. And rubble," he said.

"What's special?"

"This was the soil on which my house was built. Right on this piece of land. That rubble? It's from my house. It's got a special smell."

Subbu took the bottle from Chandra's hand, unscrewed the lid, and took a deep sniff out of the bottle as men sniffed snuff in the olden days. It worked. The stone pillars, the shining red and white mosaic, the Indonesian white cane chairs, and the bench in the garden. He could see them all in vivid detail. The casuarina trees swayed gently in the wind, and in the inner recesses of his ear, the waves crashed sonorously.

He had to wrench himself away as he felt Chandra tugging

at the bottle. Though he didn't have the heart to give it, it was too late.

Chandra smelt the rubble and wrinkled his nose. "Nothing great. You are just imagining it."

Imagine it? Absurd. Subbu felt it in the pit of his stomach. This was not nostalgia, not sentiment. That was too banal, much too common. This was special. Very individual. This was the power of the olfactory to perform a magnificent, sensuous redux complete with its comedies, tragedies and absurdities. Bharat couldn't smell anything in the clothes, now Chandra couldn't smell the distinct soil smell.

What's wrong with people's noses?

Anyway, how could he let a fool like Chandra detect his feelings? But why should he feel embarrassed? Is nostalgia an illegitimate emotion? Should one repudiate sentimental feeling? Was he getting to be more like Chandra and the others? Embarrassed by feelings?

Subbu was confused, but it was important to rebuff Chandra.

"Poetry is dead," Subbu declared.

Not knowing exactly how to react to this Nietzcheian declaration, Chandra shot back, "Deserves to die. It bored me so much during school."

They stood glaring at each other. Chandra's outrage gradually changed to resignation as he prepared to go the living room.

"You want to call me an 'old fart', don't you?" Subbu asked.

Chandra appeared startled. "Well...no...why would I?" he stuttered. "Got some urgent work to do."

Subbu returned the bottle to its place behind the photograph.

•

Back in the living room, Subbu, from behind his book, looked through the corner of his eye. Chandra had fished out a card from his bag and was chewing his pen in intense thought.

"What's that?" Subbu asked.

"Oh, this? It's a Valentine's Day card. For my girlfriend."

"Who's Valentine?"

"I have no idea. Some guy who got me into trouble. All I know is I got to send one."

"What's the compulsion? Don't send the card if you don't want to."

"If I don't send it this time, my girlfriend would leave me. Didn't send one last year, too."

"She would leave you?" asked Subbu with disbelief.

"Man, you are surely smarter than that. Which girl would stay with you if you forgot two Valentine's Days? Got to find a courier."

Subbu got a profound doubt. "You met your girlfriend this very morning. Why didn't you give it to her then? That way, you can make sure she gets it."

Chandra smirked. "Man, you don't have an eye for surprises, do you? Hand over the card? What kind of a surprise is that?"

•

By the force with which Indu slapped the air-conditioner on as she stepped in, Subbu guessed that something was wrong. She methodically closed window after window. Bharat watched her with apprehension. After fixing herself a drink, she accused Bharat of shirking his responsibilities.

"What did I do?" Bharat asked.

"The problem is that you aren't doing enough. Why do I have to go the Parent-Teacher association meeting every time? Why do I have to listen to the music?"

"What's wrong?" Bharat inquired.

"What else? It's Maya."

Subbu had left unobtrusively to close the door of Maya's bedroom. She was busy talking to one of the dolls that she had recently purchased. He slunk back to the living room.

"...her class teacher says her attention in class is poor. She not only doesn't talk much and play with other children, she now doesn't do her lessons well."

"All right. I'll go the next time," Bharat placated.

"You'd better. And I am not talking just about that. You also better do something about her studies. She appears to have become weak in mathematics."

"What can I do? I've forgotten school mathematics," Bharat whined.

"The best thing is to find a math tutor for her. I know a woman who teaches..."

Subbu's blood froze. One more class.

Indu look quizzically as Subbu cleared his throat.

"I have nothing better to do," Subbu began. "After all, I teach her science. I can teach her math..."

Indu cut him short. "I am sure you can, *pantu-thatha*. You are a good teacher. But most of the time you'd talk to her about how learning math is stupid, unnecessary for life. How mathematical equations don't really help. How homework is stupid, how classes are stupid."

Subbu was determined to rescue Maya.

"I promise," he said with the earnestness of a first-time job applicant, "to teach her math, and math alone. I'll take care of this."

Indu hesitated for a moment. "All right, *pantu-thatha*. Then you have to make sure that the next time she is given her grades, math does not become a subject of discussion."

Indu was happy to let go, and Bharat was relieved.

The doorbell rang.

Bharat and Indu froze.

"Are you expecting somebody?" they asked each other. Neither of them looked like moving to the door.

Maya peeped out of the bedroom door and said, "The doorbell rang."

Subbu got up. "Now, don't get started. I'll see who it is."

A lad of about eighteen was at the door. He was smartly attired and had a name badge pinned to his shirt pocket. He carried a box in each hand.

"Sir, any supplies for you?" he asked with a polite grin.

Subbu blinked. "What supplies?"

"Computer supplies."

Not too long ago, if the bell rang, you would have vegetables or milk at the door.

"We don't need anything," Bharat announced from inside.

"Nothing. We don't need anything," Subbu repeated redundantly.

The lad almost clicked his heels together. "Very well, sir. Have a good day."

As he turned to go, something about the lad's name attracted Subbu.

"Excuse me," he called.

The lad turned with surprise. Subbu could read the name badge. "Ramaswamy."

"Ramaswamy. Is that your name?" he asked doubtfully.

"Of course," the lad said with the slightest hint of indignation. Why would I be wearing somebody else's name badge?

"Why is that your name?" Subbu asked, and felt foolish about the question.

"Why's that my name? Uh..." the lad grinned uncomfortably. "That's...that's what my parents named me."

"No. I didn't mean it that way. Why this name? Why not some other name?"

"Oh. Some old custom. My grandfather was apparently a Ramaswamy. They—my parents—want the name to go down the generations. So, here I am. Ramaswamy."

"Oh. Thank you."

"Is that all, sir? Do you need something?"

"Oh, no," Subbu said hastily. "I was just curious."

The lad looked disappointed and turned to go away.

"Wait," Subbu said. "Haven't you forgotten something?"

The lad had the look of "now what?"

"Shouldn't you say 'Have a good day' before you leave?"

The lad grinned sheepishly. He clicked his heels again and said, "Have a good day."

Subbu responded with a smart naval salute.

This was thrilling. A Ramaswamy after how many years? He instinctively felt like calling after the boy, "God bless you," but gave up since it would be inappropriate for a sworn agnostic to say that.

Instead he called out, "Best of luck...Ramaswamy."

The lad looked up from the stairs, a bit surprised. His smile disappeared as he said, "My parents must hate me, don't you think? Otherwise why would they name me Ramaswamy?"

•

Friday evening, Maya was dropped at the Second Home from her dance class. She had been restless ever since. If Indu went out today, Subbu had promised he would take her to the park and to the swing. As expected, Indu left at five to attend an office party.

Maya's friends from the fishermen's settlement had come by. They were playing hopscotch.

"*Pantu-thatha*, can I play with them?" Maya asked.

Subbu was hesitant. But the imploring look made him yield.

Maya scoured the soil for a perfectly flat pebble. She managed to locate a piece of ceramic tile. Picking it up, she waited by the girls to be invited.

"Come on. Join us," they cried.

Maya played vigorously, but was no match for the girls. The girls were generous enough to lose once or twice. Not everyday did they get to play with somebody like Maya.

When it was almost seven, Subbu called out for Maya to finish her game. It was time to go home and also, the light was fading.

With a gently perspiring face, Maya ran excitedly to him and said, "Please, please. Five minutes more."

Subbu was grown-up enough to understand that a child's time of five minutes was approximately fifteen minutes of adult time.

"All right. Five minutes only. Okay?"

The children continued with excitement under the street light. The girls had ended their concessions to Maya and had become all business. They bickered now and then whether the stone fell on the line or inside the box. The girls argued insistently, but in friendly tones with Maya. Maya surprised Subbu by being resolute and maintaining that the stone fell inside the box.

When the fishermen's girls showed no pressure to end the game, Subbu sternly called out to Maya. She understood the tone and completed the game.

"She has a lot of homework to do," he apologetically explained to the girls.

They nodded, but it was clear that they were going to continue the game.

"Don't you have homework?" Subbu asked them.

"We do. But we don't complete it every time," the older girl replied, not taking her eyes off the ground, hopping carefully. "When we feel very bored to complete homework, we just take a punishment. A beating, standing outside the class. Whatever."

The younger girl, who had just finished her turn, walked up to Subbu and said, "*Thatha*, do you know? I learn computers at school. I can do it quite well."

"Really?" said Subbu, lifting his eyebrows.

"Yes." The little girl fluttered her eyelids. "But there's no computer at home. Can I come to your home to work on it?"

At this, the older girl, who was playing, stopped.

"Come back here," she ordered the little girl.

Her peremptory tone suggested that she was the older sister of the little girl.

The little girl cowered away, but persisted with her question. "Can I come?"

She appeared surprised by Subbu's answer. "Everybody doesn't have to learn computers."

As Subbu and Maya were leaving, he could hear the older sister chide the little girl. "How many times have I told you not to embarrass people by asking that kind of question?"

Subbu felt sorry that the older girl had mistaken his remark as his reservation about the little girl coming home.

That night, in bed, Maya asked Subbu to read *Karna* for her again. Half way through the story, all the hopping told on her. She was fast asleep by the time Subbu got to the point when *Karna* incurs the wrath of Saint Parashurama.

What was Maya doing that she should be called a "problem child"? She was doing only what he did as a child. What Krishnan did. Why, what even Bharat did as a child. What every child he knew did. What did they see wrong in what Maya did? You could not see that if you are yourself. You had to become one of them. Which was impossible. Something changed. But what? Exactly when? And why? How did the ringing of the doorbell become a disturbing event?

Lying down in darkness, Subbu wondered why his armor of insensitivity with its Teflon patina of humor didn't seem so strong anymore. Hadn't he used it successfully for so many decades? Why had aversion suddenly taken on a new importance? Had it? These days when he came to sleep, he sensed that things were no longer a part of the great continuum of the even existence he had had until now. The rhythm of his life was now positively disturbed. The nagging thought of what he could do to change his life was a new experience. Until now, he assumed that he had settled down in a pattern to spend the rest of his life. Now he wasn't so sure.

He tossed around restlessly for a while before falling asleep. The mewing sound awakened him. It first appeared in his dream. How much ever he shooed the cat, it wouldn't go away. He came awake with a start. In seconds, he realized that he had left the window open. There was a dim light in Marianne's window. The moans had started. At first soft, they poured out one after another in quick succession, one mew telescoping into the next. Even though he darted to the window to shut it close, the mewing had reached the base of his spine. He stood panting after the rapid effort to close the window. His alarm clock showed 2:30. He reached out for his betel-nut box and tucked a little under his molars. Whenever he awoke in an unscheduled manner, he chewed a little betel-nut. Its juices had a mollifying effect.

The mewing was now muted. Aaya's snores from the corridor seemed louder than ever, but Subbu didn't complain. They helped drown the cats' shrieks. And, Subbu had to admit, the snore did have a lulling effect.

•

Bharat had requested the contractor to bring the granite samples to the farmhouse site. These days work pressure did not allow him too much free time. The architect had informed him that the granite for the floor had to be chosen in the next few days. The farmhouse was already running two weeks behind schedule. Both Bharat and the architect were keen on eliminating further delays.

By the number of cigarette stumps under the architect's foot, Bharat knew how late he was. He ostentatiously glanced at his watch and apologized. The architect wore jeans, and was pacing up and down. He held an unlit cigarette in his mouth.

The contractor laid out the granite samples in the half-constructed foyer. The architect was a man of imagination. He had gone to the trouble of instructing the contractor to bring samples that were two feet by two feet. Most often granite flooring chosen with a palm-sized sample turned out to be a thorough disaster when laid over large floor spaces.

"Do you think granite's a good idea?" Bharat asked the architect.

He asked this question because one of his colleagues had remarked to him that farmhouses should have rugged materials. That polished granite was overkill. Maybe fired granite would be okay, one said. Use terracotta, said another.

The architect displayed a sign of impatience and removed

the unlit cigarette from his mouth. "Bharat, we have been through this before. If you are thinking of rugged materials, my advice is—forget it. The so-called rugged materials are the ones that require a lot of maintenance. They collect a lot of dirt. How often would you use this house? During week-ends?"

"Yes, and maybe during the holidays."

"See. Most of the time you aren't going to be here. Your servants may not clean the floor well when you aren't here. Granite is the only stuff that becomes clean as new even if you haven't cleaned it for weeks. If it's a question of money, let me know. We can use some cheaper material."

The mention of "cheaper material" and money made Bharat bristle. What was the man talking about? The cost of granite would affect the total cost of the farm in the second decimal place.

"Of course, money is not the issue. Just want to make sure that I get the most appropriate things."

Most of the granite samples were garish. There was a red with tiny chips that was attractive. Then there was a grey with black chips that charmed Bharat.

"That," he said, pointing to the grey sample, "is my first choice. And the second choice is that red."

The architect hesitated. "Bharat, I must tell you that the red and the others fall in the same price range. But this grey is expensive. It costs…"

Bharat hushed him. "I don't want to hear about it. Let's go with the grey. Shall we do a quick progress review?"

As they started walking into the farmhouse, bending and leaning to avoid the scaffolding, Bharat made a mental note to check on the markets in the next few minutes. When he left after lunch, the National Stock Exchange was about twenty points plus, and was expected to rise more. Economic

126

data indicated that GDP grew at 9% annualized, much beyond market expectations.

The gymnasium was shaping up well. He had a corner for the aerobics equipment with the billiards table coming up in the centre.

"Shall I confirm the order for the granite, Mr. Bharat?" the contractor asked.

"Of course, my man," Bharat said impatiently.

"How about the bathroom fittings?"

"I thought we were done with that last week?"

"Just checking to make sure." The contractor looked meaningfully at the architect.

"He will need some funds in advance for the bathroom fittings and granite," the architect said briskly.

"I'll transfer the money into your account when I go back to office."

Reassured, the contractor grinned.

"Can we have a cobblestone path from the gymnasium door that goes all over the farm? For walking or jogging?"

"I'll have to check. Give me a couple of days." The architect pulled out his organizer and keyed in this request.

When they were reviewing the progress of construction on the next floor, Bharat suddenly noticed that it was well past 4:30. Trading must have been over. He cursed himself for not noticing. Anyway nobody called. He had left enough instructions for his colleagues to call him if there was a change in the market conditions.

"Excuse me a minute. Let me do a quick call to the office." Bharat pulled out his phone. He was immediately struck by the display. "13 missed calls and 20 messages."

How did he miss so many calls? He recalled with a sense of alarm that he had put his phone in the silent mode during a client meeting that morning and had not reset it.

Don't get excited, he told himself. These must be some of the many dud calls he received during the day. While he nervously punched the keys to retrieve the messages and the numbers of the people who had called him, the display started flashing, "Incoming call."

"This is Bharat," Bharat said.

"Mr. Bharat, this is Sunil..."

"Which Sunil?" Bharat demanded, a little disoriented.

"Sir, Sunil, your bank manager." Sunil sounded surprised.

"Yeah, Sunil, what's the matter?"

"Mr. Bharat, we need to meet and talk urgently."

"About what?" Bharat's voice was rising.

"After today's developments..."

"What do you mean, today's developments?"

"Mr. Bharat, I am sure you know. Where are you? Are you not in your office?"

"Just what do you mean? Don't talk in riddles." Now alarm began to grip Bharat. He took a step backwards, and stepped into a puddle of water and cement. He cursed viciously at the puddle, "Oh shit!" and then glared at the architect.

The architect and the contractor steadied him. He shook off their hands angrily.

At his curse, Sunil asked, "So, do you know?"

The architect asked, almost at the same moment, "Is something wrong?"

"Don't everybody speak at the same time. I don't know yet."

The contractor had shrunk back and was earnestly requesting Bharat to step out of the puddle and continue speaking.

"Oh, shut up," screamed Bharat at the contractor. "No, not at you, Sunil." He continued to stand inside the puddle.

The contractor watched the expensive trousers and shoes of

Bharat soaking in cement and water with a worried expression.

"Sunil," continued Bharat, "I have been out of my office after lunch. What the hell happened?"

At the other end, Sunil sighed. "Mr. Bharat, you mean you don't know anything?"

"I don't know anything. Out with it."

The contractor thought Bharat would have a nervous breakdown and fled to fetch some water. Meanwhile, a sheen of perspiration had appeared on Bharat's forehead.

"Mr. Bharat, there was a huge crash on the National Stock Exchange. Confused picture. Apparently, some broker, Gupta, couldn't pay up. The situation is very muddled."

"How bad is it?"

"Mr. Bharat, I am sorry." Sunil's tone contained genuine grief. "Your share price is down by forty percent. And the worst may not be over yet."

CHAPTER 7

One number—the stock price—came to dominate Bharat's entire existence. Everyday he watched it obsessively. If the universe was a universe of numbers, all he required was for one number to be right. Was that asking for too much? He was so hypnotically caught up with his stock price that he did not buy and sell for his company when he should have. Looking at the ticker tape of stock prices, he willed with all the energy he could summon, "Rise, rise." Momentarily, his prayer seemed to reach the ticker tape through the universal consciousness. The price would show a minor inflection upward of two or three rupees, and would fall without sustaining energy. Like a very sick man, in a moment of strong will, rising from the bed, only to be taxed so much by his rise that he fell back dramatically.

Junk food and coffee became Bharat's staple. He ate a meal whenever he turned up at home for dinner. Even though he ate little, the junk food thickened him all over and around the waist, in particular. If somebody attributed it to his happiness and prosperity, he snarled. Most of the time, he was preoccupied with BOREBO, computing his asset values as of the minute, and trying desperately to make some decisions on the numbers he saw on the display.

By now, his stock price had sunk by more than fifty percent. Very regretfully, Sunil had requested him to pledge all his remaining shares to let him continue his loan for the farmhouse. A great consolation to Bharat was his salary from which he managed to pay the monthly interest on his loan. If somehow he managed to pay interest for a while, the stock prices would revive. This was, of course, a passing moment. Even if the old glory wasn't restored, surely things would soon look at least half as good. Or would they? He noticed that Sunil, struggling to continue his past courtesies, had moved away to other customers. He was only following the inexorable chart that indicated Bharat had moved down considerably on the list of high net worth clients. Bharat missed his courtesies, his servitude. He cursed the evanescent values of people like Sunil: "Mercenaries."

A general air of tragedy hung over his office. His colleagues had all lost money. The exuberant millionaires' club now had suddenly sobered down. People barked and hissed at each other all the time and had suddenly turned cost conscious. To what extent, Bharat realized only when he saw two of them quarrelling over splitting lunch expenses.

"We had agreed to go Dutch," one was arguing.

"Nonsense! You said you would buy me lunch," the other was retorting.

They were arguing about a few hundred rupees. A small number maintained the equanimity of monks. They had not bought anything. Their languor had prevented them from thinking too intensely on subjects such as investment, personal assets and the like. Being single, they didn't have needs that exceeded an apartment space. A peep into their apartments would have revealed their revelry with squalor. To them this tragedy was a joke. Discomfiture of idiots, to be laughed at. Idiots who pretended to be smart when they acquired assets, who had then looked down upon the languorous as the idiots.

More importantly, Fusion Investments was suddenly not in very good shape. The investments that Bharat and scores of his colleagues had made on behalf of their company, which had turned all of them into millionaires, had suddenly depreciated. There was a distinct possibility that, far from the thumping profits that the company expected at the end of the year, it could end up making minor to major losses. When not glued to his terminal, Bharat's life had become a series of never ending meetings with his bosses and colleagues, despondent, helpless, frustrated.

Fusion Investments headquarters in America was particularly perturbed. Since returns in America were peanuts compared to the potential returns from the Indian market, more than forty percent of the firm's global investments were now in India. The CEO was forever seeking opinions on the phone, and everybody in India had to be readily available. This meant that Bharat didn't get to go home most nights, enacting repetitively an absurd sequence of clutching paper and files, navigating the computer's databases to answer the CEO's questions with his local bosses, and snatching a few winks of sleep between conference calls with his head on his desk.

Indu was of no help. She was clear that it was his money and his assets. Just as she did not consult him extensively on how she would use her stock options, she did not offer any advice on how he should. He wished that she would order him on how to act, like with other things.

Indu, rescue me please? Tell me what to do.

She did not want to bear the burden of making decisions on his behalf. Who would live with the guilt that would haunt later, she asked. She sold most of her stocks and now had close to a million dollars in cash. To everybody who congratulated her on her prescience, she offered a dismissal, "Just luck, and maybe containment of greed."

Bharat's fits of paralysis had him alternating between two screens on his computer. The stock prices and soothe-your-mind.com. When the price fluctuated wildly, unable to bear the tension he clicked on the soothe-your-mind.com icon. It would zoom unfailingly with the announcement, "The best online psychiatrist."

The stock price really worries me.

OH, DOES IT? TELL ME MORE ABOUT IT.

I am really upset.

IS IT TOO LOW?

I don't know about that. I only wish it would stop varying.

THESE THINGS HAPPEN. OVER A LONG PERIOD YOU WOULD SEE NO VARIATION. ONLY A SMOOTH CURVE.

These conversations on soothe-your-mind.com were not salve enough. Bharat soon realized that the only effect they had on his life was the not-so-inconsiderable entries on his credit card bills. Indu advised him to see Dr. Rakesh, the psychiatrist she had been seeing from time to time to mitigate her angst. He hesitated momentarily, then agreed. Indu was successful and mostly composed. Perhaps Dr. Rakesh helped her be that way. Maybe he should see him. He had to see the doctor stealthily since *pantu-thatha* would be very upset. Subbu had reconciled to Indu's sessions with the psychiatrist since he saw an otherwise great resolve in her. She wouldn't listen to *pantu-thatha* anyway. But he would never forgive Bharat seeing Dr. Rakesh.

"Psychiatrists are for mad people. And most of the psychiatrists are themselves nuts," he had repeated many times.

Visiting Dr. Rakesh on the sly was not very difficult since Bharat always took a break from his work for the appointments. Dr. Rakesh had almost abandoned the psychiatric couch. Most of his sessions were in the conversational mode, and like many young men of the current breed of professionals, he had taken pains to master his lessons. Bharat noticed that he kept himself up to date by reading technical journals of repute.

Bharat reported that his blood pressure was high. Dr. Rakesh attributed it to lack of sleep. Besides prescribing a mild sedative, he asked Bharat to pursue some hobby, some passion. It could be anything—collecting stamps, listening to old music, tennis. The last bit of advice was the hardest for Bharat to follow. He racked his head for what he liked to do. Besides drinking with friends, working late, and weekend fun that did not fit any particular definition, he found himself unable to name any one avocation he fervently wanted to pursue.

The conversations with Dr. Rakesh were soothing since he knew a bit about the stock market. He had invested a significant sum in shares, the future of which was now uncertain.

He sought advice from Bharat, and himself offered some theories for market recovery. Bharat found a strange camaraderie when they both could talk about their potential losses. How the country, despite repeated catastrophes, had not installed a proper governance system. How a rogue trader, like the Pied Piper, could lead an entire country's investment community to unredeemable disaster.

The stock market continued to take wild swings during the day. Many times, to escape the ruthless tyrant of the stock price, he wandered the streets of Madras. The scorching sun burnt his skin. A masochism persuaded him to enjoy the singeing like a devotee enjoys a religious ordeal. This was expiation. Atonement for investing his life's faith in a fickle number. The burning sun was the price for temporarily escaping the specter of the market. He could not escape it unless he was in the middle of the streets, walking unstoppably, for he could not afford the briefest of stops. He cursed the electronic revolution. Wherever he stopped, a TV or an electronic display showed stock prices and the index values. If he wanted some coffee, he had to peer into the coffee shop to see if there were any displays. Only on assuring himself that there were no displays, could he enter the coffee shop.

When the stock prices, immanent in the universe, thus chased him, he was overcome by an urge to sell his stocks whenever they became a little positive. To start life again, canceling out all notions of confirmed affluence. The one thing he yearned for most now was emancipation from the slavery to the stock price—to escape this Satan that had embraced his entire conscious. Just when he decided to create certainty, to put paid to the capricious stock price, by selling all his shares in one go, his doubt interfered. Masquerading as prudence, it warned him not to do anything reckless. Just when he had gathered gumption and raised his sword to slay the demon, his doubt pricked his balloon of courage. The sword was returned dolefully to its sheath. Many times during a day, the sword came out in a rage and made its docile retreat. At the end of the day, not having won or even fought a battle, Bharat was a tired man.

•

For once, Chandra looked disturbed. He was channel surfing, but without his usual nonchalance. He was pressing every button with tension, and seething at the TV regardless of what he saw. Subbu could see that he had already finished half the bottle next to him. He was sporting a faint stubble, which was very unusual, and his lips were set in a thin line.

Subbu cleared his throat and sat in the cane chair next to him.

"Good morning," he greeted.

Chandra grunted.

"Would you like some coffee?" Subbu enquired.

Chandra looked up and said, "I have a drink already."

"Oh, throw it away," Subbu commanded. "Try fresh, aromatic south Indian coffee."

"Well, all right," said Chandra grudgingly, but was almost grateful that somebody suggested abandoning his drink.

Aaya was still sleeping since it was Saturday, and Subbu did not have the heart to wake her. He made the coffee himself, drew a deep breath to make sure that its smell was right, poured out the coffee into two cups and walked out of the kitchen.

"Here," he handed it over to Chandra. "When did you get in?"

"About two o'clock."

"Unusual for a Friday night."

"Yeah," Chandra replied and fell silent for some time. "Man, I got a problem."

Subbu did not ask what. He knew Chandra would continue.

"Had a fight with my girlfriend."

Subbu said "tut-tut" without any sympathy.

"It was bad."

"Oh, she'll get over it. I am sure you'll both head out for dinner this evening."

Chandra shook his head. "I don't think so. She says it's over. Asked me to pack my goods and leave her house. We broke up."

"Surely she got your Valentine's Day card?" Subbu asked with concern.

Chandra nodded.

"Yet she broke up?"

Chandra nodded again.

The first rays of the morning sun entered through the Venetian blinds. Stung by their sharpness, he shifted seats and started brooding.

"Why did she become so angry suddenly?"

"She didn't become angry. I was the one who became angry."

"Why did you become angry?" Subbu now showed some interest.

"Because she said it's over."

"But why?"

"Oh, she says she is bored. We have done it now for almost three years. She said it just like that. Recently she changed jobs. Also because she was bored. Doing the same thing again and again. She's now become an event manager. Says public relations bored her. It paid well. She was even due for a promotion. But she throws it away. Says it's kind'a boring. The same way she says I am kind'a boring. She says it so suddenly, I thought she was joking."

"Didn't you try talking it over?"

"Like I am dumb, man. Of course, I tried. No joking? I asked her. She doesn't get excited at all. Had been meaning to tell me for some time. I was the one who got angry. I stomped all over the place. No use. Her mind's made up."

"But you had been thinking of marrying her?"

Chandra sighed. "Thank God, it didn't happen. She would have walked away with half my money. Just when I was beginning to put away some."

When he fell silent again, Subbu started wondering whether he should sympathize with him. Maybe offer some advice? Just then Chandra started gathering his things and started to leave.

"Are you not saying hello to Bharat?" Subbu asked.

"No. I'll come back later. Got a lot of my stuff in the car. Let me dump it in my apartment."

"What are you going to do?"

Chandra did not comprehend Subbu's question. "Huh?"

Subbu repeated his question.

"What else? Gotta look for a new girlfriend. Starting over, it's very difficult. Hard to find somebody who isn't in a relationship. And I am not that great at snatching." He slung his bag on his shoulder and left.

As soon as he had left, a thought struck Subbu. He followed Chandra hastily.

Chandra was still outside by the elevator. There was no one else in sight.

"Chandra, Chandra," Subbu called.

Arching his eyebrows in surprise, Chandra asked, "What?"

Subbu hesitated. "Something occurred to me. I thought you might be interested."

"Out with it man," Chandra said impatiently.

Subbu suggested that since he was looking for a new girl-friend, he might as well look in his apartment complex itself.

"So you don't have to drive in the terrible traffic when it's evening time, you see," said Subbu.

"Good idea." Chandra was genuinely grateful. "Let me see. I can't remember even one girl in my block who is not booked."

When he was turning the ignition key, it occurred to him that finding a girl in his apartment block may not solve the problem forever. She could change apartments anytime.

•

Subbu and Maya had just returned from their evening visit to the park. Today they had spent some time wetting their feet on the beach before going to the park. Maya squealed with delight at the ludicrous, sideways running of the crabs. She was game to climb the stairs because the Second Home elevators were not quite as exciting as the elevators of The Home. Surprisingly they saw somebody ahead of them climbing the stairs.

As Subbu was trying hard to guess who it could be, the woman turned. It was the Stick Woman. Like them, she also had an apartment in the complex of the Second Home to which she shifted during most weekends. She was the type of woman whose rear appearance was quite deceptive. It conjured up the image of a nubile teenager. But when she turned around, you got the same shock that you did in horror movies when a figure turned and unexpectedly it had a skull-revealing, half eaten face.

"Hello, *pantu-thatha*," she greeted and waited for them to catch up.

"Quite surprising to see you on the stairs," Subbu remarked.

With her sad face, skin stretched taut, she said, "What can I do? I have put on one and a half kilograms in the last two weeks. I am so upset. Decided to increase work-outs and climb stairs."

Subbu studied her face carefully, and then her body. Who or what, except a sensitive, accurately calibrated weighing scale, could tell where the tiny excess weight was stuck to her body? How old could she be? The least was forty-five. Perhaps it was a teeming and competitive world for women to find men and for men to find women.

"You look quite fit," Subbu said. You are a stick, can't you see that?

"Do I?" The Stick Woman smiled radiantly, letting herself into her apartment. After a moment, she stuck her head out, and said, "Oh, you are so kind, *pantu-thatha*."

That evening, at the park, the girls from the fishermen's settlement hadn't turned up. Maya was disappointed. She swung for a while before she asked Subbu to take her back home. It then struck Subbu that Bharat wanted to see the maid to check if she could take on the additional duty of washing the cars. Aaya had become quite weak in recent times. She had been tending to this weekly chore, but the last few times she became breathless. Indu had ordered Bharat to ask the maid if she could undertake this duty. She didn't want "any trouble on my hands if Aaya fainted or something."

Subbu asked Maya if she wanted to go to where the girls lived. Maya was thrilled. Clapping her hands, she cried, "Oh, let's! Let's please." Holding her hand, Subbu walked with her to the Dark World. Though the light was just fading, the lone sodium vapor streetlight was already on. Beyond the light's glow was the incomprehensible darkness. They stood on the edge of the Dark World.

A dark man walked towards them and nodded to ask, "What do you want?"

Subbu referred to the maid by name.

The man walked back without a word. Then a very sophisticated communication system went to work. It not only promptly fetched the maid, but at her heels were the girls who came prancing happily.

"*Saar* wants to see you. Can you come now?" Subbu asked the maid.

She thought for a moment and then said. "Go. I'll follow you in a little while." Then she disappeared into the darkness.

The girls hesitated with shyness. The older sister then invited, "Come home, please."

Maya looked up at Subbu with hope.

"Not now. Another time," he said quickly. The light in Maya's eyes disappeared.

The girls also looked disappointed. "One nimit," said the older sister and ran into the darkness. She was back in the promised minute and handed over a candy to Maya. Maya took the candy, but made no attempt to eat it. She had been conditioned by prior instruction.

"Will you come tomorrow to the park?" Maya asked.

"Exams. We will come Saturday evening," the girls cried in unison.

While they returned home, Maya mulled over how she would narrate this thrilling experience to her select friends at school. The forbidden land. She had been taken to its border, had been permitted an exclusive, searching look at its interiors. Not an easy privilege for her friends. She turned back once or twice to see the lone light and the mysterious world that lay behind it. Meanwhile, Subbu had taken the candy from her, checked whether it was wrapped and branded, wiped it clean with his *veshti*, and handed it back to Maya.

"You can eat it," he permitted.

Bharat, with a drink in hand, was watching TV. He sat with a hag-ridden expression barely acknowledging the entry of Subbu and Maya. Subbu was worried that he drank a little too much these days.

"She'll be here anytime now. The maid," Subbu said.

Bharat grunted.

"What's worrying you?" Subbu asked, after some hesitation. "The stock price has stabilized somewhat. Hasn't it?"

"That's right. But nobody knows who'll keep his job and who won't," sighed Bharat.

"Bharat, you are a professional. You are well-qualified. I don't think you should be so bothered. There must be enough jobs going for people like you."

"Maybe. But this is a good job. It pays well. Only if I keep my job, I get a lot of my options after a while. At least for now, my life is tied to this job, not any job. I have to keep this job. Somehow."

There was a knock on the door and the maid entered.

"Yes, Master." She waited.

Bharat explained to her why he called for her.

"Did you say I have to wash the cars daily?" she asked.

"No, just once a week. I already said that," replied Bharat containing his irritation.

"How much extra would you pay?"

"Three hundred rupees a month." Indu had wanted Bharat to start at two hundred and close at three hundred if she haggled.

She thought for a long moment. "Not interested."

There she goes haggling, thought Bharat. "Okay. Let's make it three hundred and fifty."

"No, Master. I don't think I want this."

"Four hundred." Indu might murder him.

"No. I don't think so."

Bharat was incredulous. That was almost equal to the money she earned for all the work she did here.

"Why not?" Bharat demanded.

"It doesn't suit me," she said coolly.

"This is a lot of money. I am sure you have a need for it."

She thought about it again. "Maybe. But this doesn't suit me."

"What do you mean, this doesn't suit you? What else do you have to do?" Bharat raved.

"Master, that's none of your business."

White with rage, Bharat said with deliberate effect, "We may sack you. We'll find somebody else to do all the work."

"That's no way to talk, Master," she said.

"I mean it," Bharat said assertively.

"Well, if it's not this job, then it's another one."

So saying, she was gone.

Leaving Subbu to marvel at her unlettered insouciance.

•

Kamesh had called to say that he had some news, and asked if they would stop by that evening. He wouldn't reveal why. When Subbu, Bharat and Indu approached his apartment, they found the door open.

Kamesh was in the kitchen making *chapatis*. When he saw them, he called out, "Be seated. I am almost done. Will be with you in a minute."

They could then hear him cursing under his breath while he searched for something and did not find it. There was a loud sound as he dropped—it was hard to tell—a plate or a cup or a vessel. Indu, who was leafing through an old yellow periodical, was unperturbed. Bharat was in a trance, trying some complex mental calculation, that he hardly heard the noise. There was a moment of silence when Subbu rose to go into the kitchen. Even as he entered, he saw Kamesh switching off the stove and hobbling towards them, limping on his right foot.

"Gout." He tried to smile. "That was the only one left. There's some urea collection or something like that, the doctor says."

Indu, who was still leafing through the old yellow periodical whose pages were crumbling, remarked, "Maybe you should cut down your beer."

"It's ages since I drank," Kamesh protested.

"Nonsense. The last time I was here, I saw some empty beer bottles in the wash area."

"Oh, that. The maid uses them for storing drinking water. I don't even know what brands are sold in the market these days." He turned to Subbu. "I had been to see my cardiologist. He says I may have to have an angioplasty or a bypass. Not immediately. If things don't improve in the long term. How are you, sir?" He wiped his hands with his *veshti*.

Indu shuddered without taking her eyes from the magazine. "Why don't you use a towel?"

"I am very fine," Subbu replied to Kamesh's question.

"Will you have some *chapati* while it is hot?" Without waiting for an answer, and ignoring the protests of Subbu, Kamesh disappeared into the kitchen.

"Then just one, please," Subbu cried out.

Kamesh returned with plates that had one *chapati*, a vegetable accompaniment and some pickle.

Subbu found the *chapati* undercooked. The dough smeared over his molars, while in some parts it was burnt. The vegetable accompaniment was watery with too little salt.

Thankfully, the pickle, which was branded, was tasty. Subbu downed everything, chewing as little as possible, trying to recollect some pleasant experiences. Bharat ate like a zombie, while Indu took in two mouthfuls and went into the kitchen to presumably dispose of the rest. Without noticing it, Kamesh was eating his cooking with great relish.

"I hope it was okay," he stopped to say.

"It was fine," said Subbu, as he demolished the last piece with relief.

"One more?" Kamesh asked.

"No, no, no," said Subbu alarmed.

"If you don't mind, I'll take another two and finish my dinner."

"Oh, please." The man must be superhuman to consume two more of those *chapati*s.

When Kamesh returned with two more *chapati*s on his plate, Indu appeared a little vexed. "What about the news? You didn't ask us to come here just to eat *chapati*s?"

"News?" Kamesh scratched his head. "Of course, of course. My son, Raj? He has become the CEO of his company."

Despite her irritation, Indu said, "Wow! That's great. I knew it would happen. But not so quickly."

Subbu noticed that Kamesh never talked of Raj as simply "Raj", it was always "my son, Raj," as if he needed to be introduced every time.

"He has sent me an email that says the official announcement will come tomorrow. But the board has informed him."

Bharat emerged from his trance. "That's impressive. CEO? At his age? Of a Fortune 100 American corporation? Beating Americans and Germans and others to the top job? He will soon become very rich. I know his company is quite generous with its options. At least a hundred million, I suppose."

"I don't know about that. These days, the numbers are

very different. Anyway he will have fifty thousand people to oversee all over the world. He says he should even be stopping by India in the next few weeks."

"So you'll get to see him, I suppose?" Subbu asked.

Kamesh's face fell. "No, I don't think so. He comes only to Delhi."

"But Delhi's just two hours away. Surely he can come in the morning and go back the same evening?" Subbu was incredulous.

Kamesh shook his head. "No. He says he is flying into Delhi from Hong Kong in his corporate jet. Has a two hour meeting with some minister. That evening he has a meeting in London."

"In the corporate jet? Amazing," said Bharat.

Indu had the what-did-you-think-of-me-and-my-brother look. "I'll call him when we get back home," she said.

When Kamesh was walking them to their car, Subbu asked, "What about Raj's marriage?"

Kamesh shifted his gaze. "He's mentioned something about that in his email. He says that he's started living in a ..." He stopped to scratch his head, and after a long moment recalled what he wanted. "...a community. I don't know what community. He says it's very close to marriage. Bill and Frank are his best friends. He even sent a photograph through email. I forgot to show it to you."

He limped back slowly into the apartment and brought a print-out of the photograph. Frank and Bill had their hands around the shoulders and waist of a radiant and balding Raj. Subbu passed the photograph back to Kamesh.

"He says he is taking all precautions," Kamesh said hesitantly. "I don't understand all this very well."

From inside the car, Subbu spoke to him. "His CEO job. That sounds great. Good for him."

146

Kamesh nodded murmuring, "Yeah. I always knew it. The boy was a winner."

When he turned to head to his apartment, Subbu thought his eyes glistened. Wincing with pain in his big toe, Kamesh walked step by slow step. Silhouetted on the doorstep by the foyer light, he waved out to them as their car disappeared round the corner.

•

Subbu woke up with a start.

First, he suspected the cats. A few minutes of stillness proved the cats had not been mewing. What woke him up then? He lay back down and closed his eyes tight to resume sleeping. When it didn't work, he reached for his betel-nut casket. There was one piece of an intractable size that he focused on chewing and closed his eyes, his head in a raised position.

Chandra's girlfriend problem, Marianne and her cats, oversized biceps and suffocating cleavage, Maya's so-called problems, Bharat's morbid obsession with his stock price, the Moon Woman's gait, the Coiffured Man's haste to catch a plane with his desires satiated, tongue-twisting names, and corporate jets all swirled in a kaleidoscopic spiral with dazzling colors. The betel-nut in his mouth couldn't placate him as it usually did. Its bitter juices became a peculiar saporific backdrop, the counterpart of background music to the dazzling colors that danced before his eyes. The colors with fascinating shapes grew limbs that elongated into streaks only to withdraw and disappear the next instant. The psychedelic dazzle became too much for him to bear. As he furiously and insistently chewed, the mad shindig of amoebic colors solidified into a matrix, then disappeared from view like an exorcised ghost.

The ensuing silence was punctuated by only the grinding noise of his chewing jaws.

After a few seconds, the tiny voice spoke. He didn't recognize it initially, and was startled. This was the first time he was hearing it.

What? he asked.

Flee, it told him.

Now it became clear to him that it was the sound of this voice that had awakened him.

What? he repeated uncomprehendingly.

Flee, it repeated, still tiny but insistent.

Flee? What do you mean flee? he asked.

Flee, it said with the patience of dealing with a child.

Flee? At my age? he demanded not knowing why he was entertaining this conversation.

Yes, flee, said the voice nonchalantly

Flee from all this? What do you mean? he asked.

Flee, the tiny voice urged.

To where? he asked.

There was no response. He waited for a few minutes before he realized the voice wasn't going to respond.

•

Bharat summoned great courage to go to his farmhouse site. He drove nervously making a few clipping drivers swear at him. After a while, he had to stop the music. The drums made him jumpier.

The watchman gave him a weak salute which was barely returned.

For the last few weeks, the architect had halted construction at Bharat's request. Finances had to be carefully planned before he continued to commit more and more money to this project. Bharat had to take careful stock of his assets and liabilities before he could confidently authorize the progress of construction. In the few weeks time, the makeshift road that had been laid to facilitate construction had become undulated and had almost disappeared. There was now a thick undergrowth. All the clearing undertaken at the beginning of construction was clearly futile. Like a shaved beard, the weeds had come back with a vengeance making it difficult to walk through the site. What an irony, Bharat thought, these plants. The ones you want have to be petted and nurtured; the ones you don't want, grow so easily. Nature's perversion. Why couldn't it have been the other way round?

The earth had caked in places indicating the former moist activity for construction. Rubble, bricks and cement bags marred his path to the house. Clambering carefully over the little mounds, he stepped into the half-constructed house. A yelp greeted him. He had stepped on the tail of a stray mongrel that had been suckling its pups. The mother ran a few paces and turned back growling and baring its teeth. The pups were circling his feet without a care. He kicked at them and they yelped, but returned to his feet. Their mother growled even more loudly showing more teeth. While Bharat was wondering what his next move should be, the watchman appeared from somewhere shooing the bitch and the pups away. It was evident that the corner the bitch had occupied had been her home for some time now. The stains were telling and the stink, overpowering.

"Dirty dogs," the watchman cursed. "*Saar*, when would construction begin again?"

"Soon, very soon. Till then make sure nothing disappears from here."

The watchman's eyes jumped as he shook his head vigorously. Bharat looked suspiciously at another corner where the wood was stored. How many pieces were supposed to be left after the few windows and doors had been fitted? He couldn't recall the exact count.

"Is all the wood here?" he asked the watchman.

"Of course, Master. If you have any doubt, please count."

"That's okay," he said with authority. "Just take good care."

The granite samples were still on the ground. As they had been laid the day the stock market crashed. He picked up the grey that he had chosen and blew. Under the cover of dust, the grey beckoned him enticingly. He dropped it with a clink on the other pieces. The puddle that he had stepped into, when Sunil had called about the stock market crash, had now dried up making a grey, cement patch with his footprint intact. It reminded him of the Hollywood ritual of leaving footprints. Or was it handprints? Anyway, when he resumed construction, he would tell the architect to leave that part intact. He would then have left his footprint on the cement of time.

The porcelain washbasins that he had imported from Italy lay in a corner. Black and green slime had gathered on them. The original white showed only in small dusty patches.

"Can't you wipe these once in a while? What do I pay you for?" he chided the watchman.

The man hurriedly pulled off his turban and started wiping.

"No, not now. Later."

The watchman carefully folded the cloth, so the stains from wiping would be concealed, and tied it around his head. "Okay, *saar*."

Maybe he had chided the watchman too much. He was the only soul who guarded this property. He shouldn't be displeased too much. Bharat pulled out a hundred rupee note for him. "Keep this."

The watchman was delighted at this unexpected bonus, and he tried to dislodge his turban again.

"I told you. Not now," Bharat admonished. "And do it with a clean cloth."

The watchman shook his head faithfully and declared, "The next time you are here, I'll make sure everything shines. But please start construction soon. Before the rainy season destroys everything."

"Will do. Will do," said Bharat.

When would he be able to restart construction? If he knew for sure that the worst had happened, he could make some plans. The market did not give him any clues. It was still on its wild see-saw. Just when he thought the trough had been hit, and he would settle his assets and liabilities one way, the share price rose by ten rupees discouraging him to settle his debts.

Good news was okay, bad news was okay. Uncertainty was the devil.

Bharat's phone rang. His secretary told him that his boss wanted to see him—immediately. This was frustrating. It was Friday afternoon. He had actually packed up for the day preparing for the weekend. Now he had to drive all the way back into the city. His Linda still had to be serviced. Hopefully it wouldn't break down on the way.

"I have to go now. Just take care of everything," he told the watchman hurriedly.

The hundred rupee tip made him freeze into attention and salute Bharat smartly, in stark contrast to the weak salute with which he greeted him a few minutes back. The salute was completely lost on Bharat who was dreading the potential teleconference that night with headquarters. Indu had fixed up dinner with some friends. She would be wild if he cancelled it in the last minute.

When he reached office, it was already six o'clock. The office wore a deserted look. Lights, air-conditioning and computers were switched off in some sections as a part of the cost reduction drive. The coffee machines were in a state of ruin as free coffee had been discontinued.

His secretary was waiting. "The boss is ready to see you."

"I'll see him. Don't wait for me. I may be long coming. I don't need anything."

"It's okay. I'll wait," his secretary insisted.

His boss's secretary gave him a grave nod. "He's free. You can go in now."

Somehow, before he stepped into the boss's office, he knew it.

The moving sword had cut.

CHAPTER 8

Unwillingly, Bharat had rehearsed this situation many times in his mind. He expected to come out of his boss's office devastated. Instead he came out with resignation. A resignation that surprised him.

When his boss announced that they were letting him go, he was not shocked, but angry. "Letting him go." What a terrible euphemism! As if he had been a recalcitrant wild animal that had been forcibly tethered. Now he was untethered, free to go into the wilderness where he belonged. Making "letting him go" sound as if it were a liberation.

"What did I do wrong? I was conservative. Never took rash risks with the fund's money. I went with the majority. It's not my fault the market crashed. Everybody's in trouble, not just me. So why me?" he exclaimed with consternation.

"Oh, no, no. You didn't do anything wrong. You are a good professional. Just that there isn't a place for too many good professionals under the current circumstances. When there's too much good food on the plate, you dump it when you can't eat all of it. No fault of the food. And yes, you did go with the majority, you were conservative. But, if it's any consolation to you, we are asking the majority to leave. About sixty percent of the staff in your division are leaving. We may even close down the division. Hey, you aren't the only guy. Know something? Even the CEO has been asked to leave," his boss explained.

Bharat realized that his rage was perfectly rational, but it wouldn't take him anywhere.

"So long. And I wish you good luck." The boss stood up and extended his hand. "Er...if you don't mind, would you clean out your drawers just now? Monday morning, I'm forced to give the table to someone else."

That's why his secretary had waited despite his insistence that she go home. Without a word, both of them set about cleaning out his drawers and destroying some papers. She expertly packed most of what he had to carry home in cardboard boxes. She had gathered the boxes beforehand. It seemed a part of her training—helping people go home. Monday morning she would become the secretary of somebody else with the same fierce loyalties with which she had been his secretary, switching so efficiently. She would take care of the new person's every little menial job, protecting him from the tyranny of chores. Travel, hotel bookings, appointments, food, payment of bills, everything. He felt a pang of jealousy.

She carried some boxes, and he the rest, as she walked him to the Linda humming a tune under her breath. All the boxes were placed in the back seat and the boot.

Before closing the driver's door after he got in, she said, "Take care."

When he pressed the accelerator and the car surged forward, the last thread of his attachment to Fusion Investments broke. Monday morning, there would be no trace of his several years' existence at Fusion.

Is this the price for conservatism? For aligning with the majority? In the long term, the majority always wins. Who's the majority now? The nameless, faceless majority that had just been sacked? Out in the street? Or the majority that was doing the sacking? And anyway, what the hell does winning mean? He indignantly posed these questions to Prof. Chauhan. He could almost see the benign but cryptic smile of Prof. Chauhan from inside his grave. For the first time, he wondered if the majority view was the right one to possess. Should he start trying things that went against the majority? The very thought made him afraid. For a brief moment, the prickly ass flashed in his mind.

When he broke the news to *pantu-thatha*, he did not talk much about it. It was almost as if they had telepathically understood that this was inevitable. Subbu only advised Bharat to handle his liabilities carefully. The world could not ignore a good professional for long, he told Bharat. He just had to wait it out.

●

For the next few days, Bharat was stuck in The Home. After many years, he watched Maya go to school and return from school. She enquired curiously why he did not go to his office anymore.

"Got to find a new office," he said.

"Oh. Will you play with me?" she asked immediately.

Why not, he thought. "Okay."

She brought the well-worn snakes-and-ladders board, and dice that had grown yellow with age, that they looked like badly maintained outsized human teeth. Bharat initially objected, asking her why they couldn't play some games on the Internet. Later, he relented since it was convenient for him to lie down on the couch and still play with her, rolling the dice on the floor. They had made an unwritten pact that both wouldn't tell Indu about their paper board game adventures.

Aaya stood in the doorway of the kitchen, watching Bharat with suspicion, which gave way to approval. She was also sure that Bharat wasn't about to blow the whistle on Maya. At the sound of footsteps outside the door, Maya folded the snakes-and-ladders board or the chess board and scrambled indoors. Many times it was a false alarm. These days Indu didn't come back home until late in the evenings. Maya was asleep by then.

During the day, without Maya around, Bharat drank most of the time and watched TV. After a while, drinking, that he thought could not tire him, did. He chose, instead, black coffee that he sipped mindlessly until he swore at its bitterness that insidiously invaded his taste buds that they screamed. He tried calling some friends all of whom were at work and had time for him only during weekends.

Subbu watched Bharat with concern, from time to time, but thought it best to leave him to his ways, at least for then.

Struck by the morbidity of being in a closed, quiet apartment all day long, except for the occasional conversation with *pantu-thatha*, Bharat took to roaming the streets. On one of these aimless rounds, he stopped before the shop where he had bought his Manicini's suit for the hallowed CEO visit. He felt sick. He bought a blue suit to genuflect before God, his company's CEO. How carefully they had prepared for his visit, the decorations, the welcome boards, the attire of the two models who would welcome him, the sandalwood garland.

"Nice smell," he had said, taking off the sandalwood gar-

156

land moments after he received it around his neck. He curiously asked questions about sandalwood, and carefully stored it in his bag. "Wonderful wood."

The team was elated. The visit had begun well. His boss had given Bharat a look of immense gratitude, for the sandalwood garland had been his suggestion.

Bharat's sickness worsened, and he retched once. He had worshipped a false God, a God who did not hesitate to slay him when the use for him was over. But that God was not really a God. He himself was now slain. He had probably genuflected before the board, before his chairman, maybe before the analysts. And he was laid off.

Pathetic. A circle of genuflection.

Who was it paying obeisance to? Who was the God who was worthy of such a dramatic prayer? Nobody in any business corporation was invincible anymore. Were there no Gods left in the business world? Presumably the only God was the moving sword. Inexorable, unyielding, unsympathetic, and totally undiscriminating. The sword that helped save companies by killing people. It cared not for fancy titles like CEO. As long as the moving sword was around "employee relations," "people are our most important assets" and the like were inanities, weak flapping of wings against the strong gust the sword left in its wake. What a farce, the whole thing.

On one round, he sat on a barstool and got drunk in the afternoon, sitting next to a bald man who wore a ridiculous cap to hide his baldness and had dyed the remaining hair black. He was wearing a checked jacket when the temperature outside was close to forty degrees centigrade. He survived since the bar had good air-conditioning.

"Hi, buddy," he greeted Bharat.

In his drunkenness, Bharat could see that the bald man was also drunk.

They held a long, animated conversation, the way only drunks can. Bharat spoke about what he wanted to, and the bald man spoke about what he wanted to. Bharat's subject alternated with the bald man's subject with the twain never meeting. Looking at them from a distance, you would have got the impression that they were engaged in a coherent conversation on a single subject.

"Youngsters these days have a lot of opportunity, don't they?" the bald man slurred.

"Opportunity to do what?" Bharat asked. Despite his drunkenness, he now felt a compulsion to respond to what the bald man was saying. The two subjects of their conversation merged into one; the twain finally met.

"To develop themselves. To make India developed. To become rich."

As the bald man ordered another drink, Bharat told the bartender, "His next drink's on me."

The man grinned gratefully.

"What do you mean, make India *developed*?" Bharat asked.

The bald man belched and offered Bharat something from a plate of greasy leftovers. Bharat politely declined.

"Well...make our country like America, like Europe. Developed. You see what I mean?"

"Let's look at it like this. My friend's grandfather was a Station Master," Bharat said, suddenly remembering Keshav. "Had seven children. Sent two to study in America. On his money. I am talking of sixty years ago. Built a house in the heart of Madras. Left behind some money when he died. Didn't work one day beyond five in the evening. Everyday he went home, he was absolutely sure he had his job for the rest of his life."

"What kind of life is that? A Station Master's life. That's not a developed country job." The drunk insisted on offering him the greasy leftovers once more.

Bharat was lucid enough to decline yet again, then asked, "What do you mean, not a developed country job? Wasn't that a good life? What do you mean by developed country? I mean, he—my friend's grandfather—had no fear. You develop and develop and develop. Then you are scared. You are scared your job'll no longer be your job, your wife'll no longer be your wife, your child'll no longer be your child. Your company'll no longer be your company. Anybody can walk out of anything. You are scared all the time. You go back home every evening not sure of one thing. That's developed, huh? Feeling scared all the time? Funny. Makes me laugh."

Bharat laughed, and the drunk laughed briefly.

"Funny, really funny. Developed and scared? Very developed, and shitting bricks. Man, you got stuff in you. Very intelligent." The drunk glanced at his watch. "Got to go now. My wife's throwing a party. Sure you won't have this? Good stuff." He pushed the plate at Bharat and left, trying desperately to steady his staggering.

The greasy stuff excited Bharat's curiosity. He picked up a chunk and examined it carefully. It was hard to say whether it was vegetarian or not. It looked like chicken or potato. For a while, he tried guessing. Then with frustration, he bit into it. It was screaming hot and spicy. It set his tongue on fire. He had to down every ounce of liquid within his reach to douse it. The bald man must have been dead drunk to eat this stuff so casually. The stinging resulted in a bout of strong sobriety. Cursing the situation, Bharat paid for the drinks and left.

•

The seriousness of what Bharat said during the drunken fit struck him later. The fear of the wife leaving. The thought shattered him. What if Indu left him? She was successful and youthful. She could easily attract a younger, better looking and richer man if she wanted to. He had to quickly get back onto the rails. She would probably stand him in this condition for a month, maybe two, but surely not forever.

Such a thought didn't seem to have struck Indu. Bharat attributed this to the unprecedented rise in her career which kept her busy. Besides, he thought, she had plenty of money. And perhaps she wouldn't so easily disturb the comfortable arrangement of two apartments, Aaya and *pantu-thatha*, the works.

Actually, Indu was quite blasé about the loss of his job. It happens, and you get a new job, she said. Bharat was grateful that she took it so casually in contrast to the catastrophe he considered it was. Her actions seemed to reassure Bharat that she was not about to do anything rash. In fact, when he told her that Sunil seemed to have got wind of the news and had called him twice, she offered to meet his monthly payment commitments until he could sell his stock and settle liabilities.

Subbu was pleasantly surprised by this decision of Indu's only to be horrified by the lawyer she brought home the next day. The lawyer brought an agreement that stated that Indu would be paying, until further notice, the monthly payments due from Bharat, and that all such sums would be treated as a loan from Indu to Bharat. Bharat was liable to pay Indu the entire sum when so demanded by her.

"*Pantu-thatha*, you must sign as one of the witnesses," Indu ordered.

When he finished signing, Indu joked that since his handwriting was faltering, he must be growing old. Under other circumstances, Subbu may have managed a weak grin.

Over the next few days, Bharat sent applications to virtually all his contacts in his address book. Some of them responded apologetically that the situation was quite bad. Surely, he knew about it. At the first sign of an upswing, his application would be considered. Many of his messages did not receive a response. Befuddled that his hundreds of emails didn't receive a response, he frequently doubted that his email was working right. To test, he sent messages to himself. Like perfect boomerangs, these messages promptly came back to him. He opened his own messages and read them without feeling. Nothing was wrong with his email.

It was clear. Nobody wanted to respond.

Once, it occurred to him that it might be useful to check with Keshav, and see what he did after he got laid off. He did not have any contact details. Bharat searched for "Keshav" on the net.

"250,000 pages located," the search engine solemnly reported.

He tried filtering the search with a number of criteria. The number still remained impossible. With the Internet, it was supposed to be easier to locate a person, not more difficult. But there was no trace of Keshav, despite any number of notices he put on all sorts of bulletin boards.

The stock price remained low, but steady. Bharat decided to sell some shares and repay a part of his debt to Sunil. With Indu making the rest of the monthly payments, the thought of meeting his liabilities, for at least the immediate present, did not trouble him much. What *did* trouble him was the loss of work. He had absolutely no hobbies, no passions whatsoever. He woke up everyday dreading the monster of Time. How would he spend it? Just what could he do? He tried logging into soothe-your-mind.com. Its conversations became repetitive and more meaningless. He visited Dr. Rakesh for a couple of sessions, not that he needed psychiatric help, but that it helped him spend some time. He recalled *pantu-thatha*'s fervent pleas to him during his boyhood: "Develop some hobbies. Music, reading, writing, gardening, anything." He thought hanging around with his friends was cool. Now there were no friends to hand around with.

Until now, his work kept him busy. It dealt with Time quite effectively. Many times, during exciting days in the stock market, he would recall seeing nine o'clock on his watch in the morning and the next time he checked it would show 1:00 PM. He would shake his head with disbelief. Evenings were spent either on work or on parties. The bad times had reduced even the parties. People were careful with their money. Indu could not keep him company. She spent two nights a week in the office. The other days, close to midnight, she would come home weary and flop into bed. At the crack of dawn, she would be gone again.

Bharat tried going to the temple to pray, but he soon realized that he did not know the first thing about religion. When he obeyed Indu's diktat to close his eyes and pray, the ass appeared and just stood its ground. Howsoever he tried to see beyond it to submit his supplication, he could not. Lately, the ass seemed to have developed a halo that blinded him from seeing beyond it.

Work—how he craved to be under its dictatorship. Work—how it gave him a sense of security when, ironically, it offered no protection at all. Work, the modern balm.

He complained about this to *pantu-thatha* in the presence of Indu. Subbu paraphrased Ibsen: "Rob an average man of his work, and you rob him of his happiness in the same stroke." This thought, of course, promptly went above Bharat's and Indu's heads.

•

That night when Subbu woke up, he knew it was not the cats. He reached for the betel-nut in the dark. Expertly, he unscrewed the lid and threw some into his mouth. But even as he started chewing, the phantasmagoria of colors appeared—yet this time more strident, angrier, and possessed with an irrepressible energy. Every color flailed its limbs, inflated its head, and abruptly shrunk into its neighbors, only for a neighbor to start taunting.

This time Subbu waited more phlegmatically. The face of Indu's lawyer appeared among the colors. A color drew the lawyer's face into a thin line as if it were made of chewing gum, suddenly released its elastic force that hit him on the head, and stretched it sideways. In the fury of colors, he saw Jane from Atlanta's face floating by. The distorted face appeared to be lecturing on marital harmony.

As suddenly as the colors had appeared, they vanished. The tiny voice called out to him.

Flee, it said.

Flee, flee, flee, it called out.

Flee from Eimona before it is too late, it said ominously before fading away.

•

Joshi was the secretary of the association of the apartment complex that housed the Second Home. He had been the secretary ever since anybody could recall. Nobody wanted the job, and so year after year, after glorifying the last year's work, the occupants unanimously elected Joshi the secretary. Joshi accepted their tributes with cultivated humility and was quite pleased to be elected again. It filled him with self-importance and kept him occupied.

"I do all this only for all of you. It's my service mentality.

If one of you wants the secretary position this year, that's fine with me," he would say every time he was re-elected.

"No…" the occupants would cry with horror, and politely correct their expressions. "How can anybody do the job better than you, Joshi *saab* (or Joshi uncle)?"

Joshi was particularly pleased when somebody addressed him as "Colonel." He had retired from the army as a Lieutenant-Colonel. Those who had to get things done with him used this honorific without fail. And it worked every time.

Once a wag pointed out, "He is no Colonel. He was just a Lieutenant-Colonel. He went up the ranks automatically. Just didn't have the stuff to make a Colonel." When the news reached Joshi's ears, he threatened to resign. The apartment occupants chastised the man who had dared make insinuations about Joshi's rise in the army. The man, realizing his folly, tendered an unqualified apology (the only alternative was for him to become the secretary). Joshi then acquiesced to resume being the secretary.

The occupants of the complex secretly described Joshi variously. Eccentric, cranky, cantankerous, a gadfly. He was a bachelor with an equally cranky spinster sister who visited him now and then. The length of her stay was not determined beforehand. At some point during her stay, she and Joshi would have a noisy quarrel whose rumblings would start late evening. The next morning she would be gone.

Joshi was an efficient secretary. All association bills would be paid on time. All water tanks would be filled before 5:00 AM. The lawn areas would always have a freshly mowed appearance, and the watchmen could never doze during the day. No occupant could feign ignorance of the apartment complex's rules. He made a bold and severe poster of each rule. Each sentence had to end with an exclamation mark. DON'T THROW GARBAGE! CLOSE THE ELEVATOR DOOR!

VISITORS SHOULD PARK OUTSIDE! GARBAGE SHOULD BE THROWN ONLY IN THE GARBAGE BIN OUTSIDE! If any of the residents broke a rule, he levied a fine of a hundred rupees. Dreading the prospect of undertaking the secretary's job, they paid without a demur.

His apartment, on the ground floor, was the closest to the elevator shaft. From time to time, he peeped outside and goaded the users of the elevator to close the doors of the double-door elevator. Enforcement of the association rules ("bylaws" he corrected anybody who said "rules") was an important device for the preservation of his sanity. Everybody who used the elevator could hear him shuffling noisily inside his apartment. At times, through the walls, they could hear him talking to himself.

Joshi's military valor could not be spent adequately on the domestic happenings in the apartment complex. However, he was too old to carry a gun and fight. Therefore, he cultivated a pastime: public interest litigation. He required little provocation to file a case. He had filed a case against the garbage removal agency when they did not keep the bins locked allowing rag-pickers to pull out all the garbage and strew it on the road. There was also a case pending against the city corporation since the repaved road encroached four and a half inches into the property of the apartment complex.

Joshi received a hefty pension and had nobody and nothing to spend it on. So he spent it on the lawyer around the corner of the road. On the pending cases, the lawyer suppressed his yawns and spent an hour every week humoring the old man and himself. But in the last three weeks or so, things had become a little different.

Joshi first noticed the innocuous board on his morning walk to the beach. A few hundred meters away from the water, it stood in front a newly built fence that cordoned off a few acres area on the beach. "Property of Rangan" it said. Joshi flinched. Rangan was a local potentate. He ran a murky business group which was an assorted collection of night-clubs, restaurants, shrimp exports and software. It was rumored that none of his businesses, except his restaurant and nightclubs, were real businesses. He had acquired a reputation as a ruthless businessman who would go any lengths to suit his ends. Joshi was angry and worried about this new property. The government had forbidden the construction of any new property so close to the water.

His worries were not unfounded. Beside the innocuous board, appeared another shabby board which said, "Site for Sea Breeze — A club with state-of-the-art facilities." Joshi was filled with a vision of unruly two wheelers with leather-jacketed men and women zipping up and down the road, loud music and late-night howling beside drunken brawls. Outrage and concern filled his mind as he made his way back to the Second Home apartment complex.

That night Joshi convened an association meeting in which he spoke angrily about the invasion of their well-guarded privacy and blatant lawbreaking when there existed a government order that no new construction would be permitted within five-hundred meters of the high tide line. At the end of his declamation, he suggested that the occupants take legal action against Rangan. For once, he did not meet with indifference. Everybody was visibly upset that his quiet neighborhood was in danger of transforming into a bedlam. However, they squirmed at the prospect of taking legal action against Rangan whose reputation nobody could miss.

Joshi solved their problem. "I will be the prime litigant. We will file it as a public interest litigation suit. All I am asking of you is money. Fighting Rangan will not be like my other cases. He is a real thug. We'll need an expensive and powerful lawyer. The case may drag on for years."

Relieved, the occupants agreed to contribute the money necessary to the association funds, and empower Joshi to use the funds as he deemed necessary to fight this case. They did not want to be identified as litigants, and they did not want to get trapped in the processes of the court.

As Joshi expected, the road corner lawyer backed out of the case. He did not offer any excuses. He made it plain that Rangan was a living terror and he did not want to take him on. Joshi had to hire a lawyer in the city who was expensive, but was powerful in his own right. In the last three weeks, the new lawyer had succeeded in getting a stay order against progress of work at the club site. All activity there came to a halt. The association had a minor round of celebration where the Colonel's courage and commitment were praised.

•

Bharat and family had moved into the Second Home for two to three weeks to carry out long pending repairs at The Home. It was summer holidays for Maya, and Bharat did not have to go to work. Indu was staying at her office every other night since she had succeeded in bagging a big assignment from a French company. She did not mind the slightly longer commute.

"There would be no better time to get the repairs at the Home done," she said.

That Friday, the warning came in the morning itself. There was a depression in the bay, just off the coast, and a cyclonic storm was likely in the evening. Bharat dreaded these cyclones. The torrential and unrelenting downpour in Madras was nothing like cyclones elsewhere. A few times he had been in the midst of cyclones in Hong Kong and Taipei. Upon the first warning, the entire city shut down. He had watched the rains confined to the hotel room and remarked to his Hong Kong colleague, "What a piddle. Much ado about nothing. If you want to see a real cyclone, come to Madras." He knew for the next day or two life would be paralyzed. Power shut-downs, floods on the road—thanks to the poor drainage, stranded cars, missing fishermen.

Indu called to say that she was staying at the office. She had something to deliver the next day and wasn't taking chances about getting back to the office by coming home. Maya and Aaya were playing some board game. Subbu was in the bedroom reading a fat Sanskrit book.

The rains began as a deceptive patter around four in the afternoon. Bharat sauntered downstairs to stand in the foyer and stare, bored from watching TV all day or retrieving email, which was just full of junk. Thunder rumbled on the horizon. Peering down the road, Bharat could see the gigantic waves, now darker than ever, rise in fury like a gargantuan cobra spreading its hood.

Joshi's apartment door opened. The man was holding an umbrella. He hurriedly moved a few of his treasured potted plants closer into the foyer so they may escape the wrath of the storm. He guarded every plant in the compound with great care. Bharat had to admit that he had exquisite taste. The landscaping of the compound was entirely his handiwork. He kept moving the potted plants to break the monotony.

"Looks a real tough one," he said to Bharat.

Bharat nodded.

Joshi then hollered for the watchmen who came scrambling, holding onto their raincoats. By now the patter had become an intense downpour and the winds howled.

"Switch on the emergency lights if there's a power cut! The power will get cut off anytime now!" Joshi yelled in his broken Tamil to make himself heard.

The watchmen hurried. The battery backed-up lights would last about eight hours. They offered some reprieve against the darkness that would engulf the compound and a large part of the neighborhood if there was a power outage.

"Do you have your torches?" Joshi called after the running watchmen, one for the front gate and the other for the back gate. Without turning around, they nodded.

"No office today?" Joshi asked Bharat.

"No," said Bharat.

"Idiot," Joshi cursed at some garbage that was lying outside the bin. To a startled Bharat, he said, "No. Not you. These idiots can't throw garbage into the bin."

Not minding the rain, Joshi ran into the courtyard, picked up the garbage, dropped it into the bin, and dashed back. In spite of the umbrella, he had become wet. Water was rolling down his mostly bald pate onto his luxuriant gray sideburns. Slush had stained his white pajamas near the foot (he was always dressed in white *kurta* and pajamas).

"See you later." He ran into his apartment.

The rain became a thick sheet, and Bharat could no longer see the sea clearly. The waves moved like a lumbering giant behind the translucent curtain of the rain.

•

There was no power since eight.

Bharat could not go to sleep. It was not merely the noise of the storm. What was his future? Some debts had been settled. By selling most of his stocks, he could settle all his debts if required. Would that be the right thing to do? What if the market was at the bottom and the stock started rising next week? It was while staring at these questions on the ceiling that he heard the crash.

He initially mistook it for thunder. But it was as if something fell down and broke, perhaps in the foyer on the ground floor. He got up and looked out of the window. The emergency lights feebly lit up a few feet around them. The downpour made them twinkle like stars. He could not see much beside the rain. The luminous clock showed 12:30 AM. He decided to go down and take a look.

With a flashlight guiding him, he went down the stairs, climbing down every step deliberately. He was overcome by the middle-of-the-night anger: irrational, unreasonable, seething, unmanageable. His eyes were bleary and hurt. The tee-shirt was stuck to his back with sweat. Every step he climbed down, the unreasonableness of his plight bothered him more.

"Did you hear something?"

Bharat almost jumped out of his skin.

It was Joshi. He was standing with a flashlight shining it around.

"Yes," said Bharat, recovering.

The beam of Joshi's flashlight caught a broken potted plant. That's what must have caused the crash.

"Must have been the wind," Bharat said.

Joshi looked suspicious. "The wind is not strong enough now to upset a pot as heavy as this. Look." He pointed to a clothesline. "The rain is heavy but the clothes are barely moving." He started shining the flashlight around again.

Bharat followed the light's motion mechanically. At one spot, both the lights caught the huddled figure. It was close to the pots that Joshi had moved into the foyer in the afternoon. They could see only a gunny sack and could not tell whether it was man or woman.

"Watchman!" Joshi yelled.

The watchmen came scrambling.

The huddled figure rose and headed towards Joshi and Bharat. A streak of lightning lit up the face. It was a man perhaps in his late thirties with a thick stubble and weak eyes. His clothes were in tatters and his only cover was the gunny sack.

As he neared them and began, "*Saar*..." Joshi screamed to the watchmen, "Catch him."

The huddled figure was making no attempt to escape. Instead the man had begun an appeal which he continued, "*Saar*...just tonight let me stay here."

By now the watchmen had seized one hand each of the man and were trying to restrain him from moving towards Joshi. The man offered no resistance.

"Who are you? What are you doing here?" Joshi demanded.

"*Saar*, I am from the fishermen settlement. The roof caved in. My family's away. I have no shelter. Just tonight. Let me remain in this corner." He pointed and continued, "Tomorrow morning I'll be off. I'll do something about the roof. Can't do anything now. Many houses are damaged. There isn't space for just one more person in the settlement. Some of us men dispersed giving room to women and children."

"He's lying," said Joshi to Bharat and the watchmen. "He's come to steal. It's a good night to steal. No power, heavy rains. Nobody would see him even if he wanted to."

"No, no, no," the man implored. "I didn't come to steal. If so, I could have run away. I was still sitting there waiting for your watchmen to come. Do you think I can't escape from your watchmen if I wanted to? How did I get in?"

"How *did* he get in?" Joshi asked the watchmen. They looked at each other, puzzled.

"I tell you, I came past this man," the man from the fisherman village pointed to the back gate watchman.

The watchman stared back at him angrily.

"He was sleeping in his bunk. It's quite dark and noisy," the man explained.

"I'll take care of you later," Joshi said ominously to the back gate watchman, then turned back to the man. "I don't believe you. I think you came to steal."

"*Saar*, please believe me. I don't need to steal. I am a fisherman. With God's grace, I manage a decent living. Once the rain goes away, I will reconstruct my house. Make it stronger. I have enough money. Let me stay here just tonight. I have nowhere to go."

"Nothing doing. Rules are rules. Nobody stays here. Go away," Joshi ordered sternly.

"You make the rules, don't you? I am sure you can let me stay if you want to," the man retorted.

That stoked Bharat's simmering rage. "What insolence. I don't think we should let this man stay. Watchmen, throw him out."

The watchmen hesitated.

"If you let this one fellow in, tomorrow he will bring the entire slum. They'll then claim this building is theirs. Big practical problem. Throw him out," Joshi also ordered.

"Do it now!" Bharat screamed, his rage rising.

When the watchmen began to move, the man stopped them. "I'll go myself." He stared alternately at Bharat and Joshi. "What's the use of all your education?"

Bharat stepped forward. "How dare you..."

Joshi restrained him whispering, "Don't manhandle this kind of people. You may be in big trouble."

Again, lightning lit up the man's face. Water was flowing down his face that now made his weak eyes shine in anger.

"Go away..." The front gate watchman raised his hand in

172

a threatening gesture.

Without a word, the man walked away. When he was near the back gate he paused. The emergency light silhouetted the gunny sack around his head.

The man stooped to plough into the soil and slush with his right hand, and flung it at them in the typical fishermen's cursing style. "All of you will perish. Without a house, without food, you rich idiots!" he shouted. His words carried over to them distinctly, over the deafening downpour and thunder.

As the front gate watchman took a step towards him, a ribbon of lightning crossed the sky and a clap of thunder followed. In the lightning, they saw the man darting into the darkness.

•

Rangan—"the real thug" as Joshi called him—paid his men well. Two evenings after the cyclone abated, he gave Joshi's address to two of his men, and specified what they had to do that night. Rangan was always very precise with his instructions. He emphasized often that he paid so well only to get the job done exactly as he wanted it—not overdone, not underdone. When he had finished instructing, he asked the men to repeat what he told them. Each man independently repeated Rangan's instructions. Satisfied, Rangan nodded and dismissed them.

A little after midnight, the men effortlessly scaled the compound walls of the apartment complex. The front gate watchman and the back gate watchman were in deep sleep. Even if they had been awake they wouldn't have noticed the men. They were professionals who moved with the agility of cats. They stopped outside Joshi's apartment and made sure that they had the right apartment. One of them stood guard while the other swung into action. The entire operation did not take more than a few minutes.

The man in charge of the action brought out a piece of charcoal, and on the wall adjacent to Joshi's apartment door wrote in bold Tamil letters: "Don't fool around with us if you love your life."

Noiselessly, he broke a few flower pots and left the debris in a heap just outside the apartment door. Both men surveyed the scene to make sure that they had carried out Rangan's instructions carefully. When they left, the two watchmen were still snoring.

CHAPTER 9

Joshi found reading newspapers online an annoying experience. Even though he subscribed to one or two, he looked forward every morning to opening the door with a mug of coffee and finding the day's crisp newspaper. That morning when he opened the door, his newspaper was there, but on a mangled heap of broken clay, mud and plants. For a moment, he stood uncomprehendingly. Then he picked up the newspaper and jumped over the debris with great difficulty. His pajama seam near his crotch gave way with a telling noise. Gingerly, with one finger he felt the tear. Luckily it wasn't big or visible. And nobody was around.

"Watchman," he hollered.

The two watchmen, now well accustomed to his peremptory yelling over trivia, scrambled to the foyer. This time, however, they knew something was wrong. They found Joshi choleric with anger. He was trembling from head to foot, and his lower lip had a particularly conspicuous quiver.

"What's all this?" Joshi demanded.

The watchmen looked at each other quizzically.

"What's all this?" Joshi repeated his question.

That's when the back gate watchman, the meeker of the two, noticed the charcoal writing on the wall.

"*Saar*, there's something written on the wall."

Joshi had headed out of his apartment door, his attention engaged by the debris all over the foyer that he hadn't noticed the writing. He turned around to read it. To his frustration, he found it was in Tamil. He could speak broken Tamil, but couldn't read a word.

"What is written there?" he asked.

The back gate watchman read it out aloud with great hesitation.

"What's all this?" Joshi repeated stupidly.

"*Saar*, I don't know," said the front gate watchman and asked the back gate watchman in a threatening tone, "Did you notice something? Everything seems to happen only through the back gate."

The back gate watchman protested. "The foyer's near the front gate. You should have noticed."

"Whoever did this must have made a lot of noise entering from the back gate side. I am sure you were sleeping."

"Oh, stop it both of you!" screamed Joshi.

A few occupants, hearing the commotion, had now gathered in the foyer. They were viewing the debris and the writing with interest and concern. Each was picking up a piece, and making guesses as a self-appointed detective.

Bharat had not had much sleep. He had been up early when he heard Joshi calling out. Since he had nothing specific to do, he had developed the habit of puttering around in the compound and was often joined by Joshi. He had developed a reluctant friendship with the man who kept rambling about his old war stories. Some of them were amusing and fantastic, but Bharat suspected that Joshi just invented them. He had been one of the youngest to rise to the rank of a Major. If that was so, why did he take early retirement, or was it early retirement? At that Joshi clammed up. He would mutter something inaudible or change the subject and remark how one of the plants looked famished.

Bharat dashed down the stairs with Subbu in hot pursuit. The two now joined the others around Joshi.

"These two idiots." Joshi was pointing furiously to the watchmen. "Useless fellows."

"That's not the point," one of the occupants stressed. "We have to figure out who did it and why."

While the occupants made uncertain guesses, the front gate watchman cleared his throat hesitantly. Everybody turned to him.

"If *saar* will not get angry, I think I can make a guess."

"Cut the crap, and get to the point." Joshi was testy.

"I think it was the man."

"What man?" Joshi asked.

"The fisherman we chased out in the rain."

Plausible, thought Bharat. He recalled the man's insolence, his vicious curse. He felt the blood rushing to his face in anger. To the gathering, he explained quickly what happened the other night.

"Some of these fellows are very vindictive. They are desperadoes who'll stop at nothing. We have to be careful," the front gate watchman continued, encouraged by the interest on the onlookers' faces.

"It's your job to stop them," Joshi hissed.

The front gate watchman joined his palms in salute. "*Saar*, I'll quit my job if you want me to. Fighting these fellows as one man? No *saar*, no. Can't do. You should go to the police. These fellows are a big gang. I live in the next settlement with my family. I can't take such risks."

"I think we should sack this fellow," Joshi suggested and looked for support. None came. They all seemed to agree with the watchman.

One of them spoke up. "What the watchman says is right. I've heard of this sort of retaliation before. In the apartment blocks in the nearby streets. Nothing could be proved. Most of the watchmen are scared. They won't talk even if they knew something."

"What should we do?" Joshi asked generally.

"Let's go to the police," Bharat suggested. He was aching for revenge. The damned insolence, the fisherman had asked him what use his education was.

"Can't we find out a little bit more before we go to the police?" Subbu asked.

Indu, on her way to the office, joined the conversation. "How?" she asked. She had returned that morning to pack a bag of fresh clothes.

"Talk to the maids. Let the watchmen ask around."

"No. It's that chap. I remember the look in his eyes. It's him. We should teach him a lesson." Bharat's voice was rising in anger. Later he would wonder whether his anger was really at the fisherman.

"I think that's the right thing to do. If we don't teach these fellows a lesson, they'll think we are suckers. And they'll keep doing this again and again," Indu said with determination. "We must go to the police. Bharat, why don't you and I go with the Colonel and lodge a complaint with the police? On my way to work?"

At the mention of "Colonel," Joshi's initiative was kindled. "Indu's right. Let's go to the police."

The watchmen had been ordered to clean the debris and wash off the writing. While the debris was cleaned quite easily, the charcoal writing could not be erased so quickly. In fact, the watchmen did such a messy job, that a misty outline remained of the writing for a long time that would warn all who came to the foyer: "Don't fool around with us if you love your life."

•

"What happens after a few days?" Indu asked the police superintendent.

"After a few days, we withdraw our security to Mr. Joshi and just keep an eye on the locality," the police superintendent replied without raising his eyes from the thick register in which he continued to write something. In the dim light, it was hard to say what exactly he was writing. The guard at the entrance, with his rifle, was yawning.

When they decided to go to the police, Indu said it wouldn't work if they approached the police at the low level. She made a few phone calls to her bosses and their contacts, and eventually got through to the Commissioner of Police. He was kind enough to refer Indu to the local superintendent, and assured her that he would speak to him before Indu went to the local police station.

The superintendent had given them a cold, businesslike welcome. Indu wasn't sure if he bore a grudge that she had talked to his boss. When they were inside, he waved them to chairs still writing something. He must have been in his mid-fifties, close to retirement. He had closely cropped silver hair and was clean shaven. Rimless spectacles balanced themselves on his sharp nose. Bharat thought that if the superintendent stepped out of his uniform, he could easily be mistaken for a professor or a researcher.

His voice a deep growl, he said, "Yes?" and peered at them from above his spectacles.

When they were done, he asked them, "Would you prefer to lodge a formal complaint?"

Indu was impatient. "Of course, of course."

An officer registered their complaint. The superintendent sighed.

"So, what do we do?" Indu asked.

The superintendent thought for a long minute. "It looks like the fisherman is a suspect. But I have been in this area for many years. Sometimes, these fellows grow violent. But they are not the scheming, carefully planning types. They are impulsive and most often forget their quarrels in a matter of hours. While a quick look suggests that the fisherman might have been responsible, I am not quite convinced."

"It's him, it's him," Bharat interjected in a shrill voice.

"Well, we can get him and interrogate him, if that's what you want," the superintendent drawled.

"What do you mean? If that's what we want. Shouldn't you decide what to do?" Bharat demanded.

The superintendent gave him a cold glare. "Mister, as a police officer, I know my duties. I am trying to tell you a few things here. If you want me to speak as a policeman, I will. However, I think it would be useful to you if I spoke as myself. I leave it to you."

While Indu was also irritated by the superintendent, she wanted progress. "Please tell us what you think."

The superintendent sighed again.

"Now I speak as myself, not as a policeman," he began ceremoniously. "I have seen scores of such cases. They go to nothing. I can get the fisherman as a suspect for interrogation. I can question him. But there'll be little evidence. I'll have to let him go after some tough questioning. The case would be open for a while. Then we'll close it. Want a suggestion?"

"Yes," said Indu and Joshi in chorus while Bharat remained sullen.

"Let's give this a week or two. I'll post a watch on Mr. Joshi's apartment. If nothing happens, it means it's blown over. Usually nothing happens after that. As I said earlier, these fellows are impulsive, not calculating and scheming. If it's them, their anger lasts a few hours, no more."

"You mean we do nothing? Take no action against the fisherman?" Bharat asked incredulously.

"That's exactly what I am suggesting. I speak as myself, not as a policeman."

Joshi was uncertain, but Bharat and Indu were insistent. "No, we must bring that fellow in for questioning. How can we let him go scot-free after what he's done?"

"Correction," said the superintendent. "We don't know he's done it. He's only a suspect."

"I think we should get him in for interrogation," Indu declared, and Bharat nodded. Joshi, after a moment of doubt, nodded.

"Are you sure?" the superintendent asked.

"Absolutely," said Bharat.

"I'll need somebody to go with us to identify him."

Initially Bharat thought of suggesting that the watchmen go to identify the fisherman. He recalled the front gate watchman's reaction earlier that morning and knew neither watchman would accept the task.

"Mr. Joshi or I will come when you need us," said Bharat flinching at the idea of going into the settlement.

"No, let's not do that. Either of you can point him out from a distance. We'll take care of him. It's better for him not to know that you pointed him out."

"Won't he guess anyway?" Bharat asked.

"If he's a notorious character, then he does this kind of a thing for a living. Not attacking just your apartment. We will do some general inquiries without specifically referring to the incident in your apartment. If we think he has done it, we'll have to then refer to your case. Then we can't avoid referring to your complaint."

"But what's our protection if he gets to know?" Joshi enquired. After his military bravado, he had to make a visible effort not to ask look abashed when he asked the question. He had to stretch himself full height and work up a dignity in his expression.

That's when the superintendent offered to post a police guard outside Joshi's apartment door for a few days. It was agreed that Bharat or Joshi would try to point out the man to the police guard in the next one or two days, as unobtrusively as possible.

"What happens if they attack after you withdraw your security? What can you do?" Indu repeated her question differently.

"I say this as myself, not as a policeman. Nothing."

"What's our protection?" Indu repeated Joshi's question of a few minutes back.

"Nothing. There's no protection after a point."

"Nothing?" asked Indu outraged. "How can you give such an irresponsible answer as a policeman?"

"I speak as myself, not as a policeman," the superintendent reminded her.

"Okay, okay," Indu said impatiently. "Whatever. I still think it's an irresponsible answer."

"Do you know how many in this country are rich?" the superintendent asked.

He drew silence from his audience.

"How many are poor?"

Again, silence.

"After a while, do you think that any number of police-men or soldiers are protection? You must be kidding yourself."

"I still think you are speaking irresponsibly."

The superintendent sighed deeply in a visible effort to contain his rising petulance. "So how about the people who created the free market? Very responsible? How about educa-tion only for the rich? Is that very responsible? Go figure. You now want me to take care of all the mistakes?"

"Look here officer, all our wealth is earned lawfully. We have paid taxes on every rupee earned. We have a right to possess it. The police are here to protect us," Indu protested.

The superintendent's eyebrows arched superciliously. "You talk like the lady of sometime ago who said if people didn't have bread, let them eat cakes. You know what happened to her, of course?"

"Who's she?" Indu asked.

The superintendent returned briefly to his writing. "Maybe you should read Santayana. Those who do not know their past are condemned to repeat it."

"Who's this woman Santayana? And what's she got to do with all this?" Clearly Indu had no clue where this conversa-tion was leading.

"Santayana was a man. Surely you've read some history? Some philosophy?" the superintendent asked without raising his eyes.

"No, I have not," replied Indu vehemently. "I underwent Focused Courses. We had to learn lots of Java, XML, web ser-vices. We had no time for history and philosophy. Thank heavens for that. Don't think you can talk down to me."

Unexpectedly the superintendent lifted his eyes and

smiled. "No offence meant. I'll call for you when we need to locate the fisherman. The guard will report for duty this evening. Good day to all of you."

•

The next morning, the plainclothes police guard suggested that they take a discreet walk in the neighborhood to try and spot the man. The last evening's walk had yielded nothing. Subbu insisted that he would also go on the walk with Bharat and the guard since he had nothing better to do. When they were on the verge of giving up and returning home, Bharat spotted the man. He was scratching his stubble, buying *beedi*s from one of the small shops close to the settlement. Subbu noticed his tattered clothes, his thick black stubble, his mop of curly hair, and large mischievous eyes. The man did not notice them as he walked away into the settlement whistling merrily.

The police guard peered as well as he could and nodded his head. "I know him now. We can take care from here on." He did not let Bharat and Subbu know exactly what the police planned to do next.

That evening, Maya and Subbu went to the park to swing. The park was slushy from all the rain, but Maya wouldn't give up her swinging. She brought her last year's computer textbooks in the hope of seeing the girls from the settlement. Her school was closed, and she was going to a new class. She did not need the textbooks anymore. When she asked Subbu whether she could give her textbooks to the little girl from the settlement, Subbu, remembering the little girl's eagerness to study computers, asked "why not?" and suggested that she take it with her to the park that evening.

It was almost seven, and the girls from the settlement

hadn't turned up. Maya had been straining her eyes in the dimming light to see if they would appear at the end of the street. Now she looked disappointed.

"Why don't we go give the books to the girls?" suggested Subbu.

Maya's face lit up. "Oh, let's. Please." And then she got a doubt. "But, *pantu-thatha*, we don't know even their names?"

"Don't worry," said Subbu. "We only have to get close to their homes, and they will come up to meet you." He had complete faith in the sophisticated communication system of the settlement.

When they reached the edge of the Dark World, a little girl sped off on spying them. Subbu knew this triggered the communication system. It was unusually dark. One of the two sodium vapor lamps that lit the area wasn't working. Its glass was broken. The lone sodium vapor lamp and the dim lights from the little shops and tenements barely provided enough light to outline the moving figures. Subbu took Maya right under the sodium vapor lamp while they waited. She waited with excitement, her finger in her mouth.

It was then that the police van arrived. With little warning, the van screeched to a halt forcing Subbu to hastily pull out Maya from its path. In a moment, the van disgorged what seemed like dozens of policemen, some of whom cordoned off the area by blocking the street to the settlement. Subbu looked anxiously since he was inside the cordon with Maya. The other set of policemen set off into the settlement with torches and searchlights.

It was only when Subbu recognized the plainclothes police guard in uniform did he realize what was going on. The plainclothes guard, who now appeared very burly in his uniform, gave a grim nod to Subbu and headed into the settlement with an inspector who seemed to be in command.

The flashlights were swinging, and inquisitive beams from torches started searching the corners. Subbu started to go back with Maya, but he noticed the cordon had grown stronger since the police were holding back many settlement dwellers from getting in. He watched helplessly as his blank mind refused to think. What should he do next?

"*Pantu-thatha*, what's happening?" asked Maya, fear in her eyes.

"Oh, nothing. I think we should go home now."

"What about the computer books?"

"Another day, darling. We'll come back soon."

The police cordon appeared firm. It seemed the best thing to stay under the sodium vapor lamp for the present.

One searchlight, within a few seconds of the commencement of operations, picked up the face of the man. There was no mistaking it. The thick stubble, the curly hair, and the mischievous eyes. He had perhaps been heading out of the settlement without an inkling of what was in store.

"That's him," the plainclothes police guard, now in uniform, cried.

The man, trained by instinct, knew they had come for him. In that brief moment, Subbu saw panic set into his mischievous eyes. He turned around, and with the sleekness of a leopard, disappeared into the settlement. The rest of the settlement moved with surprising speed. Dozens of people, men and women, had gathered to block the way of the police—the well-conditioned, chlamydomonas-like response against a perpetual threat. The entry to the settlement was narrow, and it took only four to five people, standing side by side, to fully block any entry.

The inspector and the police guard stopped in their tracks with the rest of the policemen behind them. A few feet behind them stood Subbu and Maya, and further behind the police cordon restrained the other dwellers from entering the settlement. Heads had started peering from the balconies and terraces of the neighboring apartments.

The crowd inside the settlement parted to let a corpulent man, about fifty, to come to the front. The unbuttoned shirt revealed a black *banian*, which was drenched in sweat, and his handlebar moustache masked most of his face. His red, authoritarian eyes passed over the inspector and the guard.

"What do you want?" he drawled. He reeked of toddy, and there was a fresh whiff every time he spoke.

"That man," the inspector pointed vaguely towards the dark inside of the settlement.

Subbu watched the settlement with admiration as the few lights were turning off one by one as if a commander had given a blackout order. The shops had dimmed their lamps. The sodium vapor lamp, the torches and the searchlights were now the only sources of light left.

"What man?" the corpulent man asked.

"The man who ran away just now," the inspector said.

"Who ran? There are many people here. Who's the man you are talking about? Do you know his name?"

The police guard looked ridiculous. "No."

"See if he is here."

The policemen shone their lights on the crowd. Every face was scanned from a distance. No, he wasn't there.

"Oh, don't kid us. We know he wouldn't be here," the inspector said. "He's somewhere inside."

The corpulent man made no attempt to move. "What do you want him for?"

"We don't need to tell you that," the police guard retorted. "Just move out of our way, and we'll take care of the rest."

"Maari," called out the corpulent man to a second man

who appeared from inside the crowd.

"Yes, brother," said Maari to the corpulent man.

"They just want us to move out of the way."

"How's that possible?" asked Maari. "Many families live here. You are upsetting them. If we let you in, you'll damage all our property."

"We don't want to damage anybody's property or cause disturbance to anybody. We just want the man," the inspector replied impatiently.

"Why don't you leave us a description, and we'll make sure that he's delivered at the police station in the morning?" Maari offered. The fat man nodded his assent.

"You think we are idiots?" the police guard asked. "To go away without him? If we move away for five minutes, he will disappear from the face of earth. Nothing doing. Get out of our way."

The fat man, Maari, and the rest of the crowd stood stonily. Subbu couldn't help contrasting the bourgeois fear of the policeman that caused a tremor in the knees, and the cold indifference of the fishermen.

Maya had become silent from the recognition that something was wrong and asking questions wouldn't help. When Subbu stretched his arms and hoisted her to his waist, she was neither surprised nor offered any resistance. Carrying Maya, he started edging towards the police cordon.

The inspector raised his *lathi* and spoke deliberately, "I will give you one minute. If you don't move away, we will start *lathicharge*. What's your decision?"

Even in the dark, the bamboo stick in the inspector's hand had an ominous sheen.

"No way." "Do what you please." "Not going to move." The men and women conveyed their determination to stand their ground.

The dwellers outside the police cordon were becoming restless and were throwing questions at their folks inside the settlement. They had now started demanding angrily that they be let inside. Some were suggesting that they take on the policemen, the fiends. The policemen at the cordon joined hands and stood grimly.

At the end of the minute, the inspector cried, "Charge!"

The policemen close to the settlement unleashed themselves upon the crowd. The dark night was punctuated by the thumps of the *lathi*s followed by screams. Strangely like lightning and thunder—the same lag between a thump and an accompanying scream. Men and women fell to the ground, some with broken limbs, some with the intent of impeding the police.

The cordon could hold no longer. The police at the cordon began beating up the dwellers who rushed to the assistance of their inmates.

Subbu now closed the eyes of Maya with his palm, and decided not to move against the surging crowd from behind the cordon. Instead he leaned against an asbestos wall by the side protecting Maya by turning his back to the street. His hair was pulled and his *veshti* was almost wrenched away. He held on to his *veshti* by stamping on it with a foot, wasting precious energy in the deal, all along cursing man's primordial instinct to cover his shame even in dire distress.

The shops now had switched off their lights. The only lights that remained were the sodium vapor lamp, and the policemen's lights. Subbu's slippers were now gone, and a sharp stone was testing his sole. He held on to Maya gritting his teeth. Most of the settlement dwellers, and the police were now into the settlement. Under the sodium vapor lamp, Subbu saw the little girl who had sped off to carry the message of their arrival. She had fallen down and was making a desperate attempt to rise and run. A policeman approached her and another woman near her.

"Get out of the way," he screamed and beat the woman on her back. She fell down screaming.

The little girl was making an attempt to rise. The policeman moved towards her.

"Stop, don't" Subbu cried, but he could barely hear his own voice. The policeman cracked his *lathi* on her leg below the knee. Above the melee, Subbu could hear the telling crack of the twig. The girl doubled up in pain, and tried to rise. Her fractured leg caved in, and she fell back, her face twisted in torment for she had no strength left to cry. It was then that Subbu realized that he no longer shielded Maya's eyes and that she had seen the little girl.

Piece of God fractured. Piece of God with broken leg. Piece of God being trampled over.

The colors threatened to strike Subbu right then. He forced Maya's head on to his shoulder and jostling, pushing and kicking he managed to get beyond the cordon. As he steadied Maya and tried to secure his *veshti*, he felt the warm trickle of Maya's urine on his left leg.

•

"Did they get him?" Subbu asked.

"I think so. That's what the police guard told me," replied Bharat.

"We don't know if he did it," Subbu said watching Indu.

Promptly Indu said, "He must have. These rascals. Even that night, he must have come here to steal." Her chest was heaving, and her eyes flashed her rage.

"What if he didn't?" Subbu asked.

"What if he didn't what?" Indu shot back.

"What if he didn't break the flower pots? Write the warning?"

"Well, then he deserves to be punished for intruding here that night."

"What about all the others who were beaten? I don't know how many will get up and walk again."

"*Pantu-thatha*, you are grossly underestimating them. This is not anything to fell them. They also pretend and make a big noise."

Pretend and make a big noise. Subbu's ears were constantly replaying the thump of the *lathi* and bones breaking. Big noise.

"But they didn't do anything wrong. The others, I mean."

"They blocked the police. The law. Anyone who does that has to be dealt with firmly. After all, they were warned. It's the destiny of the law-breakers."

"You weren't there. Do you know they broke the leg of a little girl, barely Maya's age?"

"*Pantu-thatha*, her parents, her elders, should have been more responsible. All the more reason they shouldn't have protested."

"You weren't there," Subbu repeated. "I still can't understand why."

Indu's eyes flashed anger. "*Pantu-thatha*, you seem to be implying that we and the police are wrong. Let me tell you something. We haven't broken the law in any manner. We have worked very hard to earn every rupee. I have never heard this theory before that law-abiding citizens could actually be in the wrong."

"I wasn't implying anything," Subbu muttered and left the room.

Bharat sighed with relief.

The feared reprisal did not happen. It appeared that the

superintendent was right. The anger of the settlement seemed to be momentary. The morning after the police raid, the settlement wore its usual look, with men hanging around languorously. The urchins had started their game of cricket with a broken cricket bat and a well-worn tennis ball.

After a week, the police guard was withdrawn from the front of Joshi's apartment. The front gate watchman and the back gate watchman received fresh instructions and fresh job threats from Joshi. The other residents didn't seem to care much about this incident. The damage was limited only to Joshi's apartment. Most of them believed that it was a personal message only for Joshi. Some actually enjoyed it.

"His fines and his Colonel rubbish. Good for him," somebody remarked.

Till the next apartment association meeting happened, Joshi could not order the painting of his disfigured wall. The expenditure, being sizeable, had to be authorized in an association meeting. The residents passing through the foyer remarked how ugly the wall had become with the paint peeling off under the industrious scrubbing by the watchmen. Visitors to the apartment complex could not miss reading the ominous warning in the foyer: "Don't fool around with us if you love your life."

"This must be some arrogant avant-garde interior decorator's idea. These days Harlem-style graffiti is in real fashion. This actually comes close to that," one visitor remarked to another.

CHAPTER 10

They would be the last to see Dr. Rakesh. His assistant, a woman in her late twenties, fluttered her eyelids at Bharat and said, "The doctor will see you last. Doesn't have to worry about other people waiting, you see." At eight, she packed her stuff, waved to them a "bye," and left.

Maya, unaware that she was the patient, was leafing through *Arabian Nights*, her favorite book for some time now. Bharat and Maya were sitting with a cross look. They had quarreled the previous day. There had been a Parent-Teacher meeting at the conclusion of the year, and Bharat had played truant on some excuse. After the meeting, Indu had stormed in, far angrier than ever.

"See what happened," she said slapping the air-conditioner switches on.

"What?" enquired Bharat without shifting his gaze from the TV. He was peeved that afternoon since two job opportunities that he had been pursuing hopefully had come to naught.

Subbu had appeared in the hallway discreetly.

"You sit here and ask what? Why don't you attend these meetings?"

"You said you would go."

"Know what the teachers are saying now? They will not promote Maya to the next class unless we get a psychiatric evaluation done," Indu fumed.

"What's wrong?" Bharat asked. It was clear to Indu that he wasn't receiving what she was saying. Indu grabbed the remote control and switched the TV off.

"Why don't you listen to me?" she said in a high-pitched tone.

"You better turn the TV on," Bharat said menacingly.

"Why don't you listen, Bharat?" Subbu called out from the hallway. This was it. The day he had dreaded had arrived. The bad manners of Bharat or Indu mattered little to him now. He wanted Bharat to listen, so he could know as well.

With opposition mounting, Bharat gave up his efforts to watch TV. "So tell me what happened," he demanded.

"What I told you. Maya has done okay in her studies. I think *pantu-thatha* taught her the lessons as he promised. Her grades have improved a lot. Bharat, why couldn't you have taught her the rest of the stuff? Instead of sending useless emails and watching TV all day?"

"Look, I can't understand what you're saying. Don't talk in circles."

Indu dropped her bag on the dining table and pulled up a chair. "She's not done too badly in her exams. Nothing great, but will do for her to go to the next class. But she still can't log into her exam papers online. Or won't maybe. Once she's there, she completes many questions. *Pantu-thatha* can't teach her that stuff. He has taught her to answer questions once she gets there. Most of her teachers feel that she isn't communicating well with her classmates. She refuses to log into chats. Her classmates call her neurotic, strange, a nut—all sorts of things. The teachers think she is pleasantly obstinate. That's the term her teacher used. They think her behavior is not what it should be. Withdrawn, resistant, loner. They used all kinds of terms."

"Now what?" Bharat asked.

"They want a psychiatric opinion. While on subjects she has improved a lot, they think her behavioral development is not up to the mark. Until a shrink says that she is all right to go to the next class, they don't want to confirm her promotion."

Their argument extended into the night. Fortunately, Aaya and Maya were playing in her bedroom for the most part, and Maya went to sleep early. Subbu issued clandestine instructions to Aaya for all board games to be put away for some time. The teachers had complained of Maya's explicit fascination for playing board games, spinning tops, and flying kites. Forever playing with dolls and building houses with mud. Not quite in keeping with her demographic background, they felt.

"A bit...um...philistine, don't you think?" one teacher had asked. "Besides, with everything becoming electronic, how can anybody hope to stay from it almost completely?"

During admissions, they sent all the children for a routine psychiatric evaluation. Nothing wrong in getting another done, they had assured Indu.

The next morning, Bharat fixed up a meeting with Dr. Rakesh. Subbu had made it clear that he was not seeking anybody's permission in the matter; he was going with them. On learning this, Bharat had to make a hurried second phone call to Dr. Rakesh to warn him about Subbu: "My grandfather cannot be told of my sessions with you... Yes, he is aware that my wife visits you occasionally... No, that doesn't seem to bother him."

Waiting to be called in by Dr. Rakesh, while he was tending to another patient, Subbu wondered about his family. There had been no insanity in his family that he knew about. Insanity was a strong word. In the remotest branches of his family, nobody had ever been assailed by any mental problem. His family had been known for its robust cheer, its plentiful garrulousness, its serious and intense arguments about trivia, and its backslapping bonhomie. Their neighborhoods had always remarked about the family's zest for life and longevity. Almost everybody had lived into his or her eighties when medicine had hardly developed.

Wait a minute. Subbu suddenly recalled a second cousin's wife who had suffered from depression that was then not known as such. "The devil had possessed her," they said. Even that was not such a serious case. On occasion when Subbu met her, he thought she was extra demure. Devils were not demure.

And how silly, how could that woman's genes affect my descendants?

Subbu recalled that when the woman was taken to the mental hospital for a check-up, that was neighborhood news. "The mad doctor is treating her," they said as if it were the doctor who was mad. They spoke about it for such a long time after the incident. After all, one didn't hear of somebody going to the mad doctor often. And certainly, not from "decent" families.

However much he racked his brains, Subbu could not understand what about Maya was so wrong. What were her teachers objecting to? He was very confused about electronic

196

exams and chatting and video games. All he knew about computers was switching one on and checking his savings bank account balance. This he learned to do out of the necessity to handle the fixed deposit and the savings bank account that gave him his monthly allowance. He had also learned to operate the machine that gave him cash. Admittedly, he had coping problems with the disappearance of the check book, the cashier, and the teller's counter from all the bank branches around him.

Surely computers were simple to learn? He had learned it after he became eighty. Maya was intelligent enough to pick up these things. She was still young. You didn't have to see a psychiatrist just for that.

"Seeing a psychiatrist doesn't make you mad," Indu explained to him. "It's now like seeing a dentist. Don't I see one? Don't all my colleagues see one?"

Subbu wanted to respond that they deserve to see one, therefore they are seeing one.

Dr. Rakesh's head peeped out. "Come in."

Subbu was taken aback by the doctor's appearance. With well-groomed hair, a pastel shirt and a fine-printed tie, he looked more like a smart, cultured executive.

"Hello, Indu," he said.

Keeping up his act, he shook hands with Bharat as if he were meeting him only then.

"My grandfather." Bharat pointed to Subbu.

"Hello, sir." Dr. Rakesh extended his hand to see Subbu with his palms joined in greeting. He quickly withdrew his hand and returned the greeting. "*Namaste.*"

He waved them to chairs. His clinic was brightly lit, with tasteful furniture and tapestry. Why did I expect a dimly lit clinic and a depressing couch, Subbu asked himself.

"Hello," Dr. Rakesh said to Maya and produced a chocolate from nowhere. Maya grinned, looked doubtfully at Bharat and Indu, decided to take the chocolate, but made no attempt to eat it.

"What are you reading?" Dr. Rakesh asked.

"Arabian Nights." Maya held it up.

Dr. Rakesh took the book, stroked its leather cover appreciatively, and said, "Used to be my favorite. Never seen a binding like this. Leather? Where did it come from?"

"It's mine," Subbu said. "It dates back to 1910 or so."

Dr. Rakesh lifted his eyebrows in surprise. "What's your favorite story? Sinbad?"

"No. Caliph Haroun Al-Rashid," said Maya. "Sinbad's only my second best in the book."

"Really?" asked Dr. Rakesh.

"Yes. Karna is one of my favorites. *Pantu-thatha* tells it so well."

"Who's *pantu-thatha*?"

Maya pointed to Subbu with her index finger. Looking at her doe eyes, Subbu felt angry and sad that she was sitting here for an examination. An impotent rage seized him, which to calm he had to grind his big toe into the floor.

At the mention of *Karna*, Bharat's interest perked up. *Karna* had been his favorite as well. He could recall *pantu-thatha*'s dramatic gestures: his hand stringing an imaginary bow, cruel, merciless arrows being dispatched, and *Karna* dying for friendship, which he had escalated above all blood relationships. The tender sorrow that gripped him then came back for a tiny moment.

"All right, Maya, do you want to be reading while I talk to your parents?" Dr. Rakesh asked.

"Yes," nodded Maya.

"Can we talk there?" Dr. Rakesh pointed to a door that led to another room. He glanced through the corner of his eye at

Maya. She was busy reading, and didn't seem interested in the private meeting the doctor was about to have.

When Subbu got up to join them, Dr. Rakesh suggested, "Why don't you stay with her, sir?"

"No, I am going with you," Subbu said with determination. He was worried sick that Indu and Bharat might use some inappropriate words to describe Maya's condition. "Maya, I will be back soon."

Maya, lost in her reading, nodded perfunctorily.

In the adjoining room, Dr. Rakesh heard out Indu and Bharat taking turns talking. Indu talked more than Bharat, and Subbu interjected once in a while to make a remark that nothing was wrong with that or to ask why something was wrong with that. Every time Subbu interjected, Dr. Rakesh gave him a patient look.

Finally he asked them some questions about Maya's age, her general health, Aaya, and then interrogated Subbu about the family history.

"Let me talk to her," he said and stood up.

Subbu was relieved that Dr. Rakesh effortlessly put Maya at ease. He doubted if Maya even knew that she was being examined by a doctor. He hoped that everything would remain this way, and things wouldn't be as bad as he imagined them to be.

Maya was led to a stool in front of a computer. Dr. Rakesh clicked its mouse. The modem squealed and moaned in amorous tones establishing the connection between the computer and the Internet.

"Sorry, outdated technology. This dial-up connection." Dr. Rakesh smiled apologetically. "I have been meaning to upgrade. Haven't found the time yet."

In the silence punctuated by the moaning of the modem, Bharat asked, "How's your business doing?"

Dr. Rakesh smiled. "Business is booming. Knock wood."

The connection was now established.

Dr. Rakesh led Maya through many sites: games, sports, and movies. Maya sat with a decidedly indifferent expression. There was a flicker of expression when the Barbie site appeared and again when the doctor loaded a chess site. She played chess avidly with Dr. Rakesh. Subbu could easily see that Dr. Rakesh was not being indulgent; he was playing hard and getting cornered. After a while, the game was aborted, and Dr. Rakesh switched abruptly to a porn site.

Subbu held his breath, while Indu and Bharat flinched. It was only for a few seconds, and Dr. Rakesh switched to a fashion site. Maya registered indifference. He then pointed to the chats going on.

"Are your friends there?" Dr. Rakesh asked.

Maya was now gazing out of the glass window of the clinic, which opened into a small, green courtyard with a solitary mango tree. She did not answer the question.

"Do you know the chat IDs of your friends?"

"I don't know any IDs." Maya's statement caused dismay on Indu's face.

"All right. Tell me the names of your friends."

Maya thought for a minute. "Oh *pantu-thatha*, we don't even know their names," she said desperately. "We went to find out, but couldn't. There was the police...so much confusion..."

Indu raised her eyebrows and Bharat frowned.

"That's okay," Subbu said hastily. "Tell uncle the name of your school friends."

With great reluctance, Maya named two girls and a boy and then abruptly rose to go to the window. Her face was suffused with radiant excitement.

"What are you looking at, Maya?" asked Dr. Rakesh.

Maya silently pointed to the tree. Subbu, Bharat and Indu, who had followed the doctor, noticed the squirrel. The glass was see-through only in one direction. The squirrel could neither see nor hear them. It was perched carefree, only a few feet away from them, on a slender branch which rocked gently under its movement, unaware that it was under the gaze of so many eyes. It held something between its forepaws which it nibbled at furiously.

"Beautiful isn't it? Look how it runs up and down now," whispered Maya.

Soon the squirrel was joined by another, and they held a tiny but serious conversation. They then ran up and down in patterns, crossing each other now and then, and stopping for exchanging coded secrets.

"Do you like the squirrels running up and down?" Dr. Rakesh asked.

Maya shook her head vigorously. "Yes, I do."

"Maybe I can make a video of that? I have a digital camera here. You can then make it your screen saver. You can see it all the time," Dr. Rakesh offered.

"No!" protested Maya. Then remembering her mother's stern instructions on courtesies, said, "No, thank you, uncle."

"Why not?" probed Dr. Rakesh gently.

Maya, who was now completely mesmerized by the squirrel pair, did not hear the question.

Dr. Rakesh repeated the question.

"Huh?" said Maya. "Oh, if the squirrels became a screen saver, they would be doing the same thing again and again. Boring. See, see, see. How he tumbles now? Oops, he almost fell. And squirrels, they should be on trees outside. Squirrels on computers? I think that's idiotic."

"Mayaa..." Indu admonished her at the sudden irreverence.

Dr. Rakesh discreetly silenced Indu with a finger on lip.

"May I talk to her alone?"

Dr. Rakesh led Maya to the adjoining room. Bharat, Indu, and Subbu could hear the muffled, soft conversation.

The door opened after fifteen minutes or so. During the fifteen minutes, every other minute Subbu bothered Bharat why it was taking so long until Bharat snapped at him to shut up.

"Maya, you can continue your reading. Or you can watch the squirrels if you want to," Dr. Rakesh said.

Maya went to the glass window and peered. The squirrels had gone. She waited for a few seconds, then returned to her chair. "I think I'll continue reading."

Dr. Rakesh beckoned to them to join him in the adjoining room.

"I hope there's nothing wrong," Subbu said without waiting to sit down.

Indu glared at him.

"Yes and no," said Dr. Rakesh. "There's nothing seriously wrong now. But left untended she could have grave adaptation problems later."

"What exactly is the problem?" Indu asked.

"It's a sense of alienation. If you want the technical term for it, it's the early stages of what we call anomie."

"What's anomie?" Bharat asked.

"It's an affliction that causes the victim to have social interaction that's lower than the usual standards in a group. Or the social interaction is markedly different from the usual social norm. It is a sort of rootlessness. You can't identify yourself with what goes on around you. Usually it happens to adults, but now we understand that children show early signs. It can be individual, or it can be a collective affliction. There can be many triggers. Large economic changes, cultural changes. Like the fall of communism. The fall of the Berlin wall. Lack of parental attention. Lack of early attention to coping problems. It's hard to locate the exact trigger."

"You say our daughter has it?"

"Not yet. She is showing a noticeable tendency towards anomie."

At this, the suppressed rage of Subbu could no longer be contained. "Don't use foul language about my granddaughter. Anomie? What nonsense! Junk finding. Tell you what, all of you want to complicate simple things. Anomie? My foot."

"I didn't mean any offense. Anomie is perhaps not what you think. It is…"

"Look here young man, don't take me for a fool," Subbu hissed. "I did a bit of sociology when I went to school and college. And I have been keeping up with my reading. Merton, Durkheim. Read some of them." At the mention of these names, Dr. Rakesh's eyebrows went up, but he did not interrupt Subbu.

Subbu continued with a tremor in his voice. "I know about anomie. You can't communicate with anyone very well. You feel alone. You can't connect with the world around you. Sometimes you even feel that the world's working against you. You don't know or you aren't convinced why you should be doing what the world asks you to do. Gradually this could lead to alienation. Let me see, if I can remember this right. There are four reactions to anomie. Innovation, ritualism, rebellion, and…"

"…retreatism," completed Dr. Rakesh quietly.

"Thank you. Now stop using such nonsense on my granddaughter."

"Sir, may I speak now?" Dr. Rakesh asked.

Subbu turned his face away in anger. His fair skin had turned red, and he was breathing heavily.

"Sir, Bharat, Indu. Please don't get upset about this. That won't help us deal with the problem. And sir, you seem quite well informed about anomie. You should help, not stop the process of repair."

Bharat was looking puzzled, and Indu irritated.

"Will you please include us in this conversation?" said Indu petulantly.

"I am sorry," Dr. Rakesh apologized. "Maya seems to be developing at least two of the reactions. Retreatism and rebellion. Retreatism makes the person pretend that there's no problem. Makes the person turn away from the problem. Rebellion is stubborn opposition. I can see some signs of both. And if you force her, she goes through everything ritualistically. These are not positive reactions. We have to deal with these reactions, not run away."

"What happens if you don't do anything?" Bharat asked.

"More serious psychological disturbances. A lot of crime is the result of unattended anomie. A sort of an individual isolationism. An acute inability to interact with anybody or anything. Loneliness. Depression… Look. There's good news. Maya has no problem communicating and commingling with people so long as it is direct. When it comes to communicating with people through computers, electronics, playing group games with children over long distances, learning lessons online, she is unable or unwilling to cope."

"What's wrong with that? I can't do many of those things," Subbu interjected before returning to his heavy breathing sullenness.

"At your age, you don't have to," Dr. Rakesh said gently. "People don't expect it of you. They are willing to adjust to it. That's not the case with Maya. People expect it of her."

"Playing board games, watching nature, wanting to play games on the road with other girls. Is all that wrong? Maybe old fashioned, not wrong surely?" Subbu fumed.

"We are not talking of right or wrong. We are talking of norms, social norms. After all, in your age, you did things differently. Nothing wrong with that. Things are just different now. We are talking of what most people do. And the fact that Maya is not doing what most people do. This is not about right and wrong."

"If what she is doing is not wrong, then why bother?" Subbu asked. For once, Indu seemed to agree, for she also nodded.

"When you don't do as most people do, it leads to many problems. I am not saying that everything that people do today is necessarily right. My job is to tell you that if Maya continues to do things very differently from how most people do them, she is in danger of facing some problems later. People sitting next to one another are emailing each other rather than getting up and talking. Many people know others only as their email IDs or as their chat IDs. I know people who send each other SMS messages when they sit a few feet apart in meetings. Children from America, Canada and India play collaborative games on the net making distance irrelevant. They don't know each other except as IDs. This has become the social norm. You can take it or leave it."

"The problem is with all of you. You have become electronic junkies. You can't keep away from your computers and cell phones. You can't talk to people directly. You have a disease. Now, what's it called?" Subbu thought hard. "Yes, I remember. Bandwidth Separation Anxiety. That's the disease all of you have. Your addiction to these moronic computers, and email, and all this gadgetry..."

"Bandwidth Separation Anxiety was dismissed as a spurious disease long ago," Dr. Rakesh said quietly. "I have to remind you. You are arguing with an accepted social norm."

"Do *you* think that everything that's happening is right?" Subbu asked, tired and resigned.

"That's not what we're talking about. We are talking about what most people are doing. If you ask my personal opinion, I'm not sure everything that's happening is for the good. But that's my personal opinion."

"Are you saying that in a land of the blind, it's wrong to have sight?" Subbu asked deliberately.

Dr. Rakesh gave a wry smile. "Precisely. Yes, that's what I am saying. Sir, you seem quite learned. I am sure you have read the story of being sighted in the land of the blind. You know who won, don't you?"

Subbu nodded reluctantly, and then his anger, insuppressible, outraged, helpless, came back. "For all you know everybody else could be suffering from anomie, not Maya. You're saying that doesn't matter. The norms matter. But who sets these norms?"

Dr. Rakesh pouted his lips. "I don't know. The world. The rest of them, I guess."

"Why can't we set the norms?"

"There's nothing wrong in trying that. It's a rebellion. That's how the existing order changes. When people rebel, and it becomes a revolution. But do you want to lead the change? You have to be aware of the risks. And be prepared to pay the price. That's all I am trying to tell you. It's not about right and wrong."

"What should we do now?" Bharat asked.

"Counseling. I'll see her once a week to begin with. Bharat and Indu, parental attention is very important." This was the only statement of Dr. Rakesh that had some assuaging effect on Subbu.

"Bharat is between jobs. He can spend some quality time with Maya," Indu said.

Bharat frowned, and then nodded.

"I'll give her some medicines also." Dr. Rakesh quickly gestured to placate the alarmed Subbu. "Just vitamins and some calcium. Her general health needs improvement. She doesn't seem to be eating well. Make sure she does."

During the drive back, Maya almost did not take her eyes off her *Arabian Nights*. When she did, she was not the least bit curious to continue a conversation about her meeting with Dr. Rakesh. Retreatism, pretending there was no problem. Was Dr. Rakesh right? Subbu decided to suspend any further thinking on the subject. Maya helpfully distracted him with a question about the big bird and Sinbad.

That night when she was given the first of the vitamin pills, Maya asked unperturbed, "Am I sick?"

So she *was* aware that she underwent a medical examination. Until now, she betrayed no trace of this understanding.

"No, darling. These are just vitamins. To make you strong." Subbu rushed to reply before anybody else could.

"Oh," she said, and swallowed the pills. After a moment's thought, she said, "*Pantu-thatha*, squirrels should be on trees, don't you think?"

"Yes, absolutely."

"Not on computers."

"You are right. Not on computers."

For a long time, he gazed at the ceiling fan, lying in bed.

Anomie. Alienation.

Very complicated terms. Very simple child.

That night, minutes after he fell asleep, the colors danced with unusual fury. Once or twice, Subbu reached out with his hands to swipe them away from his vision. His hands just passed through them. The vanishing colors brought the tiny voice in their trail.

Flee, flee, before it gets you.

Before what gets me?

Before Eimona gets you. Can't you see it, you idiot?

What did you call me?

An idiot. That's what you are.

Mind your language, Subbu growled.

What a joke. My language? That's fine for you to say. You *are* an idiot, or are you deaf?

•

Indu was having important customers from Spain the next day. She downed a glass of juice hurriedly, packed an overnight bag, kissed Maya goodbye, instructed Bharat to spend time with her and make sure that Aaya gave her the medicines, and left.

Bharat wandered downstairs for a while. Joshi had taken the association's approval for painting the foyer. He was standing in the foyer throwing instructions at the painters. Every time a painter started to do something, Joshi stopped him with a counter-instruction. He grunted a greeting to Bharat when he saw him.

"That fellow is out. The police couldn't get anything out of him. These fellows, even they have a lawyer. How they can afford one, I don't know."

"You mean the fellow's out on bail?" Bharat asked.

"Bail, what bail? The lawyer argues that the police don't have *prima facie* evidence to detain the chap. Our superintendent orders him to be released. I saw the fellow gallivanting about in the market."

"As long as they don't cause more trouble to us, it's okay."

"Hey, I have to tell you this. This chap Rangan got our stay order cancelled. Must have bribed the judge. Our lawyer is now fighting to get a stay on different grounds."

For a minute Bharat wondered what Joshi was talking about. Then he recalled the property close to the sea that Joshi had been fighting about. There were so many cases he was involved in that it was difficult to connect a sundry reference with the appropriate case.

"Any luck with finding a job?" Joshi was genuinely solicitous. There were not many souls who stopped by to talk to him, especially during the day. Though no explicit communication had passed between Bharat and the residents, it was now well known that Bharat was between jobs. Some of the business newspapers had reported his departure.

"Still trying. Anyway, no hurry," said Bharat with studied bravado.

"Of course, of course. You are young, and you have done well for yourself financially. You can take a break. In fact, you should."

The reference to his financial health reminded Bharat to look at his watch. It was 9:45. Stock trading would begin in the next few minutes. Today would be an important day, a day that he dreaded. Both the NASDAQ and the Dow Jones had taken an alarming plunge overnight. This was the eighth consecutive fall in American markets. His stock price had held steady, though still low, for the past three weeks. Last night's fall on the market had been quite bad.

"I am going to teach this Rangan a lesson. Our lawyer is also keen..." Joshi began.

Bharat was impatient to leave and had to try to cut off Joshi without offending him. "Sorry, Colonel. I have to make an urgent phone call..."

"Oh, all right. You take care."

Joshi watched him go, wondering why somebody would saunter down with apparently no purpose when he had an urgent phone call to make.

The business channel was full of black portents. The fall in the American markets had been quite bad. The Indian markets had held for long, but shares such as Fusion Investments, whose parent was listed in America, were particularly vulnerable in today's trade.

"Shit," cursed Bharat loudly.

"Don't use that word. It's inelegant," Subbu repeated what he had been telling Bharat since he was ten.

"Okay, okay, *pantu-thatha*," Bharat said impatiently.

"Daddy, I have to eat my medicines." Maya walked in to remind Bharat.

"Come in a little while. Not now." Bharat dismissed her without taking his eyes off the TV. The trading would begin in another minute.

"It's already late. I should have eaten the pills soon after breakfast." Maya seemed to have developed a stubborn compulsion about taking her medicines.

"I told you. After some time."

Subbu rushed into the living room, calling for Aaya. She didn't know where the medicines were. Bharat had purchased them and stored them somewhere else, not in the usual place in the medicine cabinet. Existence in the Second Home, this time, was slightly disruptive due to the extended stay. They had never spent more than weekends here.

Subbu hushed Maya and asked her to return after her father became a little free. Meanwhile, trading had opened. The market had already plunged four percent in the first ten minutes of trading and seemed to be headed for the worse. Bharat's stock price was eight percent down forcing him to bite into the tender skin of his middle finger nail. He cursed involuntarily at the share price, and then at the thin streak of blood. Sucking his finger, he stared transfixed at the screen, as commentator after raucous commentator, was excitedly screaming at the stock market's performance. Nobody seemed to share Bharat's anxiety. How can people be excited when the market is going down so rapidly? What kind of people are these commentators? If good happens, they are excited. If bad happens, they are excited. Bird-brained titillation seekers.

"Daddy, my medicines," Maya reminded.

"I told you to come back in a little while."

"I have come back after a little while," Maya insisted quietly.

"They are just vitamins. It doesn't matter if you don't eat them on time. It doesn't matter even if you skip a dose."

Subbu who was watching this, tried to intervene and call her away, but it was too late.

"Mummy said I must eat the pills after breakfast. I can't skip."

Without getting up, Bharat stretched his arm out and slapped Maya across the cheek. A rainbow, but only of red, appeared on her cheek. Her eyes filled up as she clutched her beaten cheek with disbelief. The slap seemed to have petrified her.

Piece of God slapped. Piece of purest God, slapped and hurt.

Subbu's rational brain lost control. With a speed that belied his age, he moved forward in two strides, and slapped Bharat on the face with such force that his throbbing palm hurt long afterward.

CHAPTER 11

Subbu had now decided to flee.

From Eimona, before its long tentacles could grasp him and choke him in rapacious greed.

The colors and the tiny voice did not have to remind him.

He had had enough. He had been reduced to the ignominy of doing something he had never before done in his life. Something he had whole-heartedly abhorred. He had beaten a helpless man—his own grandson. A hapless child in some sense. A child already beset by the loss of his job.

Piece of God as well.

Subbu's palm was red, and still stinging from the beating. Rage is blind, but even in blind rage, he had intended for the blow to land only on Bharat's cheek. In reflex, Bharat had turned his face, and the blow landed partly on his ear. It was almost like a scene in a stage play. The dialogues had been spoken, the blows delivered, and each character had exited through a different door. Subbu, Maya and Bharat to their respective bedrooms. If a callused palm hurt so much, how much would an ear lobe hurt?

Lifelong, Subbu had advocated non-violence towards children. He made instant enemies of parents who beat their children. He had picked up quarrels with parents, known and unknown, when they beat their children. Once, when traveling with a young Krishnan, he saw a Finnish man pull the hair of his three year old daughter because she refused to eat anything. A little imagination would have revealed that the girl was jaded by the long journey from Finland and was distasteful of strange Indian food. He walked up to the Finnish man, much bigger than himself, and threatened to call the police if the man ill-treated his child in public. At the mention of the police, the man, who looked like he was ready for a fight, quieted down with a surly look. But Jaya reminded him that he might take it out on the child later. No matter, Subbu said, he could not take such behavior, and had to react to it.

Though Jaya and Sharada were themselves not given to beating children, Subbu made it amply clear to them before they became wife and daughter-in-law respectively that one of the few conditions he would impose upon them was not to beat children in his home. Even to Indu, with whom he had reservations about laying down conditions, he made it clear that Maya shall not be touched on any account.

"Of course, parental programming teaches it," she had agreed readily based on some class she had attended the previous week.

He recalled a speech he gave once at Krishnan's school that quite shocked the teachers since candor and criticism were not expected of invited speakers, particularly not of the chief guest inaugurating the School Day.

"The one master stroke through which we became more

civilized, more elevated than the west, was embracing non-violence as an expression of protest. All war, all violence, we realized is barbaric. No strife belongs in the civilized world. You, teachers, teach this Gandhian ideal all the time, yet you beat the children. What hypocrisy, what a tragedy. I would have been a happier man inaugurating the School Day if you, teachers, had embraced the Gandhian ideal. And taught children non-violence at school. Practiced it yourselves. Then watch war-mongering go down. Until you do away with corporal punishment, don't teach Gandhi to children. If we beat our children, we have no hopes that war will end. World peace will then remain wishful thinking."

The headmistress and the correspondent had been shocked. They even expressed their displeasure about this speech to Krishnan, who came back from school, and got angry with his father. He was only seven years old. Jaya, who normally had no criticism for her husband's acts, was mildly critical as she had been the day he picked up an argument with the Finnish man.

"You must be more responsible," she chided him. "Why don't you keep your ideals to yourself? You are getting the poor boy into trouble."

"Parents who beat children, teachers who beat children, anybody who beats children are sworn enemies," he repeated solemnly. In his world, there was no greater barbarian than one who beat children.

Despite his share of comedies and, what he believed was an unfair share of tragedies, Subbu had never felt defeated. He had always felt triumphant about his staunch adherence to ideals. He had almost never wavered. He had tried to practice, as fervently as possible, Vivekananda's teaching of consistency between thought, word, and deed. In non-violence towards children, Subbu felt particularly triumphant. He had never once even said that he would beat a child, let alone raise an arm. When he crossed eighty, he felt supremely confident that his lifelong adherence to this ideal could never be challenged. What would be the need to beat a child after one was eighty and had had a great-granddaughter? Was this punishment for his arrogance, a way by which the cosmos, a strange Providence, reminded him not to get too big for his boots? But it was a cruel way of teaching a man, if it was that.

With Bharat, after the loss of his parents, he had been extra careful. Even lavishly indulgent at times. Bharat was the only person for whom he had broken one of his lifelong vows: never to wear pants. Distasteful experience that it was, not merely for the few moments it lasted, but for the constant reminder it was about his transgression, it served the larger purpose of delighting his grandson. He had guarded Bharat with a paranoia from his school teachers, quite unnecessarily though. Bharat's doubts did not leave him much room for experimentation and mischief. He was almost never singled out for punishment during his schooldays.

If a man had to be defeated, it was better that he was defeated in his forties. Or fifties or even sixties. Not in his eighties. Why did Bharat have to beat Maya? If he hadn't beaten Maya, the lifelong pledge wouldn't have been broken. Subbu's anger at Bharat lasted only a short while. He reminded himself that any idiot could adhere to ideals in the absence of provocation. Adherence was adherence only in the face of provocation and adversity.

He was no longer confident about his Teflon-coated armor of insensitivity. How would he react if he saw a drugged Maya? What if Dr. Rakesh started a new chapter in sophistry with jargon that he may not understand? How would he continue to look Bharat in the eye and offer him advice? Even if he could, would Bharat consider his sincerity unquestionable?

His mind circled these questions obsessively.

The persuasive power of the dancing colors, of the tiny voice was overwhelming. There was not a moment to be lost. He had to flee. Skedaddle and renounce. In the advanced years of your life, you had to renounce, he had been told as a lad of ten. Renunciation was the ineluctable last phase of life, he had been taught. He did not believe in it then. Even now, one part of his mind was examining sharply whether this was escapism masquerading as renunciation. No, it isn't he concluded firmly. Or was it repentance for breaking his vow?

My mind falters. It shouldn't. A dithering mind is an impediment to action.

He had decided to flee. He would do it that night.

It was a Friday. He had overheard Indu arrange a dinner meeting for her and Bharat starting at ten. It would go well into the early hours of Saturday morning. If he had to flee, that would be the time. All those nights when the colors had danced before his eyes, his mind had toyed with the thought of fleeing. He was surprised how much clear detail these idling sessions had created. It was almost as if it had been a military drill. With each session, the details had become sharper, the plans more focused. All of this had been unconscious. Now the details seemed to shine under a light. He knew what he would carry in his bags. He knew, almost precisely, the time at which he would leave, where he would head to, and how.

He would, of course, tell not a soul that he was leaving. He could not bring himself to tell even Maya. He couldn't bear the thought. When the police came, he did not want to see the bodies. He did not see his house come down. Now, he did not wish to say goodbye to Maya.

He glanced at his watch. It was 11:30 and the bright sun had started streaming into the room. He could hear the sound of Bharat moving around in the living room. The TV was not on. Ever since the incident last morning, Bharat had not switched on the TV. In fact, neither Bharat nor Subbu appeared at the dining table for lunch. They ordered Aaya to serve them lunch in their bedrooms. Earlier he had heard Bharat give Maya her pills. Soon after she took her pills, Maya asked Aaya to tell her a story, and Aaya responded promptly, sensing the tension, but not sure exactly what happened. Subbu skipped dinner, not coming out of his bedroom that evening. He did not see much of Maya except when she came in to ask whether she could play snakes and ladders. No, said Subbu. She should try to read something. Maya went away quietly without her usual childish protests. He did not see Bharat at all the rest of the evening.

In the morning, he saw Indu and Bharat in the living room.

"Good morning," Indu called out.

Had Bharat told her? Apparently not, since she was coolly mixing herself a cup of coffee. But Indu could be very cool even if she knew everything. In this case, however, she didn't seem to know.

"Good morning, *pantu-thatha*," Bharat greeted with a smile sending a fresh pang of shame and guilt surging through Subbu.

Shuffling awkwardly, Subbu grabbed the newspapers and retreated to his bedroom. He had heard Indu leaving for her office telling Bharat to be ready for the dinner that evening. "Not today, darling," he overheard her telling Maya.

His watch now showed 12:00 noon. Another twelve hours from now, he would be gone. Perhaps he would never see Bharat, Indu and Maya again. He was going to leave forever a man he had brought up, with his last interaction being a resounding slap. A man who had, for most of his life, been inseparable from the meaning of existence. A man whose hand he had held firmly, sometimes gingerly, through every step.

What would his son Krishnan think of such treatment of his son? Of abandoning his (Krishnan's) granddaughter at a time when she perhaps would need her *pantu-thatha* the most? Flesh of his flesh. Blood of his blood. But then, who could guarantee whose life? Who could eternally protect whom?

I am mortal too. I have done what I can. Now I can stand this no more.

Into his eighties, even if a man does not have the choice of doing what he likes, he must at least have the choice of not doing what he dislikes.

He rebuked his mind. There it was, dithering again. Suddenly his father flashed in his mind. He had narrated to a young Subbu, a parable of Saint Ramakrishna that helped surmount the dithering mind. Though the story was about asceticism, and not about handling the dithering mind, his father had taken the liberty of making it a parable of the dithering mind. He could see the old man, sitting under a hurricane lamp, and reading haltingly. Electricity hadn't yet invaded the village. He could hear the old man's voice inside his ear, a hoarse whisper, as if passing a trader's secret.

"A wife once said to her husband, 'Dear, I am anxious about my brother. For the past week he has been thinking of becoming an ascetic and has been busy preparing for that life. He is trying to reduce gradually all his desires and wants.' The husband replied, 'Dear, be not at all anxious about your brother. He will never renounce his life and become an ascetic. No one can become an ascetic that way.' 'How does one become an ascetic then?' asked the wife. 'Thus' exclaimed the husband; so saying he tore his flowing dress to pieces, took a piece and tied it round his loins, and ran away."

Do something good, do something bad. Do something

wise, do something foolish. But if you have determined to do something, do it immediately. Dithering was the bane of humanity.

It was one of those rare occasions when Subbu remembered his father. He hadn't thought of the old man in several years. Subbu was the last of fourteen children. He always knew his father as a silver-haired old man. A towering personality with a thick, long white beard. Penury had forced him to grow a beard since shaving could not be accommodated with bringing up fourteen children. When he looked at himself in a mirror, Subbu was sure that if he grew a beard he would look indistinguishable from his last recorded image of his father. There were no photographs or pictures of the old man. He seldom spoke to Subbu or to his siblings, even rarely to his wife. When he did, it was to offer a piece of concise wisdom, after which he clammed up again.

It seemed like an eternity, but his watched showed 12:07. Subbu shook it hard to check if it worked. It was a Swiss winding watch of the 1960's. He took the watch to his ear. Its secretive ticking reassured him that it was working. *Good.* One of the precious possessions of a fleeing man is the watch. You couldn't stop every passerby to ask time or rely on seeing a clock tower when you wanted to.

At quarter past noon, he decided to step into the living room and talk to Bharat.

Bharat was stooped on some report. He did not notice Subbu. After a long minute, Subbu cleared his throat. Bharat looked up, smiled, and went back to his reading.

His mind is pure, Subbu thought. He doesn't seem to think anything went wrong. Subbu searched Bharat's face for any mark from the blow. Thankfully, there appeared to be none.

All the guilt is mine. I must apologize.

He cleared his throat again. He was muted by the choking effect of contrition. He knew he couldn't apologize. How could the mind want something so desperately and the mouth rage against it?

"Has Indu gone?" One of those irrelevant, inane questions that got conversations started in awkward circumstances.

"Yes," said Bharat without looking up.

Silence again. Where is my loquacity? Where is *his* loquacity? What do you do with this terrible silence?

"What's happening with your job? Any responses?" Subbu asked.

"Yeah, some. But I am not sure which ones to pursue. I am not sure at all. I don't know who to check with."

"Why not your colleagues from Fusion?"

"Fusion? My ex-company?" Bharat smiled wryly, and after a moment's thought added, "I don't exist for Fusion anymore. As far as they are concerned, I am dead."

"What about your previous companies? Your colleagues?"

"Even worse. They aren't there any longer. Probably laid off. Even if they are, it's like with Fusion. I'm dead. They don't want to talk to me. The day you clean out your drawers, your association ends. Nothing ever stays. Not colleagues, not bosses. Not the companies themselves. Quickly they are closed or bought these days."

"Some of your teachers from the management school?"

"No point. I had a professor. I used to talk about him. You may remember. Professor Chauhan. He's dead now. I used to follow his advice whenever I had a doubt. When in doubt, do as the majority does. In the long run, the majority always wins. That's what I did all the time. See what it's done to me now. I am doubtful about even Chauhan's wisdom. I don't know if it pays to follow the majority."

Bharat returned to reading the report.

There was silence again.

Tell him, tell him now, Subbu's mind urged. This is your last chance.

"Bharat," he called gently.

"Yes, *pantu-thatha*."

"Bharat, you know what your problem is?"

"I know," Bharat replied. "My doubt. I am unable to make up my mind."

"Not really. All great men have had doubts. That's not your problem. Your problem is that you think doubt is bad. You think uncertainty is a villain."

"Isn't it? Doubt doesn't take you anywhere, does it?" Bharat asked. He had now closed the report and raised himself to sit erect.

"Doubt doesn't take you anywhere if you think doubt is bad. If you think doubt is good, it takes you lots of places."

"I can't believe that," Bharat said. Even though he said it, it was clear that he was getting interested in this conversation. Some papers flew away in a sudden draft, but he ignored them. "I thought doubt petrified, didn't allow you to move. Explain to me," Bharat challenged Subbu.

"No knowledge about the world, about the universe, about existence is certain. That's well accepted now by philosophers and scientists. The problem with certainty is that you've got to be absolutely right. If you aren't, certainty does not allow for other possibilities. It cuts out speculation. And we all know that speculation about the possible and the impossible, adventuring with thought, that's what leads to advances in economics, science, medicine, you name it."

"Never thought of doubt this way," said Bharat. The report slid from his lap to the floor but he made no attempt to retrieve it.

Subbu said, "I was a physics student. We were all taught

Newtonian physics, which reasoned with a definite, certain world out there. That world behaved according to Newton's laws whether you or I existed or observed. The universe had an existence of its own. That's not what's accepted today. Newtonian laws are now challenged by quantum physics, which believes the world may exist only for our observation. Its behavior is influenced by whether you or I see. That all experience is subjective, and not objective, as we believed once. Physics has moved from certainty to uncertainty."

A child's glee had appeared on Bharat's face. "*Pantu-thatha*, this is very exciting. Tell me more."

"Take my agnosticism. It's doubt about whether God exists. This doubt hasn't paralyzed me. On the contrary, it has allowed me to speculate. Does God exist or not? If he does, what's his form? What's his duty? Why go to the extent of creating the universe and running it? If I had pursued any one religion with complete faith, complete certainty, it would have not have permitted me to contemplate so many possibilities. My experience about God has been much richer than the experience of many people who believe in God firmly."

Bharat wouldn't let go. As he asked more and more questions, Subbu felt sorry for Bharat's starvation. From doubt being abject and abominable, Subbu had made doubt honorable. He introduced to Bharat the concept of Skepticism as a philosophy whose very basis was doubt. At Bharat's instance, he repeated in various forms, the ideas he dwelt on earlier. That it was certitude which was scary. Doubt was comforting. Doubt ended up creating infinite possibilities, rather than certitude that sealed possibilities. Doubt always left room for hope. Doubt did not seek confirmation. It created alternative paths. Let doubt be. It was not such a bad thing.

"*Pantu-thatha*, is something different about today?"

"Why, nothing," said Subbu alarmed. "Why do you ask?"

"It is just that you seem to talk differently. Maybe I am just imagining it."

"I have some work now. What time would you leave in the evening?" Subbu had to make an effort to sound casual.

"Seven or so. I have some work on the way to the dinner. That won't start until ten. It'll be late by the time Indu and I return. As usual, tell Maya some bedtime story."

"I will," said Subbu and rose to leave.

Before Subbu could leave the room, Bharat stopped him. "*Pantu-thatha*, another day you must continue this topic. Maybe I'll have some questions."

Subbu paused. "I think I have said whatever I had to say. You won't need any help on this subject. If anybody can help you, it's yourself."

Bharat poured out a drink, but made no attempt to consume it. The ass still seemed to be stubborn, but it had moved to the fringes. It had become a little faded and the smile didn't seem so sharp. In fact, its prickly sides didn't seem so prickly. It had started becoming yellow at the edges like how a newspaper sheet deteriorates with time.

When Subbu left the room, he could hear Bharat whispering softly, "Doubt is not all that bad."

•

Around five thirty, Bharat grew impatient and drove away in the Linda. This gave Subbu an unexpected hour and a half hour start on his plans. He quickly mumbled an excuse to Aaya, and left for The Home in the electric train. When he let himself into The Home, the workers had left. Most of the repair work appeared complete. Perhaps another two to three days to the end of the three week repair period. The Home would then be ready for occupation.

Subbu was going to take only two bags with him. One for his clothes and one for all the other things that were important to him. During the idling sessions, his mind had prepared a list of what he should carry. He didn't have to pause much. He kept ticking items off the list in his mind as he packed them into one bag or the other. When he had taken what he wanted, he went to every room in The Home. Its stillness was remarkable, as remarkable as the stillness of the corpse which moments before had been actively moving. He locked the door and checked it.

He walked in a quick stride to the nearest ATM to draw the remaining cash from his account. He had created another account in a fictitious name with an address on the Kerala-Tamil Nadu border where his father's home once stood. An address that could not easily be verified, an address that may not come up for verification at all. He had withdrawn all but a small sum of cash from his existing account and had physically deposited the cash into this new account from a remote branch in Madras. Nobody in the branch was likely to recall an old man who came to deposit money amidst the scores of transactions they handled in a day. He was thankful that he had retained a not inconsiderable sum of money. Hopefully, the interest from this new bank deposit could take care of him for the rest of his life. He destroyed all trace of his original bank accounts. He could now draw money from any city in Tamil Nadu—why, anywhere in India, as long as he had access to the Internet. A small mercy of the abominable electronic world.

It was dusk by the time he returned to the Second Home. As he walked from the train station to his home, a doubt started torturing him. What if he ran out of money in some way? What if he fell ill, and had to pay for medical expenses? Of course, he wouldn't be using the entire monthly interest for his expenses. He didn't need that much. Would the surplus cover illnesses? He had no idea what medical treatment costs might be. It had been a very long time since he had been to a doctor for any significant ailment. Maybe healthy people like him died suddenly in their sleep. There wouldn't be any protracted illness and hospitalization. But what if there was?

What if he had to pay an advance for renting a house? What did they ask for these days? What if he had to pay for clothes? For years now, Bharat had been paying for clothes. Maybe he wouldn't buy shaving cream and blades. Like his father, he could grow a beard. While saving money, it would obfuscate his appearance as well. From his shopping experiences at *Foodmania*, he struggled to recall the price of every item as he mentally assembled a monthly expense statement. Though he made purchases daily, he hadn't studied the prices of individual items, paying the bill mechanically. Should he have investigated this a little more? Was he inadequately prepared? His father appeared again with his counsel about conquering the dithering mind.

No, it wasn't as if he was changing his mind about fleeing. The only question was, had he done adequate financial planning? Did he have enough money, or was he imagining he had? He had no plans of turning into a beggar. This doubt so preoccupied his mind that he stopped ahead of the gate to the Second Home, under a lamppost, and scratched the stubble that was making an appearance now that it was evening.

The gentle touch on his shoulder startled him. He turned around to face a man almost as old as himself. At first sight, naked to the torso, and dressed in tattered ochre robes, he seemed like one of those regular mendicants looking for alms. But his close cropped hair, in silver spikes, seemed clean and well kept. His silver beard and moustache were not apologetic and straggly, they were luxuriant. His robes were tattered, but starched and clean and strangely refulgent. In the dim light, Subbu could make out his eyes were piercing and powerful, yet benevolent. The rest of his face seemed hooded due to the bad light. Subbu instinctively fished for some money in his pocket. On seeing the man gesture, he stopped with his hand still in his pocket.

With his eyes still boring into Subbu's face, the man spoke with a drawl that seemed to emanate from the deepest recesses of his throat. He spoke only a sentence.

"*Koupeenavantaha khalu bhagyavantaha.*"

The man's Sanskrit diction was flawless.

Koupeenavantaha khalu bhagyavantaha—He who owns only a loincloth has all the benediction. *How did this man know?* He hadn't asked a question. And Subbu hadn't spoken a word yet. He was overjoyed. No man needed material possessions beyond a loincloth. Yes, he had all the money he needed. Everything could be easily taken care of.

His hand was still in his pocket, and when he drew it out he found a hundred rupee note in it. He handed it to the man. The man turned it over slowly and returned it wordlessly. As soon as he had given the man the money, Subbu realized his thoughtlessness. He cursed his unforgivable folly. The man broke into a laughter. He raised his hand and pointed it towards Subbu with complete disdain, still laughing. Peer as he might, Subbu could not get a sharp view of the man in the shadows under the lamppost and in the poor light from the weakly winking streetlight. As the man's laughter turned sharp and bitingly contemptuous, the front gate watchman appeared imagining that the man was bothering Subbu.

"Go away," he shooed the man. "No begging allowed here."

The man had started walking towards the beach. He did not even acknowledge the existence of the watchman. He broke his steady stride once or twice to turn back and point his disdainful hand towards Subbu. The front gate watchman made some threatening gestures which were singularly ignored. With his laughter piercing the evening's stillness, the man walked towards the beach gradually disappearing from sight.

"Who's he? Have you seen him before?"

"No, *saar*. Must be one of the thousand beggars around here." The front gate watchman didn't think the man was of any special interest.

A shame flooded through Subbu. How could he have worried so much about money?

"Are you sure you haven't seen him before?" he asked the front gate watchman.

"Oh, now you have started worrying. He won't come back and bother you. If he steps this way again, I'll give him a sound thrashing."

•

Maya was asleep. She took longer than usual to fall asleep. Children were supposed to know instinctively when something was unusual. Had she sensed something? She was difficult and cried a little when Subbu suggested that she go to sleep. She had insisted that he tell the story of *Karna* again, complete with all the histrionics. He could not emote like he did usually. His mind was straying to what else he had to collect from the Second Home to complete his list.

"*Pantu-thatha*, you are not acting well. At this stage, Karna's mother has to cry a lot more when she tells him the truth about his birth. What's the matter?"

Subbu had to collect himself many times before he could complete the story. He realized it would have been an unsatisfactory experience for her. Finally, holding his hand, she fell asleep. He gently extricated his hand, and put the unruly hairs on her forehead back in their place. At an eternal parting like this, what else does one do? He could think of only the usual things. Lowering the air-conditioning draft, pulling her blanket, removing one or two cuddly toys to make space for her to turn to her sides comfortably, and drawing the blinds so the morning sun did not wake her up early during her summer holidays. There wasn't exactly an established human history of running away from one's great-granddaughter that one could refer to, to see if one had missed something.

He paused near the door, and took a final look at the angelic face that was serenely laid on the pillow. It was a mistake, turning back to see. The grief was paralyzing. He had to steady himself by holding on to the door frame. It was one of those rare moments when all his eighty plus years told on him—when his infirmity reminded him that he was a very old man.

Hobbling a little unsteadily out of the room, he diverted his attention to the list. Most of what he wanted was already in his bags. He had carefully packed Krishnan's trousers that he had worn just once in his life to amuse a little Bharat. He had to finish the last round of packing, and wait a while to leave. He had decided to leave close to midnight, when the activity in the apartment complex died down. With bags like that, he could not conceivably leave any time during the day.

He waited for Aaya's snoring to reach a steady state. She was already fast asleep. He had to take the elevator downstairs. The stairs were a risk. The stair lights, which were never switched on after nine, would then have to be switched on. Also, however softly he climbed down the stairs, his feet would make a noise. That could alert the watchmen. He would leave the apartment complex by the back gate. It was darker there, and the back gate watchman, being the lazier of the two, would be asleep. Besides, the autorickshaw stand was closer to the back gate than the front. Many autorickshaw drivers were known to him, or rather he to them. He had a story ready for them, that he was leaving for his village. Wanted to be dropped at the electric train station. Worst case, he could always walk to the electric train station. With the bags, it would take him more than the usual ten minutes.

The last train was at 1:00 AM.

The bottle. It was on his list. He held it under the light to take a look at the soil and rubble. Jaya, Krishnan, Sharada, and even a little Bharat were genies in the bottle. He picked up the family photograph. Everybody resolutely stared back at him. Were they leering at him? He picked up Jaya's statuette purportedly dating back to the Chola period. What was he going to do with it? He shouldn't be carrying any unnecessary burden. After long thought, he decided to carry it.

He stiffened as Aaya coughed noisily, but soon the snores resumed.

The only piece left on the table was a copper and bronze plaque that his father had given him before his death. Did he need that? Again, he was stricken by indecision. Couldn't lose time now. He picked it up and stuffed it into his bag.

The plaque said in Sanskrit:

> Lead us from the untruth to the truth.
> Lead us from darkness to light.
> Lead us from mortality to immortality.

The human aspiration. Nothing more needed to be said.

•

He was dark, wiry and medium height. His face would be the face that an American cartoonist would draw if asked for a caricature of the stereotypical Indian. He could easily dissolve in a crowd. His clothes were as nondescript as his personality—grey trousers, a dark soiled shirt and Hawaiian slippers. He was a professional in his work. His impressive repertoire included everything from bombing offices and assassinations to arranging petty accidents. He could be so meticulous in his execution that he could exercise precise control over the damage that his clients sought. If it was a broken arm, it would be a broken arm, it would not be two broken arms or an extra broken leg, let alone something as vastly extravagant as a lost life. If his client ordered loss of life, then surely loss of life it would be.

Rangan was his usual customer and an important one. He had indicated that a certain Joshi had been troubling him about his proposed restaurant and club on the beach. Rangan had given him Joshi's address and told him very clearly that he wanted a bomb exploding close to Joshi's apartment. Material damage was okay, but no loss of human life. That would lead to very difficult inquiries. The purpose was to scare Joshi. A gimmick had been tried, and it didn't seem to work. Joshi was still actively pursuing the case. Rangan wanted something more impressive this time. If this failed, too, then he would get serious about dealing with Joshi. By exploding a bomb in the premises close to Joshi's apartment, Rangan hoped that he would scare the other residents also. Apparently they were lending financial support to Joshi.

A few days ago, the dark, wiry man had studied the apartment complex very carefully. Rangan had been particular: the whole building shouldn't come down. The strength of the bomb had to be just right to cause significant damage to a part of Joshi's apartment, but it shouldn't damage any other apartment. After a few hours of intense scrutiny in the wee hours of the previous morning, when the security guard was in drunken sleep, he had concluded that the best place was in the elevator shaft. The bomb could be tucked out of sight, and it would serve the purpose of scaring Joshi, maybe bring one of his apartment walls down without causing damage to the whole structure.

Now he had returned to execute his plan.

He would wait until close to midnight. It was the right hour—too late for office-goers to return, and too early for the weekend revelers to come back home. Besides he needed an interval of only four to five minutes between lighting the fuse and the bomb going off.

He arrived about half an hour earlier than expected. A few hundred meters from the gate, he parked his getaway motorbike under a tree in the shadows. His equipment was in a bag strapped to the motorbike. He sat on the bike in the shadows, chewing a toothpick, and decided to wait a while.

Except for the dim lights on the compound wall, the apartment complex was dark. There was however a solitary light in an upstairs apartment. The man fixed binoculars to his eyes and focused on the window. The curtains were drawn. It was a clear night. A silver-haired old man, dressed in white, was moving inside the window. It appeared as if he was busy packing something. Through the powerful binoculars, he could see the old man dropping things into an open bag.

•

Oblivious of the dark, wiry man's scrutiny through his binoculars from across the street, Subbu was, indeed, busy packing. He wasn't adding anything new, merely rearranging things so they fit nicely.

He surveyed his handiwork, but it didn't quite satisfy him. He recalled his mental list, and checked the items again. As he stepped back to reconsider his packing scheme, he felt a tug on his *veshti*. He turned around, and the hair on his nape bristled.

Maya!

"Maya, what are you doing here?"

"Couldn't sleep," she said, leaning to her side and staring beyond him. "Are you going away somewhere?"

"Come. I'll put you in bed."

Maya didn't budge. "Are you going away somewhere?"

Time was running out. Maya *had* to go to sleep.

"Are you going away somewhere?" Maya was insistent.

Subbu sighed. "Yes."

"Are you going away for a long time?" she asked.

"Yes. I am running away. Fleeing." *From Eimona.*

While he braced himself for the obvious questions that would follow—"where to" and "why?" and the like, Maya surprised him.

"Will you take me with you? I hate to be alone. Without you, I would be alone." She looked intensely at his face with large, appealing eyes.

In spite of his steadfast agnosticism, Subbu wanted to cry out, "Oh God! Why are you doing this to me?" In a moment, however, he found himself seriously considering this question.

Why not? Could it be worse than leaving her behind? How ridiculous. You are past eighty, you have no home, no roots, at least for now. How would you support a child?

The perfect tiny fingernails on the clenched fist, the "hands-up" position and the tender brown eyes crossed his mind's eye.

Why not? Don't be foolhardy. What's your age? You might die anytime now. That provoked Subbu. He looked at his constant companion, Death. His companion seemed profoundly disinterested. He was, in fact, looking away. Good. But then, remember, you aren't immortal. You won't live forever. So what? Nobody does. And anyway, there are only uncertainties, no certainties.

He spoke decisively. "Yes, you can go with me. Why not? I wasn't able to save your father. Maybe I can save you." *From Eimona.*

Again, she did not ask him, save me from what?

She surprised him with another question, "Will you have enough money?"

One who possesses nothing but a loincloth...

"Enough to buy you and me a loincloth each," said Subbu.

Maya giggled, tickled by the thought of both of them going around dressed in nothing but a loincloth.

"Shhh..." said Subbu with a finger on his lip. "Quiet."

"Okay," whispered Maya who was now thrilled by this midnight adventure.

"If you are going with me, we need to pack a few things for you."

Subbu hadn't planned on this. He did not have a list for Maya, only just for himself. He quickly constructed one: toothbrushes, change of clothes, her favorite snakes and ladders game... In a few minutes, a small bag, small enough for Maya to carry by herself, was packed and ready. Maya slung it on her back.

"Let's go, let's go," she whispered excitedly.

They had to cross a snoring Aaya. They tip-toed to the shoe rack and picked up their sandals. The shoe rack creaked a little, and Aaya stirred. They held their breath and waited. Aaya turned over and went back to sleep.

Subbu signaled to Maya to wait. He entered the bedroom and switched off the light.

They opened the front door gently, stepped out, and closed the door. They were unaware that Aaya opened her eyes when she heard the front door opening. It always made an unavoidable creak. Even in the darkness, in the blue shaft of light that came through the window glasses of the living room, she saw Subbu and Maya step out. That wasn't unusual. *Pantu-thatha* and his great granddaughter were always up to nighttime pranks. She didn't realize that it was close to midnight, she had the impression she had been asleep only a few minutes. But what puzzled her was that both of them appeared to be carrying some bags. Or was it her failing sight that was misleading her?

"The elevator, the elevator," Subbu whispered as he veered Maya away from the staircase.

●

A few minutes before Subbu switched off the bedroom light, the dark, wiry man deftly scaled the wall of the apartment complex. Having carefully placed the explosive pack in the clearance between the floor of the shaft and the elevator level of the ground floor, he surveyed the scene to make sure that everything was in order. Once he lit the fuse, he wouldn't have time to do anything else.

He lit the fuse.

The bomb would go off in approximately three minutes or so. Exactly thirty seconds after he lit the fuse, in a professional sprint, he noiselessly scaled the wall and dropped back into the street, and then made his way out of the premises. He would have to wait for the bomb to explode before he started his bike for fear of waking up the neighborhood too early.

About two minutes to go.

As a professional, he always stayed back to ensure that his

job was well done. This was not going to be a long wait.

Precisely at the moment he looked up at the apartment window inside which he sighted the old man, the light went off.

Good.

In a few seconds, however, he heard the purr of a car engine. The car was coming down the road. The dark man prayed for the car to go straight. It didn't. Instead it turned into the apartment complex. It was playing music loudly which startled the watchman, who woke up from his sleep, hurriedly saluted the car, and went back to sleep. Seeing the watchman's familiar salute to the car, the dark man realized that the people in the car must be residents of the apartment. He swore loudly enough to shock himself.

There were five people in the car, two young men, a gray-haired man, a woman, and a girl who must have been seven or eight. He could tell from their gait that all except the little girl were drunk. A few seconds lapsed before they got out of the car after turning off the noisy stereo. The dark man could see one of the young men say something to the woman. She pecked him on the cheek while the other young man tried to pull her away. The grey-haired man tried to pull the second young man from the woman. Holding each other and swaying, they headed towards the elevator.

Since the elevator was tucked away into the foyer, the dark man could no longer see them, but he could hear their giggles and screams. Above the giggles and screams, he could hear the unmistakable hum of the elevator descending. The revelers were close enough to the elevator, but clearly it had started descending before they could press the call button.

Somebody was coming down the elevator!

This was one of those rare occasions when his plan was surely about to go awry. No human damage, Rangan had specified. Twenty seconds or so to go.

It was too late.

The dark man became nervous and started sweating. He shouldn't have been so conceited, so damned overconfident. In his early days, his professional preparation was meticulous. His success had made him arrogant. Nothing could be done now. Things go wrong once in a while. Rangan would be angry. Very angry.

The elevator had descended. Who was getting out? Were the people from the car getting in? It wasn't clear.

When the explosion happened, the giggles turned into brief shrieks of pain that abruptly lapsed into silence.

Had he packed too much power into the explosives? Smoke billowed out of the elevator shaft and flooded the compound. The watchman stared without rising from his chair, turned to stone by incomprehension, sleep-filled stupor, and sheer terror.

The dark, wiry man gunned his motorcycle to life seconds after the explosion. As his motorbike heaved and moved, lights started coming on in a random sequence in the apartment complex, and the first signs of commotion appeared.

CHAPTER 12

Though Aaya was a little hard of hearing, the explosion was loud enough to wake her up. She was not sure what had happened. Soon an acrid smell assaulted her nose and throat causing a coughing fit. It was coming from the window overlooking the road—the window through which the dark, wiry man had seen Subbu moving around.

Aaya saw the front gate watchman running towards the foyer, soon to be joined by the back gate watchman. From that window, she could see the foyer only at an angle, but the billowing smoke could not be missed, even in the dim light. She drew her breath in horror. As she saw more and more residents gravitating towards the foyer, she decided to go down herself.

By the time she got downstairs, descending every step with painful arthritis, the fire engines had arrived and the firefighters were getting ready. The wail of a siren announced the arrival of a police jeep. Aaya had to stand on the stairs, for there was pandemonium in the foyer. There was no standing room.

Joshi was screaming hysterically, "My living room wall's gone! There's no wall left! Who did this? I demand to know! Who did this?"

Nobody seemed concerned about his demand.

"It was a bomb. It was, it was." The front gate watchman was making an animated announcement to somebody.

The neighboring apartment residents had a bucket of water each which they were throwing at the elevator to douse the fire. The firefighters were ordering the people to move away, to leave the site. The residents didn't seem to care. They kept throwing buckets of water. Some of them were bodily removed by the firefighters. The smoke seemed to be coming from the elevator.

Aaya wondered for a moment why people were walking gingerly near the elevator. Then she saw it. Blood. Pieces of human flesh. With shreds of cloth on them. Shoes strewn all over. She rubbed her eyes in disbelief. It was real. She retched and felt sick. Her last memory came flooding into her, and she froze.

Where were *pantu-thatha* and Maya?

Unconscious of her age and arthritic leg, she climbed up furiously.

She looked in Subbu's bedroom. It was empty. So was Maya's bedroom. What a time to engage in mischief! At eighty, the man was so irresponsible.

"*Pantu-thatha*...Mayaa..." she called weakly outside every bathroom. The doors opened without resistance, and all of them were empty. She acted silly and looked under the cots, opened the wardrobes to see if Subbu or Maya would jump out to scare her. Silence greeted her in the whole apartment.

The trembling in her legs became more intense. Her blouse was stuck to her back with sweat. A wave of the pungent smell wafted in causing a fresh coughing fit. Panic made her forget Bharat's number. Then she remembered it was programmed in the phone. She just had to press a button. It was an interminable five seconds before the phone rang. When Bharat said, "Hello," she broke down and sobbed loudly.

•

Three days after the bomb exploded, Indu and Bharat were sitting before the police superintendent. He was no longer as rigid as he was when they met him first. He was more willing to talk, and was courteous enough to offer them coffee.

"So?" said Bharat waiting for the policeman to talk.

Indu's eyes appeared swollen and suggested that she had been crying. Her make-up appeared cracked in places, and her lipstick was not applied with its usual uniformity. Her hair was not exactly distraught, but it was worn with some indifference. Her clothes were, however, immaculate as usual. The frown on her face left no doubt that she was angry.

The police superintendent stared at Bharat first and then at Indu.

"Things still aren't very clear," he said.

"What does that mean?" Indu demanded.

"Exactly that. We still do not have a good idea of what actually happened. Here's what we know. There was an explosion. Most likely a country bomb. No electronic detonator was used. It seemed to have been lit with a conventional fuse. The bomb was in the elevator shaft. It must have been placed, presumably, when the elevator wasn't on the ground floor. If the elevator had been in the ground floor, it would have been very difficult to place the bomb there. The bomb went off close to midnight according to the watchman at the front gate."

"What happened to our daughter? My grandfather? The rest of the stuff doesn't matter to us."

The superintendent was patient. "I know, I know. Just that I am trying to construct the whole story for you. So you know how we intend to proceed with the case. Maybe somebody must have got down in the elevator, or it was called down. The elevator was in the ground floor when the bomb went off. Five people—let's see, Manish, Kumar, Pratap, the woman, Sheela, and the little girl, Raveena, probably Maya's age—all residents of apartments in your block, just arrived by a car and attempted to get in when the elevator probably came down with Maya and your grandfather. We don't know who went in and came out of the elevator. At some moment then, the bomb went off. Your coffee is going cold. Do you want a fresh cup?"

Bharat and Indu said no, and asked him to continue.

"After the firefighters were done, our forensic experts scrutinized the place. The bomb wasn't exactly a weak fellow. It blew the bodies to smithereens. The fire also badly charred the remains. We don't know who, of these people, were the victims."

"How many bodies did you recover?" Bharat asked the question with difficulty.

"None," said the superintendent. "As I told you, the bodies were torn to shreds. And mostly burned."

"Did all the seven die?"

"We are not sure of that right now. According to the forensic experts, it appears like only four or five died. But hard to say which four or five. And even that number is not certain."

Earlier the police had questioned Aaya. She repeated what

she felt. That she first thought that Subbu and Maya were up to some midnight mischief. Come to think of it now, it appeared like they were running away since *pantu-thatha* was carrying some bags, and they seemed to be leaving in genuine stealth.

"Running away? To where?" Indu had scoffed.

When the police checked Subbu's bank account on the second day, they discovered that it had been cleaned out. It did seem to corroborate Aaya's theory that Subbu had planned to run away.

"So, does that mean that my grandfather and my daughter ran away?" Bharat asked hopefully.

"We don't know. First of all, we suspect that only five, maybe four, died in the incident. That's not for sure. Even if we know that for sure, the forensic experts will take some more time to determine whose bodies they were, assuming we get more information about all the people involved. These days, people live alone, they are secretive. It's hard to get reliable information about blood groups, relatives, family..."

"Let's assume for a moment that only five people died, the missing two must be Maya and *pantu-thatha*, right?" Indu asked.

"*Pantu-thatha*, who?" the superintendent blinked.

"Oh, Bharat's grandfather."

"No, we can't be sure about that."

"Why should two of the other five be missing? Why would they run away?" Indu asked.

"The two young men—Kumar and Pratap—were running a finance company. They had lots of trouble. They were financing movies and had lost most of their depositors' money. You may not know this, but they were already under investigation by us. The girl, Raveena, was..." the superintendent stopped before continuing. "...maybe I should say 'is'. Oh, damn it. Is or was. The girl, Raveena, was Kumar's daughter. Look at it this way. Kumar and Raveena, or Kumar and Pratap, ran away after this incident. It's a good chance to erase your old identity. Create a new one. Start a new life."

"If somebody's missing shouldn't it be my grandfather and Maya? I mean, they planned to do it. Kumar and Raveena. It just happened, right? People don't run away just like that, do they?"

The superintendent sighed. "People do strange things. You can never tell. This is not the most bizarre thing I have heard of in my career. People do funny things on an impulse. They do."

He stopped for a moment, and then continued. "If your grandfather and daughter did run away, where did they go? The autorickshaw drivers in the place swear they didn't see them or drop them anyplace. There was a drunk from the fishermen settlement who claimed he saw an old man leave your apartment complex with a girl. But next he says that he also saw a naked man walking hand in hand with a headless corpse. Maybe what he says is true, but according to us it's unreliable testimony."

"Who did this?" Bharat asked, absentmindedly sipping the coffee. He winced at the tepid coffee, and pushed it away.

"We don't know yet. We don't have a list of suspects. Obviously somebody who didn't like Joshi, but there must be so many people who don't like him. He's sued so many influential fellows. The man is in no condition to speak. He is hysterical. He's in hospital with high blood pressure. The doctors won't let us talk to him just now. We have to wait. The watchmen don't seem to have seen anything either. We don't suspect they are accomplices."

"I know who did it. It's them. The fishermen settlement. They are getting back at being beaten. Nobody gets beaten that way and keeps quiet," Indu said bitterly.

The superintendent shook his head. "This was done by a professional. Costs a lot of money. Those people don't have the cash to fund an operation like this. This has been done by somebody who has lots of money and is bloody angry, perhaps at Joshi. Maybe at all of you. But it's not the settlement. I told you. Their anger lasts only a few hours."

"Well you could be wrong," Indu said sternly. "I think you should not rule out that possibility."

"Lady, we are not ruling out anything." The superintendent was patient. "As a policeman, I don't take chances. We'll investigate that possibility too. I speak from my past experience. It's terribly unlikely that the fishermen's settlement had anything to do with it."

"So what's the decision on my grandfather and Maya?" Bharat had difficulty articulating.

"At the moment, missing persons. This is a difficult case. It may take days, or even weeks, for us to close. Our forensic experts are working. The field investigators, CID, are all on the job. If we have further information, we'll let you know."

"So, missing persons? Not living persons, not dead persons?" Indu asked, the frown on her face sharpening.

"That's right, madam," said the superintendent.

"Can't you do any better?"

"I am afraid not. At least, not at the moment. Good day."

•

A week later, when Indu and Bharat returned from the police station, late in the evening, the phone rang in The Home. They had vacated the Second Home. Bharat found it morbid and tiring to stay in the Second Home. And anyway the repairs at The Home were over. The Second Home never recovered from the state of disarray it reached the night of the explosion. If it wasn't the insurance investigator who wanted to ask a few questions, it was the construction contractors who were repairing the building who asked to step in to inspect your apartment, or it was the police with an odd question or two, or an association meeting that went on for hours chaotically without reaching any resolution. Joshi's stature would have moved association meetings to resolutions quickly, but he was still in hospital.

The ring of the phone startled Indu and Bharat who were lost in their thoughts.

Indu answered the phone.

Even as she spoke, Bharat could see that she was suffused with excitement. At one stage, she bit her lower lip and cried a little.

"We will be there tomorrow morning. We'll be ready by nine... Yeah, I got the address, just in case... No problem," she said and put the phone down.

Bharat stood up. "Who was it? The police? Where are we going tomorrow?"

Indu shook her head. "No, it wasn't the police. It was SNC."

Bharat blinked. "What's SNC?"

"SNC...the TV channel," Indu said impatiently.

The last thing Bharat had been expecting was a call from a TV channel, especially SNC. Many SNC shows had been topping the ratings lately.

"What do they want?"

Indu dabbed her eyes with a kerchief, and said with carefully controlled excitement, "They want us to appear on the *Madan Live* show."

Madan, the one-time matinee idol, heartthrob of millions, was a favorite of Indu and Bharat. He had practically retired from the movies. His *Madan Live* show, where he did candid interviews of personalities ranging from current celebrities to perfect anonymities, was one of the most watched shows. One of the rarities that caused Indu to lose her controlled countenance was Madan. She had watched all his movies, swayed to all the songs that he had lip-synched, and maintained that he was the handsomest of them all. So what if he had aged?

"What do they want us for?"

"Well, SNC has been covering the incident like other channels. They are as intrigued by the mystery behind the incident as the other channels. Madan wants to do a short interview of one of the residents...what it felt like to...lose somebody...who could've done it..."

"Wait!" Bharat cried. "We haven't lost anybody..."

"So where are they?" Indu demanded. "If *pantu-thatha* had run away with Maya, then he is a dirty old man...they only want a brief interview...may not last more than ten minutes. Madan has many other features on his show."

"I don't know if I want to do this now," Bharat said nervously.

Indu bit her lower lip again. "SNC is one of the world's largest TV channels. It would be impolite to say no. Besides if we have to fight, we'll need the support of the media. I want revenge. I'm not a loser. Never was. My father taught us to win. I intend to fight. I intend to win."

Bharat stared into her face bewildered. Fight? Against what? Or whom? And why is somebody fighting us, if there's a somebody. Why do we need TV channels to fight? And what is winning? And in that moment, how much Indu looked like Kamesh of yesteryear.

"Well, all right," Bharat said.

"Good. The SNC folks would pick us up tomorrow morning. They'll drop us too. We'll need to leave by nine."

•

Bharat woke up the next morning with a splitting head-ache. He glanced at the bedside clock. It was 8:15. As he stretched his limbs, he could see Indu through the connecting door, busy in front of the dressing table mirror. Through the corner of her eye, Indu noticed that Bharat had woken up.

"Quick," she urged Bharat. "They'll pick us up at nine. Get ready!"

She was pulling up the zipper of a blue skirt when Bharat walked into the bathroom, his head pounding, to brush his teeth. When he came back from the bathroom after his shower, she was in dark maroon trousers and an off-white shirt with a different hairdo. Apparently she wasn't very happy with her hair, which she was adjusting.

The coffee Bharat made himself was acidic and bitter, but soothing for the headache. He downed a painkiller tablet with his coffee, and returned to get dressed. Indu had now changed into a polka-dotted blouse.

"What are you going to wear?" she asked Bharat.

"Haven't thought about it," Bharat replied.

When he came to the dining room in corduroy trousers, and a cotton shirt, Indu had adjusted her hair yet again.

"If I were you, I'd change that shirt. Anyway the trousers don't show. The table will hide it."

"I am not changing my shirt," Bharat growled.

"Oh, really? Even when you appear okay face to face, you appear shabby on TV."

"Well, that's all viewers will get this morning."

Somehow Indu felt that if she started an argument with Bharat, she wouldn't get anywhere. "Suit yourself."

The SNC channel car reported at nine. Besides the uni-formed chauffeur, a polite, young, close-cropped suited executive came to take them.

"What time do we start the interview?" Indu asked the executive.

"Well, Ms. Indu…" he began.

"Oh, please. Drop the Ms."

"Well, Indu, as you know *Madan Live* is a live program. It starts at eleven and goes on until twelve noon. You will be on the 'Happenings' section, which should begin by eleven ten or so. We're taking you a little early so we can get you used to the settings. Introduce you to Mr. Madan. He needs to be given a briefing about you before the show. Even though it's live, Mr. Madan and a program manager will discuss the sorts of questions they'll ask you. You'll get some time to prepare."

Bharat was staring out of the window. They passed *Livewire*, the fashion supermarket.

"Can we stop for a moment? At *Livewire*?" Indu asked.

"Huh?" said the executive. "You want to stop? Just now?"

"My dress, you see. When you called last night, I hadn't quite planned on this…most of my good gowns had gone to the laundry…thought would get a nice gown on the way."

"Why, Indu, you look perfect in this dress," the executive said.

"Do we have some time? It's only 9:30. We should still be able to make it. I won't be more than a few minutes."

The executive appeared embarrassed since Indu was almost imploring.

"Turn around. Go to *Livewire*," he ordered the chauffeur.

Bharat sat in the car with the executive while Indu went to buy a gown, and the two men did not trade a word.

When Indu emerged from *Livewire*, she was in a black strapless gown that fit her like a second skin. She had quickly redone her hair so it fell in wavy strands over her shoulders.

The executive's eyes popped. "Indu, it was a good decision.

You look great. Now..." he ordered the chauffeur."...step on it."

When Madan was introduced to Indu, he remarked, "What a gorgeous person," shook hands, and gave her a light hug. Madan's six feet three inches frame towered over Bharat's as he said to him, "You've got a beautiful wife." And to both of them, "I am sorry to hear what happened."

Indu was straining to retain her composure, her poise. That was clear from her inane replies to the various remarks around her. At all other times, her responses would always be incisive or pointedly polite.

"Can we do the briefing?" the program manager asked.

"You go, not me," Bharat said to Indu.

"What do you mean, not me?" asked Indu.

"I'm not doing the interview...I'll sit around here."

"You mean you don't want to be in the interview with Mr. Madan?" the program manager asked.

Bharat nodded, and Indu looked irritated.

The program manager glanced at his watch. "Running out of time. That's fine. You can sit in the audience. We'll introduce you as Indu's husband. Maybe you can just wave out. Now Bharat, if you'll take a seat here, Indu please come with me."

The lights were on Indu and Madan. Madan was reading from a script background details about what happened at the Second Home apartment complex.

"We have here Indu, a very brave woman..." Madan announced. The cameras now focused on Indu. Watching her on a TV hidden from the cameras, Bharat couldn't help thinking how irresistibly attractive she looked.

"Her husband, Bharat, used to be an investment manager at Fusion Investments, a leading American finance company..."

The lights now focused on Bharat. In the background, a woman appeared carrying a board which said, "WAVE AND SMILE." Bharat waved and smiled.

Madan turned to Indu. "Who do you believe did this?"

"Personally I think the fishermen settlement had something to do with this. The police are reluctant about investigating this angle. I have no idea why. They had a motive..."

"Where were you when this happened?"

"At a party."

"How did you find out what happened?"

"The *au pair* of my daughter...the nanny...she called my husband..."

"Your daughter died in this incident?"

"We don't know...the police are not sure yet."

"Apparently the police are working simultaneously on the theory that she disappeared with your husband's grandfather. That both of them ran away."

"We don't know about that, either. The police are working on that angle as well. I believe the irresponsible old man and my daughter are around. Somewhere."

The lights were sharp, hurting. Indu's face appeared blanched under the harsh lights. As the questions progressed, Bharat felt a sensation in his throat which he had felt when he was a boy. In his childhood, it was a definite precursor to weeping. As a boy, it would take a few minutes for the first tear to roll down after the appearance of this sensation. He could not guess what would happen if the sensation continued for a few moments. It appeared like Indu was staring at him. Her stentorian presence made the sensation disappear. On the table, between Madan and Indu stood a flower vase. Bharat's eyes strayed towards the flowers. They were fresh, tastefully arranged, outstandingly aesthetic, but almost completely un-noticed. Strangely like Maya. Fresh, beautiful, but almost un-noticed. Here today, gone tomorrow.

"Indu, what's the future?" Madan was asking.

"Our daughter had some problems. The psychiatrist called it early stages of anomie. Later I discovered that many young children seem to be suffering from it. We know how difficult it can be. My husband and I want to start a trust devoted to the care of children who suffer from anomie. We intend putting close to half a million dollars into it. We've even set up a website, Maya-anomie-project.com"

"Half a million dollars? Wow. Give the lady a big hand."

The woman held up a board: "CLAP," for the audience to see.

The audience clapped.

"Indu, anything else you'd like to say before you leave?"

"We are there for those children who suffer from anomie. They shouldn't lose heart."

The woman held up another board: "CLAP VERY HARD."

The audience clapped again, this time thunderously.

•

Ten days after the incident, the police still termed Subbu and Maya "missing persons." Many investigative tests, including DNA tests, were either still in progress or inconclusive. Indu was quite miffed with this. She still believed that the superintendent was reluctant to investigate the fishermen settlement angle.

"Opinionated idiot," she cursed him.

On the eleventh day, Bharat could see a distinct restlessness in her.

"I think we must hold a grieving party," she said.

"But nothing's still concluded...the police are still searching. Should we do it now?" Bharat faltered.

"It doesn't matter what we believe. Or that nothing's concluded. It won't look good. Already I have a tough time answering questions. At the office, at the parties. Nobody takes ten days usually. We are already a few days late. I think we shouldn't delay it."

"Well, okay," said Bharat.

"Can you make the arrangements, please?"

"When do you want to have it?"

"In two days. Or three. Whenever the caterers are ready. No, no. Don't get to the caterers directly. Better contact my usual event managers. They might do a better job."

Before leaving for work she called out from the door. "By the way, the lawyer's sending the draft agreement for the trust. Take a look at it, will you?"

"Okay."

When Bharat checked his email, the lawyer's draft agreement was waiting. While junking most other mail mechanically, he noticed a message he almost deleted. It was from Sagacity Investments, a British finance company. He opened it listlessly. What would it have to say? He expected: While your profile is most impressive, we regret, at this time, we do not have a suitable opportunity for you. Or, at the moment, we are not hiring. We find your resume attractive, and have filed it for later use.

However, Sagacity's email read: "We considered your application, and are happy to offer you the position of Senior Investment Manager. The terms and conditions of your offer are attached. If they are acceptable to you, please let us know by mail. We welcome you to the Sagacity family."

Bharat read and re-read the mail a dozen times. What was the joining date? The coming Monday. What day was today?

251

Already Thursday. Did he have proper clothes? Anyway, he had plenty of time until Saturday evening to prepare. Some stores were open even on Sundays. Senior Investment Manager. Back again, only in a different place. In a different family. The Sagacity family.

•

At 2:00 AM on Monday morning, Bharat closed the front door of The Home with relief. The grieving party was over. It had started Sunday evening at 7:00. A few minutes back, the last guests had left. There had been about fifty of them. By moving some of the furniture to Maya's bedroom, and Subbu's bedroom, they had made standing room for the guests. When their legs ached, the guests took turns sitting. Fortunately nobody got drunk, and there were no ugly episodes. Whenever he went in to fetch liquor bottles, he saw Aaya sitting in a corner with a tearful look. She hadn't spoken much in the last ten days. She hadn't eaten much either

"Don't be difficult," he chided her once or twice when he went to fetch the bottles. He had been chiding her thus for the past few days. But she was ignoring him completely. He decided to ignore her, too.

As soon as the guests had left, Indu had gone into her bedroom. She wanted to wash and change before going to bed.

There was a lone, unopened bottle of whisky on the center table. Let it be. Can be taken care of in the morning. He was heading to his bedroom when the doorbell rang.

He froze and half-expected *pantu-thatha* to answer the door. It took a whole minute for his limbs to become free.

Who could it be, at this hour?

With great hesitation, he opened the door.

On the head of the stairs stood a woman, a little hesitant,

with a cat in her hands, stroking it mechanically.

Marianne realized that she had to introduce herself. "I am Marianne, your neighbor...I live upstairs...one floor above."

She had a Cheshire Cat's smile, a middle-aged, haggard, Cheshire Cat's. Was this the Cat Woman *pantu-thatha* talked about now and then?

"Oh," said Bharat with mock remorse at not recognizing her. "Of course, of course. Do come in."

She stepped into the apartment. "I...I heard about your daughter and Mr. Subbu. She was an angel, and Mr. Subbu was a great man. I...I thought I'd give you this."

Oh God! Another grieving card. He opened the envelope. The card said, "I am sorry that this had to happen to you." It was handmade paper, and Marianne had scrawled the message in a neat hand. He had received maybe another twenty cards that said the same thing. At least this woman had class. She had brought a handmade paper card with a very personal message. Handmade paper cards were a luxury. Like handkerchiefs. Most of the other guests had been cheap. They had sent custom versions of electronic cards from free sites.

"Thank you, thank you very much. Won't you have a drink?" Bharat asked.

Marianne hadn't shed her hesitant manner. "You must be tired..." She trailed off, staring behind Bharat, eyeing the bottle on the table. Then she plucked up courage to say, "Can I have that bottle if you don't mind? I'll take it home and...drink it."

"Oh, certainly," said Bharat, anxious to end the conversation immediately.

Marianne stared for a long moment at her toes. "Must have been a long day for you. You go to bed now. I have to leave, too. Alan will be waiting."

"Of course," said Bharat, glad to get rid of her. Who was

Alan? Boyfriend or husband? Might be a mistake to ask.

She was gone the next moment, awkwardly clutching the bottle and the cat, and managing her stroking at the same time.

By the time he had a wash and came to bed, it was nearly 3:00 AM.

Indu kept the connecting door between their bedrooms open. He lay down in her bed, switched on the night lamp, and switched off all other lights. Indu stood by the window gazing. The light from the window highlighted her perfect, hourglass figure against the window frame. Like the Eiffel Tower is highlighted in night photographs of Paris. He couldn't help thinking how attractive she looked. The years passed, but she never aged.

As his eyes trained to the dark, he could see her profile as she turned to look at something. She managed to maintain her stunning resemblance to Nadira, the actress who had won the Miss World title. He was reminded of the incident in an airport, years ago, when she had been pregnant with Maya. One of the many times when she had been mistaken for the famous actress. He could vividly recall that day when there was an announcement airing that David Johnson, a lost boy, claiming to be American, had been located by the airport authorities. They were searching for his parents. How they had argued with each other that day, the young men and the woman who mistook Indu for Nadira.

As he was gingerly rubbing the Z-shaped scar under his left eye, a result of a childhood injury, he heard it for the first time. He wrinkled his brow and aquiline nose in curiosity. The strange noise.

"Is it cats?" he asked her.

"Looks like it. But then very strange for them to mew like this. Wonder where it's coming from," Indu said.

"Let's get some sleep. Got a long day tomorrow," he said. "I mean, today. My first day in my new job. Don't want to screw it up."

"All right," she said, and continued after a moment's silence. "I think the party was well attended."

He agreed, almost absent-mindedly. "Yes. It was well attended."

A new day was dawning in this part of Eimona.

The cats mewed on.

LaVergne, TN USA
17 August 2009
154999LV00002B/41/A